Dear Reader,

Writing *Frozen in Time* was such a fun experience for us. Every element of Anne's latest adventure brought new challenges to us and to her as she figured out how a life-size bronze statue of a famous Blue Hill citizen seemed to vanish overnight into thin air.

Much like Ben and his treasure-hunting collection in this story, both of us have mementos from the past near and dear to us. As with Anne and her aunt Edie, it's the memories of the person attached to the things that mean so much.

In addition to solving the mystery of the missing statue, which contained a time capsule, Anne and her friends also renew their faith in how valuable those closest to us are.

Lois Stover, our fictional Blue Hill architect, was inspired by the real-life Anna Keichline who was responsible for many great developments in architecture, including an unglamorous but very useful hollow clay brick that was an early form of the now commonplace concrete block. Lois is quite different from her real-life inspiration, but we loved learning about how Anna made a big difference in her profession.

We hope you enjoy this trip to the cozy community of Blue Hill and the secrets Anne reveals.

Happy Reading!
Pam Hanson & Barbara Andrews
writing as Emily Thomas

Secrets of the Blue Hill Library
Nowhere to Be Found
Shadows of the Past
Unlocking the Truth
Theft and Thanksgiving
The Christmas Key
Off the Shelf
Gone in a Flash
All Sewn Up
If Walls Could Talk
The Rightful Owner
Cracking the Code
The Valentine Visitor
Without a Trace
Stagestruck
All That Glitters
Lights! Camera! Action!
Mum's the Word
Sidetracked Suspicions
For the Birds
Finding Home
Agree to Disagree
Frozen in Time

Frozen in Time

Secrets of the
BLUE HILL LIBRARY

EMILY THOMAS

Guideposts

New York

Frozen in Time

CHAPTER ONE

A re you ready for the big reveal?" Anne Gibson asked Wendy Pyle as her friend raced up to the checkout desk.

"I sure am," Wendy said, depositing a stack of books on the varnished surface. "And sorry I'm late. We're running out of fun summer things to do. How long until school starts?"

"Not too many weeks now," Anne said sympathetically. Her own two children, Ben and Liddie, were getting antsy. She could only imagine what things were like in the Pyle household with seven children to keep occupied.

"Good thing!" Wendy said. "Oh, Maggie Sloan is going to meet us at the park. She said she had an errand to run first." The wife of Reverend Tom Sloan was the chairperson of the celebration committee both women were on.

"Just let me get my purse and let today's helper know I'm leaving, and we can go."

"I'm so excited to see the final result," Wendy said, leaning her elbows on the counter.

A few minutes later Anne joined her dynamo of a friend, and they headed out to Wendy's red SUV.

"Sorry about the sticky seat belt. I'm not sure what spilled on it," Wendy said.

Anne felt a pang of sympathy mixed with admiration for Wendy. In addition to raising her large family, she was wife to the local high school football coach, and she was a whirlwind organizer and a voracious reader. A mishap with what may have been a juice box was a small thing compared to what she dealt with on a daily basis.

"Oh, that's fine," Anne said. "I'm so curious to see the cleaned and restored statue of Blue Hill's most famous citizen."

Wendy laughed. "Some people would argue that your aunt Edie should have a statue erected to her. She was definitely one of Blue Hill's most interesting residents."

"She really was. I still marvel at how talented she was."

Anne's beloved great-aunt had been a woman of much mystery and many talents. Aunt Edie's bequest to turn her old Victorian house into a library for her small Pennsylvania town had allowed widowed Anne and her children to return to her childhood home. The money from her late aunt's estate provided enough funds to remodel the house and library and establish a trust for Anne's salary.

"I remember when I was a girl, Aunt Edie talked about what an inspiration Lois Stover had been to her because she'd done so many interesting and exciting things," Anne mused.

"Here we are," Wendy said, pulling into a parking spot adjacent to Rosehill Park.

Anne got out of the vehicle and joined her friend on the walkway leading to the statue.

"I loved playing here as a child," Anne said, watching as a little girl pumped her legs to make her swing go higher while her mother pushed her.

"My kids have sure enjoyed it," Wendy said.

Anne admired the small pond and the lovely rose garden as she and Wendy walked toward the newly restored statue of well-known architect Lois Stover. The Blue Hill native was the first woman to be certified as an architect in Pennsylvania and was also a secret agent during World War I, a fact Anne found fascinating. Anne strongly suspected that her great-aunt had done intelligence work during her many travels. It was a fanciful notion, Anne knew, but she wouldn't put it past Aunt Edie.

"I've learned quite a bit being on the statue rededication committee," Anne said. "I've passed that statue dozens of times without really thinking about the town's most famous citizen. Her connection to my great-aunt makes it that much more fascinating."

Two young boys on scooters whizzed past them, and Anne shielded her eyes against the bright August sun shining through the trees. "I can't believe in two weeks the time capsule hidden in the statue will be opened in honor of the twenty-fifth anniversary of the dedication of the statue."

A puppy dragging its leash followed closely behind the boys and dashed right between Anne and Wendy.

"Oops!" Wendy said, looking after the scampering pooch. "Looks like somebody is trying to keep up."

Anne turned to look too and was gratified to see one of the boys had stopped to pick up the dog's leash before it tripped itself.

As they neared the chain-link fence attached to granite posts that surrounded the statue, Anne was happy to see the draping still held in place by the scaffolding. She and Wendy had wondered about the possibility of some mischievous teens tugging at the covering. Anne didn't see Maggie Sloan waiting for them. "She must still be running that errand," Wendy said, checking her watch. "Whew, it's warm out today."

Anne and Wendy had learned through their research that Arlen Buchanan, the local sculptor who created the statue, did the initial design work of the statue back in the 1950s and that Lois Stover worked with him on it before she died of cancer in 1955.

Buchanan, who currently resided in the local nursing home, had gotten the start to his stellar career in the 1950s designing the Stover statue. But he had been unable to complete it for more than thirty years because of murky donor-funding issues.

What I've always liked is that the time capsule contains items Lois herself put in before her death," Wendy said. "I wonder what secrets will be spilled out when the capsule is opened at the anniversary celebration? It's too bad the time capsule wasn't opened in 1990, on what would have been Lois Stover's hundredth birthday."

Anne nodded. "I know. But they couldn't very well open the time capsule the year the statue was put up, could they?"

"And waiting to open the time capsule until the twenty-fifth anniversary of the dedication of the statue means we get to be around for it!" Wendy said, waving to Maggie.

Anne turned and waved too as the reverend's wife hurried toward them.

"Ladies, I'm so sorry I'm late. My errand took much longer than I thought it would."

"That's just fine," Anne said, noting the usually elegant older woman looked a bit flustered.

"I was running late too," Wendy said sympathetically.

"Is everything all right?" Anne asked with concern. "You look a bit…"

"Rattled?" Maggie finished for her. "Actually I am. I stopped at the bakery department at the grocery store out by the highway to place the order for the pastries being served after the ceremony and the opening of the time capsule. Because of the heat wave we've been having, I'm rethinking the menu."

Anne listened patiently with Wendy as their committee chair recapped her conversation with the head baker about the merits of custard versus cream as a filling for éclairs to be served under the hot summer sun.

She was itching to take a look at the cleaning and restoration work done by Harold Buchanan, the sculptor's older son, an art teacher retired from Blue Hill High School. And she wanted to get back to the library to check on her new volunteer before she needed to pick up Ben and Liddie from their friends' houses.

"So the pastries are out and cookies are in on the menu now," Maggie finished with a satisfied smile.

"Cookies will be nice," Anne agreed.

"And I'll make sure my kids only take one apiece," Wendy said, grinning.

"Excellent," Maggie said, her efficient demeanor restored. "Now, shall we remove the draping and take a peek at the restoration Harold did?"

The statue was draped to prevent damage during the cleaning and restoration. Anne knew they just intended to take a peek at the foot of the statue and replace the protective covering.

"Last time I talked to Mr. Buchanan, he mentioned he still might want to do some finishing touches before the rededication ceremony and opening of the time capsule," Maggie said.

"I wonder if the rumors about the time capsule are true," Wendy said thoughtfully.

"You mean the stories about the alleged map showing where the family gems that Lois Stover smuggled out of Europe are hidden, or even the jewels themselves?" Anne asked.

Since serving on the committee, she had heard vaguely about the rumors but hadn't paid that much attention. She'd been too concerned with rounding up enough folding chairs for the ceremony.

"Yes, wouldn't that be exciting?" Wendy said.

"I'm sure whatever is in the time capsule will be of historical significance," Maggie said, stepping carefully over the chain-link fencing that surrounded the draped scaffolding.

"Why would the architect give the sculptor family gems to hide in the time capsule?" Anne asked. She thought it was more likely blueprints and notes were going to be revealed when the time capsule was opened. She didn't know what kind of container held the objects, but why would anyone put valuable jewelry in a place that didn't have security? She'd heard the rumor, and no doubt most of the townspeople had too.

Wendy laughed. "Good point! There goes that theory."

Anne positioned herself at one corner of the tented scaffolding, and Maggie and Wendy did the same at the other corners. Together they gently lifted the hem of the protective canvas covering to get their first look at the restoration work. The scaffolding was too high for them to remove without assistance from a park worker.

"Oh my!" Maggie gasped.

"What?" Wendy echoed.

Anne stood shocked and speechless as she stared into the emptiness under the tarp.

How could a one-ton bronze likeness of Blue Hill's most famous citizen disappear from its base?

CHAPTER TWO

Anne stood in the park with other committee members who'd heard about the theft. Their murmured comments showed how shocked they were. A group had gathered at the base where the statue should have been.

"Where could our favorite statue be?" a newcomer asked.

"Maybe she's taking a walk around the park," Wendy joked weakly.

While she appreciated her friend's attempt at humor, Anne remained dumbstruck. She was alarmed to see all the color had washed out of Maggie's face. Dealing with refreshment issues was one thing, but now the "guest of honor" at the ceremony was missing.

"Who on earth could have carted off the statue without being seen? And why would anyone want it?" Anne asked, talking mostly to herself.

"Well," Maggie said, "let's contact Harold Buchanan and find out the last time he was in the park…and whether the statue was still in place."

"Good idea," Anne said. "He might have some idea of what the thieves could do with something that heavy and bulky."

Wendy nodded in agreement, but none of the three moved to leave. Anne, like her friends, couldn't seem to take her eyes away from the empty base of the missing statue.

"The theft must have happened in the small hours of the night," Wendy said.

"Yes, but even then it's surprising they got away with it. The thieves must have made a lot of noise getting it down." Anne gave a lingering look at the looted site, then turned away.

"Judging by the bolts lying around the base, I wonder if they just pounded them out with something heavy like a crowbar?" Wendy suggested.

"It looks like they took out every last bolt. Maybe that means they didn't want to damage the statue," Anne said. "Let's go to the library to call Mr. Buchanan."

A small crowd was gathering in the park, all shocked by the disappearance. Apparently, someone had had the presence of mind to call the police. A squad car pulled into the parking lot just as they were getting into Maggie's car.

"Good! Let the police handle it," Maggie said. "How hard could it be to find something that large?"

Anne watched as Officer Michael Banks, a friend from high school days, got out of his squad car. She would have waved if she hadn't already climbed into the backseat of Maggie's car.

"Let's make that call to Mr. Buchanan, although I don't relish being the one to tell him the bad news," Anne said. "He must have been really proud to have his father's work on display for everyone to enjoy. Shall we go to the library to call?"

"Let's go to my house where we'll have more privacy—if neither of you needs to get home for your children," Maggie said.

"No, they're happily playing at friends' houses. They'd be disappointed if I picked them up early," Anne said.

Wendy confirmed that her offspring were all engaged in summer activities that didn't require her presence, so the three women headed toward the Sloans'.

Blue Hill was a small town, and it didn't take long to get to Maggie's. They reached her house just as Anne was wiping away an errant tear. She knew it was silly to cry over a missing statue, but so many people would be upset when the ceremony was canceled. People in town were proud of their statue and the outstanding woman who had warranted a monument in the park.

"My husband is at the church working on his sermon. I should call over there to see if he's heard about the missing statue," Maggie said after ushering them into her welcoming kitchen with the scent of spices in the air. "Then we can call the sculptor's son on my phone."

"That's fine. I wish we had some idea why it was taken, but I can't imagine what it could be," Anne said. "I wonder if your husband could shed some light on it."

"If anyone in town could figure out a motive for the theft, it would be Reverend Tom," Wendy said. "He's the best listener I've ever met, and he never forgets anything. I don't think there's anything going on around town that someone hasn't told him about."

Anne agreed wholeheartedly. Maybe he could suggest a reason for the theft. Someone had gone to a lot of trouble, but why?

She had a terrible thought: What if it was stolen for the metal content?

She decided not to mention this as a possible motive to Wendy or Maggie. They were upset enough without suggesting the statue might be destroyed for scrap metal.

"Maybe the town will get a ransom note," Wendy suggested. "Although I can't imagine Blue Hill coming up with enough to make the theft worthwhile."

"I'll call Harold Buchanan if it's okay with you two," Maggie said. "We've talked quite a few times about the ceremony."

"I imagine he has more spare time since he retired from his job as a high school art teacher last spring," Anne said.

"I was so sorry to hear about his retirement," Wendy said. "He has a reputation for being a wonderful teacher. I was hoping some of my kids would get to take his class."

"It's ringing," Maggie said, holding the phone propped under her chin. Her face was flushed and her usually cool demeanor had vanished, a sure sign that the missing statue was a major problem. "Oh dear, his answering machine just came on. Should I leave a message?"

"You could ask him to call you when he gets home," Wendy suggested.

"I wouldn't leave a message about the statue though," Anne said. "I always think bad news should be given in person."

When Maggie had carefully enunciated her phone number, repeating it a second time for good measure, she hung up and invited Wendy and Anne to the kitchen table for some freshly squeezed lemonade.

"Here you are," she said as she filled three pretty amber glasses from a pitcher she'd had in the fridge.

Anne always enjoyed being in Maggie's homey country kitchen. It invited friendly conversation. Today, though, the only thing they could talk about was the theft. She sat at the kitchen table with Wendy and sighed. Harold Buchanan wasn't answering his phone, so where did that leave them? As a committee member, she felt an obligation to clear up the mystery.

"Maybe he's in the park," Wendy suggested, sipping her lemonade.

"I'll try him again later in the day," Maggie said. "He has a little studio at the back of his house where he goes to work on his art. Maybe he doesn't have a phone there."

"You left your number," Anne reminded her. "I'm sure he'll get back to you. He's such a sweet man."

"Who's a sweet man?" Reverend Tom Sloan asked as he stepped into the kitchen.

"We weren't talking about you," his wife teased. "Did you forget something from the house?"

"No. I don't mean to interrupt your visit, but I wanted to learn more about the missing statue," the reverend said. His brow was creased, and he didn't have his customary warm smile.

Anne sat back and sipped her lemonade while the other two women filled him in. She was tempted to chime in, but her friends covered the few facts they knew.

"If I have this right, the statue vanished sometime this week?" he said. He pursed his lips and looked thoughtful.

"It must have been more than one person. I don't see how anyone could lift the statue off its base without help," Anne said. "But what will they do with it? Take it to another state and sell it to a flea market dealer?"

"There's another possibility," Reverend Sloan said. "Maybe the thieves were after something inside the statue."

"The time capsule!" Anne said. "That could be what the thieves were looking for."

"What would be in it that anyone would want?" Wendy asked.

"Probably just historical artifacts," the reverend conceded. "Nothing salable I would guess."

"That's it!" Maggie cried out. "They were after Lois Stover's treasure."

"You know that's only a rumor," her husband said, frowning.

"Well, at least half of the town believes it," Maggie said.

"I don't," Anne said. "What treasure and why would it be inside a statue?"

"I've heard several versions of the story," Reverend Sloan said, "but they boil down to the same tale about hidden treasure. I believe the rumor originated in the 1950s."

"But the time capsule wasn't hidden until 1990 when the statue was dedicated," Anne said.

"It was sealed in the fifties," he said. "That was when the speculation about hidden treasure first surfaced, I believe. The story has popped up from time to time during my ministry. That's about all I know, so I'd better get back to the church and finish my sermon. I'm sorry about the theft. I know it will ruin a lot of plans."

"It certainly will." Maggie sighed.

"I'll keep my ears open for any hints of who would do it," he said.

"I think I've heard a vague story about treasure," Anne said when Reverend Tom had left them. "Yes, I remember a neighbor telling me he was hunting for it with his metal detector."

"That was Ralph Spinner, wasn't it?" Wendy said. "I've seen him all over town with that gadget of his. Do you think he ever finds anything of value?"

"He showed Ben and me his collection of coins and odd bits of jewelry. But he hasn't been out recently, I'm afraid. He hurt his back falling off a ladder. I doubt he'll do much prospecting for a while," Anne said.

"I can see why he'd give it up. He must be in his eighties," Wendy said.

"I think he was a Sunday school teacher when I was little," Anne said. "Even then, his hair was pure white. But now, all of his little found treasures have really excited Ben, so he wants a metal detector of his own. I'm having a hard time convincing him it's not a child's toy."

"I've heard they're pretty expensive," Wendy said.

"Guess I'd better get back to the library," Anne said. She hated to leave without an answer about the theft, but she had a feeling this wasn't the end of her involvement. They still had the rededication ceremony scheduled in two weeks. Would they go ahead with the event? She could imagine a lot of disappointed people gathered around the ruined base.

"Why don't I give you a ride?" Maggie offered. "It's hot enough to fry an egg on the sidewalk."

"My kids actually tried that," Wendy said. "It cooked a little, but the neighborhood dogs lapped it up and ruined the experiment."

Anne laughed with the others, then declined Maggie's offer again. "Thanks, but I think I'll walk. It will give me some thinking time."

Less than halfway back to the library, she began to regret turning down a ride. They were in the middle of an August heat wave. Ahead of her, the pavement seemed to shimmer, and she could feel the heat radiating through the rubber soles of her tennis shoes. She was less than two blocks from the park, and she did want to take another look at the site of the theft. After debating with herself, she decided to take a short detour and see the ruined base one more time.

She hoped the police would still be there, but there was no sign of the black and white car. They'd left evidence of their presence behind, though: a long strip of yellow tape circling the area where the statue had been. Only a few spectators were gathered outside the crime scene tape, and none were people she knew well.

Denied access to the area, she had to admit she didn't have any real business going over to the base. If the thieves had left any clues, she trusted the police to find them.

A thought nagged at her all the way home, practically making her forget how hot and sweaty she was. This wasn't a random theft. Someone had carefully planned it, bringing the right tools and a vehicle to take it away. Not only that, it was timed to avoid any suspicion. The thieves would likely have had to know when the police would be cruising or answering a call on the other side of town.

Did that mean it was a local person? It was even more upsetting to think of a Blue Hill resident stealing it, maybe someone she'd passed on the street or a patron of the library.

Now the big question was, where could anyone conceal something that size to avoid detection?

CHAPTER THREE

A nne sighed and glanced at her watch for what seemed like the millionth time in the last hour. It was nearly time to close the library. After the shock that morning of discovering the missing statue, she was more than ready for this day to be over.

She was so distracted, she jumped when Remi Miller came up to her at the desk and started to ask a question.

"Mrs. Gibson, I'm sorry! I didn't mean to startle you," the younger woman said.

"Oh, Remi, that's fine. It's just been a long day." Anne smiled at her helper, who looked especially perky today in lime-green leggings and a yellow-checkered top. Although she was a twin, she never dressed in outfits identical to her sister's. In fact, they weren't identical twins, and they had differing outlooks on life. Fortunately, both were hard workers, eager to learn.

As many others in Blue Hill, Remi had already heard about the missing statue, so Anne spent a few minutes discussing the situation with Remi before her helper left for the evening. She was glad she'd planned a simple supper for her children and couldn't wait until she could lock the door and retire for the evening.

With minutes to go, she looked up as the door opened and was surprised to see Mildred Farley striding purposefully toward her, hugging a stack of books in her arms. She was wearing a blue cotton housedress, which was unusual in itself. Mildred never left home in such casual attire.

"Mildred, nice to see you," Anne said sincerely, not bothered that it was closing time. Mildred Farley had been a dear friend of Anne's aunt Edie and served, in turn, as a friend and stand-in aunt for Anne. As a longtime resident of Blue Hill, Mildred possessed much knowledge of the town's history and was good at being close-mouthed. Anne greatly appreciated the older woman's friendship and insights.

When Mildred put her books on the counter, Anne noticed something odd.

"Didn't you like any of these?" she asked. "You only had them out two days."

"I found I wasn't in a reading mood," Mildred said, sounding a bit evasive. She patted her curly white hair, perhaps as a distraction.

"Well, if you'd like me to recommend some other titles, we have some I haven't shelved yet," Anne said. By now she knew exactly what Mildred liked to read, sometimes putting new arrivals aside for the prolific reader.

"Truthfully, I hope you can tell me more about the missing statue. At my hair appointment, in the drugstore, everywhere I went today, people were talking about it. Some of their theories are downright silly, but I know I can depend on you to give me a factual report."

"All I can tell you is what everyone knows. Someone took it in the middle of the night. Exactly when is still unsure. The base and a few scattered bolts are the only things left. I did see Michael Banks arrive on the scene to investigate."

"Certainly the police can find something that large. Someone must have seen the thieves hauling it away," Mildred said.

"You'd think so," Anne said. "But the theft was so well planned, they probably had a hiding place nearby, maybe a barn or an abandoned building."

"I'm glad Edie isn't here to see it," Mildred said. "Lois Stover greatly inspired her."

"Aunt Edie would've been drawn to anyone who led such an interesting life," Anne said. "But how did she get to know Lois?"

"Your aunt was never shy, you know. We were still in school when Lois Stover was the guest speaker at a career day assembly at the high school. Edie made a beeline for her the minute she finished. For reasons only they knew, the two of them hit it off immediately. Next thing I noticed, they were deep in conversation."

"I wonder what my aunt said to someone so famous," Anne said.

"I asked her that—when she got out of detention for missing her next class. But all she did was give me that sly little smile of hers. I do know they exchanged letters. Edie was happy whenever she got one from her."

"I never found any of those letters that I know of," Anne mused. "You'd think Aunt Edie would have cherished them and kept them. Maybe the next time I go to the attic, I'll look for them specifically."

"I gave up a long time ago trying to figure out why Edie did what she did. I do know Lois Stover was an example of an independent woman who accomplished great things. I'm sure she inspired Edie to set goals and take risks to achieve them."

Mildred's deep gray eyes looked moist as she recalled her dear friend's relationship with the architect.

"No matter who inspired her, you were always her best friend," Anne said. "She needed your steady influence."

"I don't know about that, but I was energized by her zest for life." Mildred's face puckered, and Anne was afraid she'd cry. Mildred still regretted the loss of her friend, but this time no tears came.

"Edie must have been in her twenties when Lois passed away. She did show that age is no detriment to friendship," Anne said.

"I do know one interesting story about Lois Stover," Mildred said, lowering her voice, although they were the only two people in the library. "She had a wealthy aunt who went to Paris to study art at the turn of the century. When it looked like World War I was a certainty, she summoned her niece to help save her jewelry. Supposedly, Lois smuggled it into this country to hold for her aunt. As far as anyone knows, the aunt never came to claim any of it. And no one has ever seen any of the jewels. Lois never wore them in public, and none of the jewelers in town ever worked on them."

"Maybe Lois mailed her aunt's jewels back to Paris after the war was over," Anne suggested.

"Maybe." Mildred didn't sound convinced. "But there was a terrible influenza epidemic after the war. I vaguely recall Edie telling me Lois Stover's aunt was one of the casualties. I never heard what happened to the smuggled jewelry, and I don't think anyone else did either. That's why stories of them being hidden away somewhere keep surfacing. Even when it doesn't make sense, people love hidden treasure. And who knows? Maybe Lois did hide them away somewhere to keep them safe. There was a lot of mistrust of banks in the 1920s and '30s. She might not have felt comfortable putting them in a safe-deposit box."

"She must have hidden them away somewhere," Anne said. "Maybe she had a hidden compartment in the time capsule only she knew about."

"That would be a perfect hiding place. No one would think to open it until long after Lois was gone." Mildred's face lit up with enthusiasm. "One thing I know about Lois Stover is that she loved puzzles. Maybe she wanted to leave one last mystery behind. Whoever could solve it would get the jewelry."

"If someone heard the legend about the jewelry and decided it must be in the time capsule, it would explain why that person would steal the statue to get at it," Anne said.

"They must not have found the capsule. Why else would they go to so much trouble to steal something as heavy and awkward as a statue?" Mildred asked.

"I suppose it could be hidden in an arm or the head, places difficult to investigate in the park in the dark. That's only a guess," Anne said.

"A pretty good guess, I'd say. Of course, we don't know what's in it. I suppose there could be jewels, or possibly a map to find them," Mildred said. "It would be Lois Stover's final puzzle."

"Or maybe we're just being fanciful," Anne said with a light laugh. "Both those women lived such interesting lives, we can imagine them doing almost anything."

"True," said Mildred. "Now I'd better let you close the library and make supper for your children."

Anne saw her friend out, but her mind was reeling with the possibility of hidden treasure, puzzling plots, and the friendship between her aunt and the famous architect.

* * *

Anne didn't often feed her children a meal that came pre-packaged, but they both loved macaroni and cheese. It was quick, tasty, and nutritious enough when she added some mixed vegetables to their plates.

"I hate these mushy things," Ben said, fastidiously picking a lima bean out of his serving of vegetables.

"Eat it with a bite of macaroni. You won't even taste it," Anne said as she prepared a salad for herself. She added strips of red pepper, chopped onions, and baby shrimp she'd thawed earlier, then dribbled on ranch dressing.

Ben hid the lima bean under the edge of his plate, but Anne decided to ignore it if he ate the rest of his vegetables. She wasn't fond of lima beans herself.

"More!" Liddie piped up in a loud voice.

"May I have some more, please," Anne corrected her.

"Me too," Ben said, adding *please* as an afterthought.

"Eat your vegetables, and you both can have seconds," Anne said, bringing her salad to the table and sitting down.

Ben shoveled a load of veggies toward his mouth with his fork but lost most of it to the floor where Hershey the dog gobbled them up. Liddie picked away at hers with a spoon and finished first. Sometimes her children reminded her of the fable of the turtle and the hare. Ben liked to rush through things, and it sometimes tripped him up. He wasn't at all like his father in that regard. Eric had been methodical and patient.

While the children finished chocolate pudding cups, Anne put the uneaten part of her salad in the fridge for tomorrow's lunch. This wasn't the first time her appetite had disappeared when she thought of how much she missed Eric. She was growing terribly fond of her high school boyfriend, Alex Ochs, but her feelings weren't like the rush of excitement she'd experienced when she first met her husband-to-be.

"I have a new treasure," Ben said, slipping off his chair and digging into one of the leg pockets on his khaki shorts. "Ralph gave it to me."

"Do you mean Mr. Spinner?" Anne discouraged her children from calling older people by their first names.

"He said to call him Ralph," Ben protested. "See what he gave me."

Her son showed her a tiny race car on the palm of his hand. It was the kind of little toy that might once have been a game piece or a prize in a box of caramel corn.

"Nice," Anne said.

"He found it with his metal detector," Ben said. "He thinks I'm old enough to have one of my own. Then I could find treasures everywhere."

Anne wiped her daughter's face and hands and let her leave the table.

"You know they're awfully expensive, way too much to be considered a toy," Anne regretfully reminded him.

"I have lots of money," Ben said. "I've been saving for a long time."

It was true that Ben had a savings account at the bank, but the last time Anne had checked, it contained less than forty dollars.

"I'm afraid you don't have enough in the bank for a metal detector," Anne said.

"But I have lots more in my piggy bank," Ben said. "Come into my room, and I'll show you."

Liddie had scooted into her own room to begin the complicated process of putting her dolls and stuffed animals to bed, so Anne followed her son to his room.

"See," he said, vigorously shaking his plastic pig until a few pennies fell out on the bed.

"Yes, but it might be better to open it from the bottom when you want to use the money," Anne said, a bit concerned that his shaking would crack the thin-skinned pig.

"Do you want to see all my treasures?" Ben asked, always eager to show his small hoard to his mother.

"Sure," Anne said. She'd seen them countless times, but she still enjoyed it when Ben wanted to show her his most valued possessions.

He took a shoebox from under his bed and methodically laid out his little treasures on the bedspread.

"What's your favorite thing?" Anne asked, although she already knew the answer.

"My puzzle box is the most fun."

Ben had worked for days to figure out how to open it. He still liked to fiddle with it, doggedly believing there might be a second secret compartment.

"These are my first favorite," Ben said, picking up a pair of Eric's gold cuff links. "I love them because they were my dad's."

Anne stared wistfully at her husband's favorite cuff links. He never wore them, but they were a gift from his father and had a lot of sentimental value. She had other jewelry from Eric: tie clips, rings including one with a ruby she'd had made for him, and other sets of rarely worn cuff links. Someday she would divide them between Ben and Liddie, but they were both a little young to be responsible for the items now.

"This is my lucky pencil," Ben was saying when Liddie ran into the room and did a nosedive onto his bed, scattering some of his precious possessions.

"Liddie, no!" he said, snatching the puzzle box from her hands.

"Ben, be kind," his mother said, taking the box. "Liddie, you know you're not supposed to play with Ben's things unless he says you can."

"You can play with Bear," Ben said, reaching for a well-loved but now ignored stuffed toy. "In fact, you can have him if you'll go back in your room."

"I don't want your dirty old bear," Liddie said. "It smells funny, like Hershey does when he's been out in the rain."

"Does not!" Ben replaced it on the shelf. "At least my room doesn't smell all perfumey like yours."

"That's my fashion doll. She smells wonderful," Liddie said indignantly.

"That's enough!" Anne said, laughing in spite of herself. Next her kids would be smelling each other's feet. "Ben, put away your treasures. Liddie, go to your room and pick out the pajamas you want to wear after your bath. It's time you both get ready for bed."

"I'll find a lot more treasure when I have my metal detector," Ben said.

Anne didn't know how else to discourage him, so she only sighed.

She went to run the bath water and idly wondered whether the statue could've been secreted away by water. No one had put her in charge of the case, but she couldn't help but wonder if there was a simple explanation as to where the statue could be. It surely wasn't far away, or someone would have noticed it tooling down the highway in the back of a truck.

"Mom, I can't find my race car," Ben cried out. "Liddie must have it."

Anne might not be able to find a huge statue, but she quickly found her son's tiny toy under his bed.

Maybe what this town needed was to enlist the help of all the mothers. Who else had more experience finding lost objects?

CHAPTER FOUR

Saturday mornings always seemed so busy, even after the library went on summer hours and closed early. Anne stood behind the checkout counter after locking up for the day and stared at her lengthy to-do list. She'd chauffeured both Ben and Liddie to their activities and wondered what to tackle next.

She hadn't needed to write down her number one concern: the missing statue. The police were looking into who had stolen the statue of Lois Stover, but Anne and her fellow committee members had a pressing deadline. How soon were they going to have to deal with canceling the anniversary ceremony scheduled for two weeks from today?

"Please ring," she said to her cell phone, pulling it out of her pocket and staring at the dark display. Anne was hoping for a call from either Maggie or Harold Buchanan. She'd left messages for both. There was nothing she could do at the moment to unravel all the problems associated with the missing statue.

The library was quiet and deserted, which only emphasized her silent phone. Without any urgent jobs to do in the library, she decided to start a load of laundry. Now that Liddie dressed herself, she liked to change outfits four or five times a day. Ben didn't have nearly as much to wash, but his stains and ground-in dirt were much harder to get out.

Anne was keeping her cell phone in the pocket of her denim skirt so she could hear it over the rhythmic beat of the washing machine. Still, it was an odd but welcome sound when it went off close to her hip.

"Mrs. Gibson, this is Harold Buchanan. I got your message."

"Thanks for calling me back," Anne said. "I understand you've spoken to Maggie Sloan. As you are aware, our committee now has a big decision to make — whether to cancel the ceremony since there's no statue."

"Let's talk it over a bit before you make your recommendation," he said in his distinctive voice.

His baritone was highly prized in the church choir, and he sounded and looked younger than his sixty-some years.

"Yes, we need your advice on what you would like us to do and what you think your father would want," Anne said.

"Tell you what, I was just going to the park to see for myself. Why don't you meet me there?"

"I'd be happy to," Anne said, forcing herself to sound enthusiastic. The empty base made her sad, and she didn't know what she could contribute to solving the mystery.

"Great. I'll see you in about twenty minutes," he said breaking the connection.

Anne thought of calling the other committee members, but until she had something concrete to tell them it seemed pointless. Anyway, Maggie had yet to return her call, so perhaps she was busy.

When she got to the park, it was surprisingly deserted. There were no couples strolling the grounds or senior citizens taking midday walks. It was still very warm but not hot enough to keep people indoors. Apparently, everyone who wanted to see the empty site had done so.

Anne checked her watch and saw that she was on time. There was no sign of Harold Buchanan, but perhaps he'd been too optimistic about how long it would take him to get there.

There was still yellow crime-scene tape surrounding the site, and Anne resisted the temptation to duck under it for a closer look. She was lost in thought when a familiar voice called out to her.

"Hey, Anne, this is good luck finding you here."

Anne spun around and saw Grace Hawkins, the editor and primary reporter for the *Blue Hill Gazette*. She was a pretty, blue-eyed blonde who'd become a good friend to Anne when Grace helped Anne find information about the town history. Today Grace looked particularly perky in a blue-and-white-striped sleeveless top and navy capri pants, but her expression was grim.

"I'm supposed to meet Harold Buchanan here, but he's late," Anne explained. "How are you?"

"Harried, but I'll be better if Mr. Buchanan does show up here. I've been trying to get a statement from him for my lead article, but he's avoided me so far."

"I imagine the theft of the statue hit him hard," Anne said. "It's one of his father's most noteworthy pieces."

"Yes, you'd think he'd be eager to put a plea for its return in the paper, but so far I haven't been able to pin him down," Grace said.

"I imagine he just needs time to process the loss," Anne said, always ready to think the best of people. "It must have been a shock to learn it was missing."

"Yes, I guess so, but maybe this is my chance to get a short interview and a photo—if you don't mind," the reporter/editor said.

"No, not at all." Anne looked in all directions expecting to see Harold walking toward them. "I guess promptness isn't one of his qualities."

"You'd be surprised how many people live in their own time zone," Grace said with a light laugh. "I could write a novel in the time I spend waiting for people to keep appointments."

Anne shared a laugh with Grace.

"That's probably Harold now," Anne said, surveying the grassy expanse. She pointed at the far side of the park where a man in shorts was ambling toward them at a leisurely pace.

When he got closer, Anne had to smile at his pink-and-green plaid shorts and purple dress shirt hanging loose. The artist and former teacher was known for his eccentric outfits, and apparently he'd gone completely off sensible combinations since he'd retired from teaching. When he was a hundred feet or so away, Anne saw that both the shirt and shorts were spattered with paint in an assortment of colors. While Anne stared, Grace snapped photos.

"Sorry I'm late, Mrs. Gibson," he said, tipping an imaginary hat in her direction. "And I know you, don't I?" he said to Grace, "But I'm afraid I've forgotten your name."

"Grace Hawkins, editor of the *Blue Hill Gazette*. I didn't know you'd be here, but I'd like a photograph and a statement about the missing statue."

"A picture in my paint clothes? I'd rather you'd take it when I'm wearing more suitable attire."

His protest was too late. Grace had snapped a series of photos as he'd walked toward them. She was nothing if not quick to take advantage of a subject.

"Do you have any idea who would steal the statue?" Grace asked.

Instead of answering, he ducked under the crime tape and the chain that surrounded the site and stared at the base. Most of the scaffolding had been removed, but a few bolts were still scattered around. Anne was glad Grace let him take in the scene before pressing him for a comment.

"My, my," he said, shaking his head. "Someone went to a lot of trouble to take it."

"Didn't they, though?" Grace said, slipping under the crime tape and taking a few shots of the empty base.

Anne watched, but she wasn't tempted to join them inside the crime scene area. She stopped at stop signs, yielded at yield signs, and always walked in the crosswalk when there was one. She wasn't about to go past the police tape, but that didn't mean she wasn't interested in anything her friends observed.

"You can see where a truck backed up to the statue," Harold said, standing between two cement posts anchoring a chain that ran the circumference of the site.

"Was this how the thieves left things?" Grace asked.

"If it is, they were tidy criminals," Harold said, slowly circling the chained area as though the posts could tell him something.

"There was still scaffolding over the base," Anne said, glad to contribute some information. "The police must have torn it down."

"Can I get you to stand on the edge of the base for a photo?" Grace asked, evidently forgetting the artist didn't want his picture taken.

"I don't think so," Harold said. "It's bad enough one of my father's most famous works has disappeared. I don't see any merit in giving the thieves the satisfaction of media attention."

"Maybe a front-page article would attract the attention of someone who saw the statue being moved," Grace said. "Even if it was covered by a tarp, it would still be visible in the bed of a truck."

Anne agreed with her friend. Even though the theft was old news to the people of Blue Hill, the *Gazette* had subscribers all over the county. An article might remind someone of seeing something suspicious.

"I didn't teach high school all those years without learning a few things," Harold said. "You know what's coming up, don't you?"

"Football practice," Anne said. It was impossible not to know about the upcoming season when her good friend Wendy's husband was the coach.

"Are you suggesting the theft is a prank?" Anne asked.

"It's pretty complicated for a prank," Grace said.

"So was letting a greased pig loose a couple of seasons back," Harold said. "If I remember right, two of our boys were suspended for that."

"The trouble is, this isn't a pig. It's a felony theft. Whoever took it won't get away with a slap on the wrist," Anne said. "What do you estimate the value of the statue to be, Harold?"

"Priceless to me," Harold said. "The town no doubt has a comprehensive policy that covers it, but money can't make up for the loss of one of my father's best pieces."

Anne heard the sadness in his voice and wished there was something she could say to comfort him.

"You're assuming the police won't find it," she said. "It can't be easy to hide something that large. Maybe we'll get it back and won't have to cancel the ceremony."

"That's a possibility," Harold said, not sounding optimistic.

"It can't hurt to put an article in the paper," Grace said, staying on message.

"All right, take your picture," Harold said. "Where should I stand?"

With a minimum of fuss, Grace had him stand between the two cement posts on either side of the track the thieves' vehicle had left. There was a lot of crushed grass, but no clear tire marks.

"That's good," the *Gazette* editor said. "I can get the empty base in the background."

Harold grunted impatiently but stayed put while Grace ran around to get in the right position. He started to walk off as soon as her camera clicked, but Anne called him back.

"We haven't talked about canceling the ceremony," she said.

"It's up to your committee," he said. "But I won't attend unless the statue is returned."

"Then we have no choice except to cancel," Anne said. She had her answer, but it didn't make her happy. So many people had worked so hard to pull off the celebration, maybe they should go ahead even without Mr. Buchanan and his father's statue.

"Wait a minute!" Harold said. He walked over to one of the posts and studied it. "I wonder if the police noticed this."

"What?" Grace and Anne both walked over and saw what he was pointing at: a very small smear of red.

"Probably not," Harold said. "It's such a small mark, it was probably easy to overlook."

"So it is possible the thieves drove a red vehicle," Grace said. "I assume it was a truck since you can't stuff a statue into a hatchback."

"There must be dozens of red pickups in the county," Anne said, unwilling to even consider that Alex's distinctive truck had been used in the theft.

"The paint can be tested and matched to the vehicle it came from," Harold said. "All the police have to do is find a truck with a scratch and test it."

Though Anne was sure Alex wasn't involved with the theft of the statue, she would feel better when she could check his truck and not find a telltale scratch.

Chapter Five

Anne put three peanut-butter-and-jelly sandwiches in Ben's battered backpack from the last school year, then added small bags of chips. Alex was taking Ben and Ryan to a softball game that began at four o'clock, so the snacks should tide them over until dinner.

"It's just you and me for the rest of the afternoon," she said to Liddie, who was busy spreading her paper dolls and their clothes up and down the length of the couch.

The trip to the park to meet Harold had left Anne with more questions than answers. She was eager to talk to Wendy and Maggie about the retired art teacher's opinion on canceling the ceremony. Maybe she could take a few minutes after church in the morning.

The rest of the day seemed to race by. She was giving Liddie a snack, apple slices to be dipped in peanut butter, when she heard the honk of a familiar horn.

"Ben, Alex is here to take you to the ball game with him. Do you need any money?"

"I'm good," he said. "Bye, Mom."

She could hear him racing down the stairs and decided against calling out to remind him to say thank you. It was a blessing that her son could be quite the young gentleman at times. He related well to adults, especially men. Which was good for Ben but sad for

Anne. It should have been Eric taking his son to a ball game, but she was grateful Alex often included Ben in family activities with Ryan.

She wasn't so sure about Ralph Spinner's influence. He was a great neighbor, always willing to help out with her garden. In winter he sometimes used his snow blower to clean out the library's parking area. He had a wonderful sour cherry tree in his backyard, and this year he let Ben pick enough to bring home for a pie. Not only that, he shared his heirloom tomatoes with her, purple-skinned and absolutely delicious.

How could he be a better neighbor?

He could stop filling Ben's head with treasure-hunting tales. A metal detector was an expensive adult toy, not appropriate for a child.

"Mommy, can we go to Mrs. Farley's?" Liddie asked. "I want to show her my paper dolls."

"That's a good idea," Anne said. "Let me call her to find out if she wants company."

"She might be taking a nap," Liddie said solemnly. Now that she no longer took naps, she was fascinated that the older woman sometimes did have a catnap in the afternoon.

"We'll see," Anne said, calling the familiar number on her cell phone.

Not surprisingly, Mildred sounded delighted to have them.

Anne helped Liddie put her paper dolls in a plastic food bag along with the clothes, some still not punched out.

* * *

When Mildred opened her front door, the paper dolls were of secondary importance. Liddie made a beeline for the kitchen where Mildred had already put her prized Red Riding Hood cookie jar in the middle of the kitchen table. Not only was it a popular collectible, the cookie jar was always well stocked. Within minutes Liddie had carefully removed the lid and helped herself to one of Mildred's homemade chocolate chip cookies. Mildred poured a glass of milk to go with it, and the two women went into the living room to chat after putting the cookie jar up high out of Liddie's reach.

"I saw Harold Buchanan in the park," Anne said. "He doesn't have any interest in going on with the celebration."

"I guess that's understandable. He must be upset about the theft. But a lot of people have worked hard to make it an important community event. I think the committee should go ahead with it, only make it a memorial ceremony."

"That sounds good," Anne said. "We can honor the town's most famous woman without having her statue in front of us."

"Who doesn't love a picnic in the park? I wouldn't be surprised if half the town turns out," Mildred said in a confident tone.

Liddie bounded into the room with chocolate smeared on her face and hands. Anne hurried to clean her up before she left handprints in places they didn't belong.

* * *

"You've given me a lot of encouragement," Anne said as they were leaving. "I'll talk about your idea with Maggie and Wendy. I suspect they'll both hate to have all their work to go for nothing."

"Well, let me know how it comes out," Mildred said. "I was going to donate two gallons of lemonade, but I can buy another jug to fill if you need it."

"Maggie has taken charge of food," Anne said. "But I'll be sure to mention your offer to her."

As she drove home with her daughter, Anne thought about Mildred's suggestion. The celebration could become a fitting way to honor the state's first female architect, or it could turn into just a big picnic without the focus of the statue. She'd have to talk it over with Wendy and Maggie, the two committee members who'd put the most effort in planning for it.

Meanwhile, it was suppertime and Ben wasn't home yet. She wasn't worried. She knew how softball games could drag on into extra innings, so she made a light supper for Liddie and herself, and she put kibble out for Hershey. Once Anne convinced her daughter that eggs weren't just for breakfast, they enjoyed cheese omelets with toast points.

Liddie went from table to tub, and soon she was snuggled into her favorite pajamas and waiting for her brother's return.

"Is Ben in trouble?" she asked.

"No, it's not his fault he's late. The game probably went into extra innings."

"What's an inning?" Liddie asked, always curious about new words.

"Three outs," Anne said, then realized that wasn't an answer that would satisfy her daughter. She spent the next ten minutes trying to explain softball.

When Liddie went back to her paper dolls, Anne looked out the window that overlooked the library parking area. After a few minutes she was pleased to see Alex drive up in his truck, the truck's crane upright in the bed.

"Stay here, Liddie. I'm just going to run down and thank Alex for taking Ben with him."

No doubt her son would remember to thank Alex, but Anne enjoyed her renewed friendship with her high school sweetheart. It brightened her day when they had a chance to talk, and she was pretty sure he wouldn't be in a hurry to leave.

"How was the ball game?" she called out as she went through the door.

"Mom, you should've been there," Ben said, dancing with excitement.

"I didn't think you'd want to ride in the bed of my truck," Alex teased.

"No, and last time I took Liddie to an event where she had to sit for a long time, it was a disaster."

"It went thirteen innings, and our team won," Ben said. "Can Ryan stay overnight?"

Before Anne could make a decision, Alex spoke up. "You guys have had enough fun for one day."

They began chasing each other around the truck, and Anne knew it was time to call a halt to their play. She walked around to the passenger side of the truck to cut Ben off, but what she saw made her freeze in her tracks.

The otherwise pristine red paint on the side of the truck was marred by an indentation that showed the metal underneath.

The boys ran around her, but she no longer gave them her attention. She was too shocked by what she saw.

"That's a nasty scratch," Anne said, staring at the indentation on the cab of Alex's truck as he came to stand by her.

"Now where did that come from?" he asked, more to himself than her.

"You didn't know it was there?" Her throat felt scratchy and constricted. The telltale red paint left on the post anchoring the chain fencing around the empty statue base seemed a perfect match to his vehicle color. "How could you damage it like that and not know you hit something?"

"Easy, I wasn't driving when it happened. It looks like I loaned my truck one time too many."

"Who borrowed it?"

He looked perplexed and paused before answering.

"Any one of several people could've had a minor scrape and been afraid to tell me."

"Who?" she asked, not satisfied with his vague answer.

"I'm not going to name names until I have a chance to talk to everyone who borrowed it recently," he said evasively.

She could understand why he wanted to get the facts before accusing anyone, but she felt sick to her stomach at the thought that Alex himself might have been involved in the theft of the statue. In her heart of hearts she knew he couldn't be and yet....

She herded Ben upstairs, torn between suspicion and worry. Even if Alex was innocent, people were going to suspect him once they heard about the paint scratch. His business was based on his honesty and integrity. Could the paint on the post bring everything tumbling down for him?

Chapter Six

"Come on kids. We'll be late for church," Anne called to Ben and Liddie.

"I'm ready," Liddie said. "Ben isn't." She smoothed the skirt of her favorite yellow dress and made sure her matching socks were pulled up.

"Ben, let's go," Anne called out.

She was eager to sit in silent prayer and reflect on her faith—and all the questions that had been on her mind since the night before. How did the scratch get on Alex's truck? Did his paint really match the smear on the post at the park? Anne had a good eye for color, and they seemed to be the same. But she couldn't believe Alex was involved in anything illegal.

"Can Hershey sleep on my bed until we get back?" Ben asked.

Ben's chocolate Labrador retriever was a one-dog disaster when they left him alone in the apartment.

"He can't sleep on my bed," Liddie said. "He chews everything."

"You know the answer, Ben," Anne said. "Now put Hershey in his pen."

Ben made a game of enticing his dog into what was actually a very roomy carrier. Anne checked her watch and was about to confine the dog herself when Hershey followed a doggy treat into his pen.

"We could put him in the car. Then I could show him to my friends," Ben said.

"You know it's too hot for him to stay in a vehicle," Anne said firmly. "Now give Hershey some fresh water. We have to leave."

They weren't late for the service, but by the time Anne walked Liddie to her Sunday school room, she had to hurry to take her place on a pew. She'd hoped to talk to Maggie before church since the reverend's wife was frequently surrounded by friends afterwards. The sooner Maggie and the other committee members made a decision about either going ahead with or canceling the rededication ceremony, the easier it would be to get the word out.

Reverend Tom gave one of his better sermons, and Anne could almost see Jesus wandering hot, dusty hills to preach to the crowds and teach his disciples. It was astonishing how few worldly goods they needed to survive. It put her small problems in perspective.

She didn't need to look for Maggie after the service. Her friend found her the minute she left her pew.

"We need to talk," Maggie said with urgency. She looked particularly festive in a chiffon print dress, an unusual choice for her, but her face was troubled. "Walk outside with me."

Many members of the congregation had the same idea, standing in front of the church to visit with friends. Maggie led Anne away from the crowd to a place on the side of the building where no one would hear them.

"Why so secretive?" Anne asked, concerned about picking up her children in their Sunday school classes.

"I just don't want to start any rumors before the committee members have made up their minds."

"I talked with Harold," Anne said. "He thinks the whole thing should be canceled, but he didn't convince me. I think a memorial remembrance for Blue Hill's most famous woman would be very appropriate even without the statue."

"I tend to agree with you," Maggie said, "but it would be nice if we could get the sculptor's son to participate. I wonder how his father feels about it."

"He's in a nursing home, isn't he?" Anne asked.

"Yes. I wonder if anyone told Arlen Buchanan about the theft of the statue," Maggie said. "My husband visits there from time to time. He's mentioned that Mr. Buchanan has some memory problems—he's better some days than others. I'm afraid if you want a Buchanan at a ceremony, you'd better persuade Harold."

'I'm not sure I can, but I'll give it one more try. Meanwhile, I'll see how Wendy feels about going ahead with some kind of event."

"Good. I'll get a consensus from the other people who've been helping," Maggie said. "If you can convince Harold, I don't see any other obstacles. Everyone loves a picnic in the park."

Anne wasn't sure she could convince Harold to participate, and she doubted his father was lucid enough to persuade him. She hurried to collect her children so their teachers could leave.

When they got home, Anne started preparing the seasoned meat for tacos. She usually gave the children some say in what they had for Sunday noon dinner, and she was pleased with their choice. Mildred had given her a large tomato from her garden, and it was perfect to chop up for their tacos.

Ben took Hershey outside and threw a ball for him to chase until Anne called him in to eat. Liddie entertained herself with her paper dolls. Both children were hungry enough that she didn't have to call them twice.

It didn't take long for Ben to get back to his favorite subject: treasure hunting with a metal detector.

"Can I go to Mr. Spinner's house when I'm through eating?" he asked as he hurriedly bit into his second taco.

"Don't stuff your food," Anne automatically told him. "And I don't think it's a good idea to bother Mr. Spinner on a Sunday. He may be expecting company or something."

"If company comes, I'll run home right away. I promise."

"When we're through eating, I'll think about it," Anne said.

"Oh, Mom, it takes Liddie forever to eat. Do I have to wait for her to finish?"

Anne didn't say anything since Ben already knew the answer.

Instead of giving him permission to go, Anne decided she really should speak to her neighbor. If Ben was making a nuisance of himself, she hoped the elderly gentleman would be honest enough to say so.

"Let's clear the table, and we'll all walk over to Mr. Spinner's house," Anne said.

"Oh, Mom," Ben moaned, but he pitched in to help clean the kitchen.

"I have to see for myself if he really wants you hanging around."

It was a pleasant day for August, not overly hot like it had been, and a nice breeze made their short walk to the neighbor's a pleasure, even for Liddie who walked hand-in-hand with Anne.

Mr. Spinner had his garage door open and was pounding on something on his workbench, but he immediately left it to greet Anne and her children.

"How's my buddy today?" he asked Ben. "Ready for a little treasure hunting?"

"About that...," Anne began. "I don't want Ben to become a nuisance."

"He's no nuisance," Mr. Spinner said. "We have a great time together, don't we, Ben? I was hoping to take him over to the elementary school playground. I've never found anything spectacular there, mostly just small change, but it's a good place to practice with the metal detector. With your permission, of course, Mrs. Gibson. You'd be welcome to come along and watch."

"Please, Mom," Ben said. He wasn't usually one to beg and coax, but it was easy to see how much this meant to him.

"All right," Anne said. "Liddie and I will come watch for a little while. She loves the play equipment at the school. Are you sure it's all right to treasure hunt there?"

"Yes, as long as the turf is replaced properly. That's one of the things I want to teach Ben."

They made a little procession, Ben leading the way at a gallop but running back to the elderly man's side at frequent intervals. Liddie wasn't a fast walker, but she was enthusiastic about playing at the school. Anne wondered if other children were taking advantage of the climbing and sliding equipment, but the playground behind the building was vacant.

"Where should we try first?" Mr. Spinner asked Ben.

Her son glowed with pride as he picked their spot at the bottom of a high slide. When the metal detector indicated a find, even Liddie stopped playing to watch Ben carefully remove a clump of grass with a small metal garden spade.

"It's money!" he called out, removing a dirt-encrusted coin from the hole he'd dug.

He began cleaning it on the leg of his shorts, making his mother sigh. No wonder getting Ben's clothes clean was such a challenge.

"Wow," Mr. Spinner said. "You have yourself a Kennedy half dollar. Don't find one of those every day."

As happy as Anne was for her son, she was afraid his success would only increase his eagerness to own a metal detector. His meager savings wouldn't begin to buy one, and her budget was a little too tight to include the purchase of any she'd seen online.

Liddie got tired and wanted to go home, but Ben seemingly couldn't get enough treasure hunting. Anne told him he could stay another half hour, then walked home with her daughter.

Ben came home on time, clutching three grimy pennies along with the half dollar.

"See, Mom, a metal detector would pay for itself in no time," he said.

"Pennies don't add up very fast," Anne said, then was a little ashamed of herself for raining on her son's parade. There was nothing wrong with his enthusiasm. He was a bright boy. He'd eventually accept that a metal detector was too expensive.

Or maybe he wouldn't. When she tucked him into bed that evening, he was still telling her about all the treasures Mr. Spinner had found.

"It's a real spike from railroad tracks," he told her in a sleepy voice. "I'd sure like to find one of those for my collection."

Anne didn't comment. Instead she kissed her son's forehead and left the room.

Today had been the children's day. She was happy to spend all of Sunday with them, but she still hadn't talked to Wendy. Anne thought of calling, then decided not to. Her friend had kids to put to bed, and her husband seemed to have a multitude of meetings and jobs to do now that football season was approaching.

* * *

Monday morning was cloudy with a chance of rain before noon. Both of her children were in gloomy moods that matched the dark gray sky. They staged a small rebellion against going to their caregiver.

"I could help you in the library," Ben offered.

"Oh, sweetheart, Mrs. Pyle is coming to help today. I'm afraid I don't have any jobs to keep you busy."

She knew how long Ben's attention span was when it came to the library. In half an hour he'd be following her like a puppy, begging to go over to Mr. Spinner's house by himself.

"I could do puzzles," he said.

"You know all the ones in the Children's Room are much too easy for you."

Anne stood up from the table just as Liddie tried to climb off her chair and managed to put her elbow in the remains of her cereal. Milk went all over, mostly on Liddie's pink T-shirt and matching shorts.

"Happy Monday," Anne said under her breath as she hustled Liddie to her room to find a clean outfit.

"I hate that," Liddie said as Anne laid out a neon green shirt and plain white shorts. *Hate* was her latest buzzword, although Anne strongly discouraged it.

"If you don't hurry and get dressed, you'll be late." It was all Anne had to say to get her daughter moving. Liddie hated being late for anything.

By the time Anne got back to the library, the peace and quiet of the old building was calming. She didn't have to wait long for her friend Wendy to show up for her turn as a volunteer. Much as Anne appreciated all her helpers, she was especially happy it was Wendy's turn. She needed to talk to her about going ahead with the ceremony.

"You can't believe what a weekend we had," Wendy said. "I haven't seen Chad so upset in ages, and I had to resolve one crisis after another with the kids."

"What's wrong?" Anne asked with concern. Wendy's football coach husband was usually good-natured and low-key.

"It's all about the missing statue," Wendy said. "Chad thinks he knows who's responsible."

"Who?" Anne asked in surprise.

"Well, he doesn't know the names of the thieves, but he's pretty sure the theft is related to football pranks." Wendy lowered her voice as an elderly man came into the library and went directly to the newspaper rack as he did every morning.

"His team?" Anne asked.

"Not necessarily. Kids from Deshler are his first guess. Apparently, our team did something involving a pig on the field during last year's game. If the Deshler players stole it, maybe it was for revenge."

"Oh dear," Anne said, realizing how complicated it would be to pin down the thieves. The statue could be hidden in a player's barn.

"Yes, oh dear," Wendy said, going through the motions of sorting through returned books. "Maybe we'll go to the away game with Deshler and see our bronze Lois Stover standing on the fifty-yard line. But it could be even worse."

"That sounds bad enough," Anne said.

"Two years ago Deshler stole a trophy Blue Hill got as league champions. You can see where this is going. The pranks keep escalating in seriousness. Stealing the Stover statue could be the latest payback."

"As head coach, Chad has to find the culprits," Anne concluded. "I can see why he's upset."

"One suspicion is even worse: Maybe some of our players stole it to frame Deshler. They're the only team with much chance of beating us this season. If they're blamed, the long-standing rivalry might grind to a halt. The powers that be would certainly cancel this year's game."

"Harold mentioned something about high school pranks," Anne mused. "There could be some truth in the theory, but how will Chad find the real culprits?"

"I don't know," Wendy said with a deep sigh. "He knows kids, but he's no detective."

"Maybe the police will come up with something," Anne said, trying to sound optimistic.

"I hope so. If kids in either town did it, sooner or later someone will slip up, maybe bragging to friends."

Anne liked Wendy's theory, but she wasn't completely convinced. It seemed like a lot of trouble for a high school prank.

CHAPTER SEVEN

The weather was pleasant, and the distance to Harold Buchanan's house was less than a mile, but Anne had only gone a couple of blocks before she wished she'd gone by car.

Because of a special summer trash pickup, Blue Hill looked like one of those community summer garage sales that went on for mile after mile, only nothing was for sale along the sidewalks of this town. On the contrary, neighbors and strangers were picking through the accumulations left by the curbs, no doubt hoping to find something of value the owners had overlooked.

She saw a man in overalls pull up and throw two broken kitchen chairs on the bed of his beat-up truck. It was already half full of sad-looking furniture. People were always out scavenging on trash days or after storms, Anne thought. A basement would flood after a bad thunderstorm, people would sadly put their ruined possessions out on the curb to go to the dump, and someone would inevitably show up to take anything that looked usable before the sanitation workers arrived.

Did the man in overalls think the broken furniture he was taking had value? Anne wondered. Would he be looking for someone's hidden money, jewels, or other valuables in the upholstery? Was he going to demolish all of it in hopes of finding a cache of jewelry, or was he just a hoarder who couldn't resist anything free?

Anne loved mysteries and puzzles, but she never could understand the treasure-hunting mentality. She thought the reality shows on cable television encouraged people to believe that secret wealth was hidden in attics, basements, and trash piles. All the talk about Lois Stover's hidden jewelry was bound to get people looking for any sort of other hidden valuables around town. Anne thought to herself that the main treasures hidden in attics and basements were the memories the items contained of those who had gone before.

What would Ben drag home if he had the chance? Anne shuddered at the thought and nearly tripped over a plastic shower curtain that had fallen across the sidewalk. She was all in favor of a good housecleaning from time to time, but this treasure hunt bordered on lunacy.

Anne continued walking, watching for debris that could trip her up. She was surprised to see an old wicker doll's buggy and was tempted to take it for Liddie until she saw its damage was irreparable.

"Mrs. Gibson," a familiar voice said. Ralph Spinner was going in the opposite direction carrying an old suitcase with lots of travel stickers pasted on it. "You caught me out picking through the neighborhood trash."

"You and half the town, it appears," she said with a forced laugh. "I was even tempted by a little wicker doll's buggy, but it was too damaged to repair."

"Yeah, I saw that. Would've brought a pretty penny at an antiques shop if it were in pristine condition," Ralph said.

"What are you going to do with the suitcase?" she asked, curiosity overcoming her determination not to pry.

"No idea, but it's from the 1920s from the look of the labels. Maybe I can sell it online. Well, say hello to my little buddy. I won't hold you up."

Anne passed several other people she knew, but fortunately they were too involved in their housecleaning/treasure hunt to engage her in conversation. She managed to get to Harold's house with only one more hazard—a coil of rusty wire had snaked its way across the sidewalk, and Anne narrowly missed getting her foot caught in it.

Harold's neighborhood was older but also more elegant than most in Blue Hill. Stately Victorian homes, cared for lovingly over the years, and only a few had been turned into duplexes. The retired art teacher's home wasn't the largest, but it was one of the most charming with gingerbread trim painted a beguiling shade of ivory to highlight the Wedgewood blue siding. It was clear that Harold had put a great deal of thought and talent into his home.

She didn't have to use the old-fashioned door knocker to get his attention. Harold was standing in the open doorway of his detached garage surrounded by open and closed boxes.

"Are you treasure hunting too?" she asked.

He laughed in response.

"No, and I don't believe in the tooth fairy either. I started weeding out things in the house shortly after my last class at the high school. It's pretty well done now, but I still have the garage and my workshop. For a long time I thought I'd try some assemblage art, so I bought every odd piece of junk I found."

"I saw an exhibit by California assemblage artists when I lived in New York," she said. "Some of the trash they used was pretty unusual. I especially remember an old claw-foot bathtub."

"Well, I've decided it's not for me. I love layering oil paint on canvas too much to waste my time on anything else."

"You even have paintings hanging in your garage," Anne said with surprise when her eyes got used to the dim interior.

"Most are my rejects—at least ones I'm not particularly attached to. My better pieces are in my workshop. Would you like to see them?"

"I'd love to!" Anne said, temporarily forgetting her reason for being there.

Harold unlocked the door of his prefab studio. It was only a long, metal building on the outside, but when Anne stepped inside she was genuinely wowed. A riot of color surrounded her on all sides. She didn't know where to look first.

"This is incredible!" she said. "When did you have time to paint all these and still teach at the high school?"

"When painting is the most important thing in your life, you make time," he explained in a kindly voice.

Anne noticed that some of the paintings stacked against the wall had price tags on them. Apparently, Harold had tried to sell them without success. She could see why. They started at a hundred dollars and went up from there. There probably weren't enough art collectors in Blue Hill to provide a market for his work.

"I'm flabbergasted," she said. "I'd heard that you were good, but these are dazzling."

She paused in front of a scene of a prairie fire, the colors so expertly applied she could almost smell the acid wind sweeping across the canvas.

"You're not by any chance here to buy a painting, are you?" he asked.

"I wish I were. That mountain scene would look spectacular hanging in the library, but unfortunately our budget doesn't allow for much besides new books."

"Too bad. As you can see, I'm drowning in my paintings. It wouldn't matter so much if I had any relatives to leave them to, but when my brother died, that left only my father and me. But if you're not here to buy, how can I help you?"

"Almost everyone who's worked on the rededication for Lois Stover wants to go ahead with a memorial ceremony whether the statue is found or not," Anne said.

"Which it probably won't be," he said with a tone of regret.

"Either way, Lois Stover is still the most famous woman who ever lived in Blue Hill. And people remember your father's spectacular statue even if it's not in the park. The only thing missing now is the artist's talented son."

"I'm sorry, but it's not something I'm prepared to do. Now that I'm retired, time is precious to me. I have to select some paintings to display in a Philadelphia gallery. And possibly I'll decide to do a few new ones before I take them there."

"That sounds great. When do you have to deliver them?"

"November," he said, busily restacking some canvases.

Anne racked her brain trying to think of a way to persuade Harold to come to the ceremony. He obviously was looking for any excuse not to attend. A few hours didn't seem like a terrible waste of time.

"I understand if your father is too ill to attend a community event, but don't you want to represent him?"

"My father has some dementia. Some days he's lucid, but more often than not, he isn't sure who I am. I assure you, he doesn't care about anything but his colored pencils and his next meal."

"I'm sorry to hear that."

She regretted Harold's refusal to take part, but she had a glimmer of an idea.

"Now that you're retired, I imagine you'll have a lot of time to paint," she said.

"I can hardly wait to get this cleaning done so I can give it my full attention. I especially like mixing my own paints, and that's time consuming."

"Do you see yourself doing a painting a month or one every week?"

"More likely one every three or four days. I tend to work on more than one at a time to give the paint time to dry properly."

"So this time next year, you may have hundreds stacked up?"

"I have high hopes for the Philadelphia gallery," he said a bit defensively.

"How many paintings are they taking?"

He looked uncomfortable but reluctantly answered, "Six."

"Six." She didn't point out how few that was given his output, but she had an idea.

"Have you ever thought of having an Art-in-the-Park show to give people in Blue Hill a chance to buy some?"

"It takes more time than I want to spend to pull off something like that," he said, standing in front of an uncompleted painting on his easel.

"Not if you have an ambitious committee to take care of all the details." Anne had her fingers crossed, not at all sure whether Harold would like her idea.

"What are you suggesting?" he asked in a puzzled voice.

"There will be hundreds of people in the park for Stover's memorial ceremony. Why not set up a nice display of your work? It's not impossible that you'll make a few sales to thin down what you have here."

Anne held her breath. Would Harold embrace her idea or throw her off his property?

"You'd arrange for tables and such?" he asked, frowning so the lines in his forehead deepened.

"Anything you need." Anne hoped the rest of the committee would go along with the idea.

"What's the catch?"

"Half the town sees your art. Maybe you sell some."

"And?"

"If you want to, you can say a few words about your father's statue—but that's strictly optional. Having your art displayed for sale will enhance the celebration."

"A one-man show, though...*Hmm*," he said, apparently still thinking about it.

Anne glanced at her watch. "I have to be going. Do think it over," she said.

"Let's do it. And if the mountain painting doesn't sell, I'll donate it to the library."

"That would be wonderful," Anne said. "We'll talk more later."

Anne felt as though she was walking on air when she left Harold. She'd enlisted him for the celebration, but a more somber thought lurked at the back of her mind. She'd just promised him a chance to sell his art in the park. Who else would come forward and want their own table or booth? Would the park be crowded with embroidered pillowcases and knit baby booties? When word got around about Harold's paintings, how many other people would want space? They would need rules—no used merchandise for a start. But the rest of the committee had no idea what she'd had to offer Harold to ensure his presence.

She had one more stop to make before she hurried back to the library. Then she had to break the news to Wendy and Maggie and hope they would go along with an art show for Harold Buchanan.

As time consuming as planning the Stover memorial was, it wasn't at the forefront of her worries. Her mind kept going back to the scratch on Alex's truck. Did the paint scraped onto the post at the park come from his truck? And if so, how did it get there? Could Alex's truck have been used to steal the statue? It was just too much for Anne to believe.

CHAPTER EIGHT

Anne liked going to the *Blue Hill Gazette*. The newspaper office had a cheerful Victorian facade, but it was the editor who made it a pleasure to visit. Grace Hawkins was young to be in charge of the publication, but her lively intellect more than qualified her for the job. In spite of their busy lives and rare chances to get together, Anne enjoyed her good friendship with Grace.

"Hello. Anyone here?" Anne called out through the empty reception area. She knew where to go and what to do to find what she wanted, but she wouldn't dream of searching without Grace's approval.

"What can I do for you?" the editor asked as she stepped out of her enclosed office. "Oh, Anne, what a nice surprise."

"It's nice to see you too," Anne said, "but I'm afraid I'm about to make a nuisance of myself."

"You could never do that," Grace said as she walked toward Anne. "What's up?"

"I need to find all the articles about pranks related to local football games," Anne said.

"How far back?"

"Three years should do it."

"Today is your lucky day. I just pulled all I could find and scanned them onto my computer," Grace said.

"Then you're suspicious of the team's involvement in the theft of the statue?" Anne was relieved to hear of Grace's interest.

"Come into my office," she said. "I'll show you what I came up with."

Half an hour later, Anne had a picture of rival schools doing all they could to disrupt their traditional enemies. The team at Deshler was mentioned the most, but Blue Hill had done their share of mischief.

Was stealing the statue the climax of a long-standing rivalry? If so, was Deshler's team responsible? Or had Blue Hill taken it to throw suspicion on their opponents?

"I see possibilities," Anne said when she'd read all that Grace had pulled from the newspapers. "What are you going to do with this information?"

"Not sure yet." Grace twirled a lock of her golden hair around her finger, a sure sign that she was perplexed. "To be fair, I probably should talk to both coaches, but no doubt they'll both try to defend their players. What makes it complicated is that the theft of the Stover statue is a felony. That makes it a police matter, and I don't want to step on their toes before their investigation is over."

"I see what you mean," Anne said. "But maybe if we talk to the players we can keep the police out of it. We just want to get the statue back, not ruin anyone's life over a stupid school prank. I think I'll call Wendy and see what she could find out."

It seemed more and more plausible that football players could be involved in the statue's disappearance, but she didn't have any hard facts to explain Alex's scratched truck. In her heart she was sure he would never steal anything, but she also didn't understand how he could not have noticed picking up such a nasty scratch on his truck.

Was there anything else she could do to establish his innocence? She knew she should ask him about it, even though she had a nagging feeling that it was none of her business. Still, they'd become close in the time since he'd remodeled Aunt Edie's Victorian house to use as a library. She didn't want to see Alex blamed for something he didn't do.

"So what are you thinking, now that you've read the articles?" Grace asked.

"Well, obviously the two teams have a fierce rivalry and they aren't above playing childish tricks, but stealing the statue is much more serious than anything they've done in the past."

"Maybe you should leave it to the police to find out who's behind it," Grace said in a mild voice.

"You're right, of course, but I still think it would be better if we could just get the statue back quietly." Anne debated whether to tell Grace her motivation for caring. "If I tell you something, will you promise not to put it in the paper?"

"Of course," Grace said without hesitation. "I'll keep it strictly off the record. I put friends first, then the *Blue Hill Gazette*."

Slowly at first, then with increasing agitation, Anne told her about the scratch on Alex's truck and the red smear on the post near where the statue had been.

Grace sat down on the edge of the desk and was silent for a few long seconds.

"There's only one thing you can do," Grace finally said.

"What?"

"Talk to Alex about the paint on the post. He may have a perfectly reasonable explanation of how his truck got scratched."

"You're right," Anne said. "I shouldn't jump to conclusions until I have all the facts. Quite a few people drive his truck. As a contractor, he hires part-time help all the time and lets them use it on jobs. Maybe the paint on the post isn't even from his truck."

"Exactly," Grace said, sliding off the desk. "And his truck could have even been stolen, then returned. It wouldn't take much for someone to get a duplicate truck key made."

"You always give me a fresh slant on things," Anne said, standing to leave. "Thanks for everything."

"If I can help you in any other way, let me know. Eventually there should be a pretty good story, 'The Case of the Missing Statue.' But I won't publish a word until you give the go-ahead."

"I can't thank you enough," Anne said, hugging her friend. "Just talking to you focused my thoughts. Now I have to get back to the library. I've taken advantage of Remi long enough."

Once she was out on the sidewalk, Anne realized what a long walk she had, complete with an obstacle course. Even the downtown merchants were cleaning back rooms and throwing out old stock and outdated displays.

In spite of her common sense, she saw an adorable pair of gold and black sandals still in the box. When she picked it up, though, they were two different sizes, neither of them hers. She tossed them on the next trash pile she passed and decided to see if it was easier walking on the other side of the busy main street.

As she waited for a car to pass, she failed to see that it was a familiar one until Maggie Sloan pulled up beside her.

"Can I give you a ride?" she called out through her open window.

"That would be lovely," Anne said. Not only would it save her time, but she also needed to talk to Maggie. Here was the perfect opportunity.

"I ran over something back there," Maggie said letting one hand flutter over her shoulder. "I'm afraid it was glass. I hope I don't get a flat tire."

"Do you want me to get out and check the tires?" Anne asked.

"No, if a tire has a slow leak, it will soon let me know. I had one once from running over a sharp stone. The man who patched it said that's pretty rare."

"I have to talk to you about something," Anne said. "It's about Harold Buchanan."

"Oh dear! He's not going to come to the ceremony, is he? I was afraid of that. I guess if the statute is still missing, he doesn't have any connection to Lois Stover."

"As a matter of fact, I found a way to bring him to the ceremony—if the rest of the committee approves," Anne said.

Maggie swerved around a box of books that had fallen off a trash pile and spilled over the street.

"I hate to see books thrown away," Maggie said. "Do you think we should go back and see it there are any you can use for the library?"

"No thank you. I'm kind of in a hurry," Anne said. "About Harold..."

"Oh, I'm sorry. I interrupted your thought, didn't I?"

"That's okay. You know Harold is a very prolific artist. He has a garage and workroom full of his oil paintings, and I didn't even see what he has in the house." Anne watched Maggie's reaction, but she seemed more interested in scanning trash piles.

"All this stuff would make such a good rummage sale for the church," Maggie said. "Now, what do Harold's painting have to do with the celebration?"

"I offered to let him set up his paintings to sell in the park that day." Anne felt a little breathless after blurting out her news.

"Art-in-the-Park," Maggie said thoughtfully. "It might actually add to the excitement of the day, but would he be the only one selling arts and crafts?"

"The committee would have to decide that," Anne said. "You're the first one I've told."

"I don't want it to turn into a flea market," Maggie said. "But a few of Harold's paintings wouldn't be bad. Let me toss the idea around, and I'll get back to you. We might need to run it by Mayor Bultman as well, in case we need special permission for this type of thing. But, I'm sure he wouldn't mind..."

Maggie's reaction was the best Anne could hope for. She got off at the library and hurried inside to relieve her volunteer.

After profusely thanking Remi, Anne saw her off and went behind the desk to do some work. Fortunately, the volunteer had checked in all the returns and left everything in good order.

Anne thought of calling the sitter to see how the kids were but decided to restrain herself and trust Ben to behave. The library was quiet with only a few people browsing in the stacks.

In the peaceful moments, Anne rehearsed in her head what she wanted to say to Alex. She knew he couldn't possibly be involved in the theft of the statue, but she wanted more reassurance that he didn't know anything about it. But Alex didn't come into the library, nor did the other person she wanted to talk to. It was closing time before Wendy came with a stack of books to return.

"I have something to tell you," Anne said. "Or rather, suggest to you. It's about Harold Buchanan."

"Is he still refusing to come to the ceremony?" Wendy was pink cheeked from a day of keeping up with her children.

"Not exactly. Let me lock the door, and we can go up to my apartment for a cold drink. I have some iced tea in the fridge."

"Sounds wonderful," Wendy said. "I can't stay long though. We're having burgers on the grill, and Chad will start them whether I'm ready or not. I have to toss a salad and get the buns ready to warm."

When they were seated at the kitchen table with tall glasses of tea, Anne told her friend about letting Harold display his paintings in the park. Wendy's reaction was almost the same as Maggie's.

"Will he be the only one?" Wendy asked. "I'm afraid if word gets out, the committee will be overwhelmed with requests from other people, and time is pretty short."

"That's a possibility," Anne admitted. "That's why we have to set up rules right away."

"The best would be to limit it to paintings and other artworks. Not turn it into a garage sale," Wendy said thoughtfully. "I can see it working if we do that."

"Good! And in exchange, I think we can get Harold to say a few words about the statue and his father. The art show was the only way I could come up with to get him to the park that day."

"It's a brilliant idea," Wendy said. "Now if we can only find out who stole the statue. Chad is talking to every member of the team, but so far he hasn't learned anything useful. I'm beginning to believe it wasn't our players."

"What about the Deshler coach? Is he checking into whether his team could be involved?" Anne asked.

"Allegedly." Wendy sipped the last of her tea and stood up. "Sorry but I have to run."

"Well, thanks for hearing me out," Anne said. "I don't know whether Harold will sell any paintings, but people should enjoy looking at them."

When Wendy had left, Anne turned her attention to dinner. In only moments she heard footsteps on the stairway leading outside. Liddie bounded into the kitchen, but she was alone, not what Anne expected.

"Where's your brother?" Anne asked.

"He went to Mr. Spinner's garage," Liddie said. "He said to tell you he'll be right home."

Anne was disappointed but didn't say anything to her daughter. Ben knew he was supposed to ask before going somewhere. She debated whether to go find him and decided to give him ten minutes.

"Mom!" he said, rushing into the apartment just before she was ready to look for him. "Mr. Spinner said he wants to sell his metal detector, and he wants me to have it."

"Honey, I'm afraid you don't have nearly enough saved up for something so expensive."

She expected arguing or pouting, but Ben seemed not to have heard her.

"We'll work it out," he said with a secretive smile.

"Not this evening we won't," she said, sending both children to wash up for dinner.

She took corn dogs from the oven and stirred the green beans on the stove. Wouldn't it be wonderful if there were a huge metal detector to detect the missing statue? She could imagine it flying over barns and empty warehouses until the signal beeped to betray the location.

But whether it was ever found or not, she refused to believe Alex was involved in the theft.

Somehow there had to be an explanation for the paint on the post. And she had to work up the nerve to ask him. If she didn't word her questioning just right, Alex would think she didn't trust him, and she certainly didn't want that.

A prank by football players seemed plausible, but it was a lot of work for teenagers. And it was a prank that could lead to a jail sentence.

Chapter Nine

Anne looked up from the checkout desk Tuesday morning to see Wendy heading toward her, an unfamiliar teenage boy in tow.

"Hi, Wendy," she said, trying to keep her tone light.

"Hi, Anne," Wendy said. "This is Derek Umsted."

Anne extended her hand to the boy clad in a football jersey emblazoned with the number 36.

"Nice to meet you, Derek," she said as he took her hand and pumped it vigorously.

"Nice to meet you too, Mrs. Gibson."

Anne smiled at his good manners. "I don't remember seeing you in here before."

He reddened, and Anne was sorry she'd embarrassed him.

"I'm not much of a reader, Mrs. Gibson," he said. "But my older brother is. Maybe you've seen him in here before, Mitch Umsted?"

The name was vaguely familiar to Anne.

"He's a big reader," Derek added. "But mostly nonfiction, like sports biographies and magazines."

Anne nodded encouragingly.

"He's a couple years older than me," Derek said. "Works a couple different jobs and does some sign lettering too."

Anne waited expectantly for more, but the teenager seemed to have talked himself out. She glanced at Wendy, hoping to see some sign that she had brought Derek to the library to talk about high school pranks.

"Derek plays football for Blue Hill High School. He's a junior," Wendy said.

"The jersey was kind of a giveaway," Anne teased.

"Tell Mrs. Gibson what you told my husband," Wendy said.

Anne waited patiently while the teenager reddened and looked down and shuffled his feet.

"Me and the guys were talking, and none of us know anything about that statue missing out at the park. Honest. So they elected me to go tell Coach Pyle. Believe me, I know we've done stuff in the past but not this."

Wendy patted the teenager on the shoulder. "Thank you, Derek."

"Yes," Anne said, "thanks so much for telling me."

The boy seemed to relax when neither she nor Wendy asked him any more questions.

"Do you mind if I get going? I have to return Mr. Ochs's truck. I picked up a load of lumber for him."

"You work for Mr. Ochs?" Anne asked, the wheels in her head turning full speed.

"Only part-time," the teenager answered. "Less now that football practice is starting up."

Anne thanked Derek again for coming in. She waited until he left to ask Wendy the question first and foremost on her mind.

"Do you believe him?"

Anne watched her friend think for a minute before answering.

"Yes, I actually do," Wendy said. "He's one of the most trustworthy kids on varsity this season."

"Me too," Anne said. "It would be much easier to catch the thieves if Blue Hill football team members stole the statue to blame Deshler. But I'm awfully glad they didn't."

Wendy sighed. "It would break Chad's heart if his boys pulled something like that. And by the way, he talked to the Deshler coach who insists his team members don't know anything about it either."

"It would take a lot of planning ahead of time and a big vehicle to haul it away." Anne was thinking out loud.

"And someone clever enough to avoid getting caught. They must have known the town's patrol car on night duty was on the other side of town whatever night it was taken." Wendy looked at her watch and said she needed to go home and put another load in the washing machine. "I want to be all caught up before the kids start bringing home smelly practice jerseys. The kids are supposed to put them into the machine rather than my having to touch them."

"Sounds like a good idea. I'll remember it if Ben gets into sports. Thanks again for helping check this out," Anne said. "I agree with you. Derek seemed genuinely baffled about how the statue disappeared."

After Wendy left, Anne started shelving books, but her mind was on this new information. If Alex had loaned his truck to a teenage boy to run an errand, who else had borrowed it? Had whoever been driving it used it to steal the statue?

She desperately wanted Alex to be innocent — and she believed he was. But if his truck was used in the robbery, he would want to know it. He was the only one who could help identify possible suspects.

The rest of Tuesday afternoon dragged by. The library wasn't busy, and she couldn't keep Alex and his truck out of her mind. She needed to talk to him before reaching a conclusion, but in her heart she was sure he was innocent.

Making dinner and getting her kids ready for bed relieved her stress. She enjoyed Liddie's story time as much as her daughter did, but it was interrupted by an odd clinking noise coming from Ben's room.

When she went to check on him, she found Ben sitting in the middle of his bed vigorously shaking his piggy bank. A small pile of coins was between his outstretched legs. From what she could see, they were mostly pennies and nickels.

"What are you doing?" she asked, then realized it was obvious.

"Counting my money," Ben said, his face a mask of innocence.

"Why?"

"To see how much I have."

"Let me put it this way: Why are you counting money when you should be brushing your teeth for bed?"

"I did that already." He did an exaggerated smile to show they were clean.

"Good," Anne said, "but that doesn't tell me why you're shaking out all your coins. It's bedtime, not shopping time."

"I just want to know how much I have." He crawled off the bed and a cascade of coins followed him.

"Okay," Anne said. "Get a plastic bag from the kitchen drawer. I'll start picking these up."

She automatically counted as she pushed the fallen coins into a pile. Since there were so many pennies, the pile only added up to a little more than seventeen dollars.

"I'm going to keep the bank and the money until tomorrow," Anne said. "I don't want you shaking money out of your piggy bank when you're supposed to be going to sleep."

"Can I have it back tomorrow?" Her son looked stricken.

"First thing tomorrow. But morning won't come until you go to sleep." She scooped the rest of the coins from the bedspread in to the plastic bag.

Once both children were settled down for the night, Anne went to the kitchen and made a cup of soothing bedtime tea. She'd brought home the latest library journal to check the list of new books. Unfortunately, her budget for summer purchases was nearly exhausted, but she liked to keep on top of new publications anyway.

Anne turned the magazine's pages without seeing anything that caught her eye. She closed it while still waiting for her tea to cool.

There was one thing on her mind, and she wasn't going to be able to sleep until she talked to Alex. She hated calling him when evenings were his time to bond with Ryan, but she needed some answers to put her mind to rest.

"Anne, what's up?" he asked, sounding happy and relaxed when he answered the phone.

"It's about the scratch on your truck," she said, trying to sound casual.

"Yeah, I'm not sure how it even got there. I should look into it before I call the insurance company. Little dings are tricky. They can cost a lot more to fix than you'd expect."

He didn't sound quite so nonchalant when he talked about the price of repairing it.

"Have you been to the park to check out the posts surrounding the site?" she asked.

"No, I've been tied up at work," he said, sounding puzzled.

Anne took a deep breath before continuing. "Maybe you should go look while it's still light enough to see. Oh, Alex, there's red paint on the post directly behind where the statue was. If it matches your truck, you could be in trouble."

"Really?"

She was relieved he sounded so baffled.

"Ryan's having a sleepover at a friend's, so I'll go right now. Thanks so much for calling me. I'll call you back after I've checked it out."

He hung up, and Anne was so happy she'd called him. If the police matched the paint to his truck, he wouldn't be caught by surprise. If it turned out he'd been involved in the theft, she would be stunned. What possible reason would he have? Her thought went back to selling it for scrap, but surely Alex's contracting business wasn't in enough financial trouble that he'd resort to something ludicrous like that.

She waited on edge for him to call her back and invented things to do. She was a bit ashamed of herself when she opened the bottom of her son's piggy bank and shook out the rest of his money. There was a crisp five-dollar bill, a gift from a grandparent, and several ones. Even with the money in his savings account, the total wasn't much more than sixty dollars. What was Ben thinking?

As tempted as she was to run a hot bath, she didn't want to be soaking in the tub when Alex called back. She was hoping he'd debunk any similarity between the two shades of red.

She was about to give up on hearing from him when there was a soft knock on the outside door. When she raced downstairs to see who was there, it was Alex.

"Kids sleeping?" he asked in a soft voice when she led the way up to her apartment.

"Supposedly. Did you see the paint smear?"

"Yes, I saw it all right."

She was afraid to hear his conclusion, so she offered to pour a cup of coffee for him. "It's decaf," she said.

"No thanks. About the paint smear, it definitely came from my truck. The brick red is pretty distinctive and it's at just the right height."

"Oh, Alex, I'm sorry," she said. "Do you have any idea who could have used your truck?"

"On the way here, I tried to think of everyone who drove my truck or borrowed it in the last couple weeks. Derek Umsted has been working for me this summer on a temporary basis. He parks it at his house sometimes when he doesn't have other transportation to get home."

"That sounds suspicious." Anne wanted someone besides Alex to be a suspect, but she felt awful it could be the earnest teenager she'd just met.

"Not necessarily. I contract out a lot of the work on my jobs: plumbing, electrical work, roofing, backhoe excavation. When

I'm really busy, I call on a couple of carpenters to help me. I'm always sending one or the other to pick up lumber or other supplies. They use my truck for that. Their pickups are too small and they don't have the lift mine has."

"So half the town has access to your truck."

"I guess you could put it that way. It's a tool of my business. I need people using it."

"Where do you keep the keys?"

"In the ignition. It's Blue Hill. People leave their doors unlocked."

"Leaving the keys in the truck seems like an invitation for someone to use it behind your back," she said gently. She had never criticized Alex like this and didn't want to now. But someone had used his truck to steal a beloved monument.

"You're right." He sat down on a chair on the opposite side of her kitchen table and looked discouraged. "If I'm working out of town and one of my men needs wall board or framing lumber on the opposite side of town—well it's a huge savings on labor costs if the keys are in the truck."

"I guess I understand. You don't want to pay someone for the time it takes to find you and the keys in your pocket."

"That's about it," he said in a weary voice.

"Have you called the police department? Talked to Michael?"

"No. It didn't seem important until now."

"They'd probably like to know who had access to your truck," Anne said.

"They won't be thrilled to know it's half the town." He looked so upset as he said his good-byes, Anne felt horrible.

She followed him down to the outside door and watched him drive away in his small pickup. Had she made things better or worse for Alex by telling him about the paint?

One thing was clear: Loaning his truck out so frequently could mean there were now dozens of suspects instead of a few football players carrying out a prank.

CHAPTER TEN

Anne poured cereal into bowls for Ben and Liddie as Hershey snuffled around, hoping some of the sweet puffs would fall to the floor, but her mind wasn't on breakfast. She was thinking about how much their lives had changed since moving back to Blue Hill. It was a wonderful place to raise her children, and she missed the hustle and bustle of New York City much less than she'd expected.

Not for the first time, she gave a silent prayer of thanks for Aunt Edie's bequest. It had allowed her to move her family to her childhood home after Eric's untimely death. Not only had the stately Victorian mansion provided a nice place to live, Anne also had a job she loved—running Blue Hill's library.

Starting over without Eric was terribly hard, and she also missed her aunt's joyful outlook on life. How would Aunt Edie have reacted to the theft of the statue? Anne could imagine her burning up phone connections until she discovered an elusive clue. She'd known almost everyone in town and wasn't the least bit shy about calling in old favors.

Anne's pleasant thoughts about her aunt were interrupted by a loud thump.

"What's going on?" she asked, hurrying to investigate the noise.

She found her children in Liddie's room looking guilty but trying to look innocent. Anne had to suppress a smile as she faced them.

"Well," she asked patiently.

"It was Liddie's idea," Ben piped up immediately.

"What was Liddie's idea?" Anne asked her son as she continued to stifle a grin. The two of them looked so solemn it was hard not to laugh.

Getting no answer, she turned to her daughter. "Liddie?"

Somehow Anne doubted that Liddie was the instigator of whatever mischief had caused the big noise.

Liddie looked down at her feet.

Ben exhaled a big sigh. "Mom, it was my idea."

"What was?" Anne asked.

"To see if we could bounce all the way to the ceiling on Liddie's bed."

Liddie looked up and in all seriousness said, "We couldn't, but Ben's finger almost touched."

Anne was happy her children hadn't been able to bounce so high they bumped their heads on the ceiling, but she realized she needed to do something to keep them active and out of mischief until school started. She knew what might work—at least for Ben.

"Ben," she said slowly. "I think maybe it's time to think about getting you a metal detector."

"Really?" He could hardly contain his excitement.

"Yes, really." Anne hoped she was doing the right thing in allowing Ben to have a beginner's instrument. She worried that he was going to buy into the treasure-hunting fever that was epidemic in Blue Hill lately. But trying to break Liddie's bed and both their heads wasn't a good idea either!

"Now come eat your breakfast, and then we'll talk about getting you the metal detector."

"Mommy, can I get one too?" Liddie asked.

"Liddie, honey, I don't think you'd like one," Anne said diplomatically, hoping her daughter wouldn't put up a fuss over Ben getting something she wasn't. "And Ben will have to pay part of the cost with his own money."

"Okay," Liddie said amicably.

Anne smiled her relief and herded them to the kitchen. As she poured milk on the children's cereal, she hoped it wasn't a bad decision to let Ben get a metal detector. Hopefully, they wouldn't have to eat packaged noodles for a month to afford it.

The only person she knew who owned a metal detector was their neighbor. Before she shopped online, she probably should ask an expert's advice, especially since he'd done much to fire up Ben's enthusiasm.

"Maybe I should talk to Mr. Spinner about the best one for you," Anne said as Ben slurped his cereal and Liddie fished one piece at a time with her spoon.

"He said he'd sell me his," Ben said. "That's why I emptied my piggy bank."

"Oh, honey, I'm sure you don't have enough to buy his. From what I could tell, it's one of the best brands."

"He said he would." Ben pushed away his empty cereal bowl. "Can we go talk to him now?"

Anne glanced at the kitchen clock. She had just half an hour before the kids had to go to their caregiver and she had to open the library.

"Liddie's still eating," Anne said. "We'll go when she's done."

Ben waited impatiently as Liddie slowly finished her cereal.

"We can go now," Anne said, grabbing a damp paper towel to clean her daughter's milky lips. "We'll ask Mr. Spinner's advice but only if he's outside watering his flowers. I'm not going to wake him up or interfere with his breakfast."

"I need my money," Ben said reaching up on the counter where the plastic bag was.

"You won't need it right now," Anne said, preparing to leave.

"Can't I carry it anyway? I promised Mr. Spinner I'd show it to him."

"Okay." She was pressed for time and didn't want to take extra time to convince Ben to leave his money home.

Outside she could see Mr. Spinner across the street watering his lovely marigolds and impatiens.

In his excitement to see his friend, Ben ran across the street without checking both ways for traffic.

"Ben, come back here and cross the right way," Anne said.

She was eager to talk to her neighbor so she could go to work. But that didn't mean she could let Ben run into the street without looking both ways first.

"Mom," he protested as he crossed again to stand by her. "We have to talk to him before he goes inside."

"He's waiting for us," Anne said keeping Liddie's hand in hers. "Now tell me when it's safe to cross."

"No one drives on this street," Ben said.

Anne wasn't going to argue the point, but she was pleased when Ben carefully looked in both directions and gave her the go-ahead. As soon as he reached the far curb, he sprinted toward their neighbor.

"I brought my money," her son announced, waving the plastic bag until Anne was afraid it would break and spill coins everywhere.

"So you did," the elderly man said. "Now Ben, I'd better make sure our deal is okay with your mom."

This was the first she'd heard about a deal. What was Ben up to?

"Here, you can count it," Ben said, thrusting the bag of money at their neighbor.

"Friends don't have to count," Mr. Spinner said. "Your word is enough for me."

"What word?" This got more puzzling by the minute for Anne.

"As you probably guessed when we went to the school yard, my treasure-hunting days are behind me. With my arthritis, it's all I can do to keep up with my garden. I know I have to give up using my metal detector." He gestured toward the interior of the open garage.

"I know a little money has to pass hands. I agreed to sell my detector to Ben for the exact amount in his piggy bank."

"I have money in the bank too," Ben said.

"Not my concern. A deal is a deal — if your mother agrees."

Anne looked at her neighbor's beaming face. He was obviously pleased to let Ben have his metal detector. As for her son, he was clearly excited, eager to put his money in Mr. Spinner's hands.

"Do you think Ben is old enough to handle yours?" Anne asked, beginning to regret her offer to let her son have a metal detector.

"If he has any trouble operating it, I'll be right here to help him."

The last of Anne's reluctance collapsed. She couldn't remember when Ben had been so excited. As long as he didn't trespass in people's yards, he should be all right using his new tool.

"Can I try it out now?" he asked when they got back home.

"No, I want to go with you the first few times." Anne knew she'd feel slightly silly tagging along with the metal detector, but she needed to do it for her peace of mind.

She was nearly five minutes late opening the library, but fortunately no one was waiting outside the door.

The first patron through the door a few minutes later brought a smile to Anne's face. Wendy put a stack of children's books on the counter and grinned at her friend.

"Your choices were spot-on for the kids," she said. "Thanks for taking the time to pull them from the shelves."

"That's what I'm here for," Anne assured her. "What brings you out so early, besides returning books? You're not on the schedule to volunteer."

"No, I just wanted to tell you the news about the Art-in-the-Park idea. Maggie's really enthusiastic about it. In fact, she spent most of last evening talking to people who are working on the ceremony. There wasn't one objection."

"Great! That means Harold will be there for sure," Anne said.

"Better than that. He agreed to allow other talented artists to set up with him. I got the impression he wants to give some of his former students a chance to show what they can do, but he's not eager to get involved with a giant project."

"Once a teacher, always a teacher," Anne said. "I'm delighted!"

"It's going to be quite a day for the community," Wendy said. "And the credit belongs to you."

"Hardly! It's been a group effort from the beginning. You haven't heard whether the police have made any progress in tracking down the statue, have you? Having it back would make the event just about perfect."

"No. Chad has talked with Officer Banks and he's promised to keep in touch if he learns anything that connects the football team to the theft. Naturally, Chad wants the thieves found so his team is definitely cleared. From what he's heard, they still don't have a clue where it is or who stole it."

"It's such a big object to just disappear." Anne frowned and started checking in the books Wendy had returned.

"Yes, but think how many barns and empty buildings there are within a hundred-mile radius. It could be anywhere."

"True. It has to be someplace where it can't be accidently found. But it sounds like we'll have a wonderful tribute to Lois Stover even without it. By the way, I have news of my own."

"About the big day?"

"No, although it's a big day for Ben. I finally agreed to let him have a metal detector. He bought Mr. Spinner's. That is, if you call paying him the contents of his piggy bank enough for the purchase price."

"I always thought he was a sweet man. This certainly confirms it," Wendy said. "Well, I have errands to do. I'll be curious to know how Ben's treasure hunting turns out."

"I suspect he'll find lost pennies and bent nails," Anne said with a smile.

Much as she liked seeing her son so happy, Anne wasn't looking forward to their first metal-detecting expedition.

When she finished working for the day, she changed into jeans, a loose-fitting pink T-shirt and sneakers. She didn't know what Ben considered an appropriate treasure-hunting outfit, but this would have to do.

She'd planned to make spaghetti for dinner, but it would take too long for her impatient son. Instead she made hamburgers.

"Can we go to the park?" he asked after wolfing down his dinner. Even his serving of broccoli disappeared without a comment.

"No, that's a little too far away even if I push Liddie in her old stroller. I thought we'd go to the elementary school playground."

"Mom, I've been there hundreds of times with Ralph— Mr. Spinner. We never found anything but pennies and a thing girls use in their hair."

"This isn't a good time to dig out clumps of grass at the park. The recreation department is working hard to get it ready for the celebration."

"Mom, I know how to put the grass back just like it was."

She gave him a look that made him give up any thought of the park—at least until later, she hoped.

"Where can we go?" Ben asked.

"I thought we'd start close to home," she said. "I don't think anyone has ever looked for treasure in our own backyard."

"Boring," her son said. "We won't find anything here."

"You don't know that. People have been living in this house for over a hundred years. There's no telling what they might have lost."

Also Liddie could play in the yard while they experimented with the metal detector. And no one need see her trailing along with a little treasure hunter.

Once in the backyard, she surveyed the yard while Ben started his search. Except for the garden area, the grassy lawn had been reseeded. Scattered blades were struggling to grow, and Anne made a mental note to run the sprinkler when Ben was done with the metal detector.

Ben was pacing the yard, looking like a scaled-down version of Mr. Spinner. She didn't know what he expected to find, but for the moment she was happy pushing Liddie in her swing.

"Here!" Ben said triumphantly.

"Here what?"

"This is the place," he said, activating the metal detector the way their neighbor had shown him.

"How do you know?" Since she'd given in on letting Ben have the device, Anne wanted to know all she could about using it.

"There used to be a gizmo right here. Look, Mom, you can see a slightly bumpy area."

He circled around it, and pointed out the slight indentations where something had once stood.

"Do you mean a gazebo?" Anne asked.

"Yeah, I guess. Anyway it was probably the place people went in the old days to sip their lemonade."

Anne had to smile at her son's interpretation of a slight irregularity in the ground, but he was too excited for her to discourage.

Ben slowly ran the detector around the circle he'd found. Suddenly the sound changed to a loud, demanding shriek. He stopped and prepared to dig a hole with the garden tool Anne had given him.

Anne admitted to herself that the circular gadget on the end of the metal rod certainly knew how to sound off. The question was whether Ben had found anything that he'd deem worth finding.

He pulled out a plug of grass with the roots hanging down and tested with his fingers to see if anything was caught in it. Then he turned his attention to the hole, feeling around in the dirt until he found something. He squealed with excitement, and Anne walked over to look at his find.

"What is it?" he asked with a bewildered expression on his face.

He held out his palm to show her the dirt-encrusted object.

"It's a bobby pin," Anne said sympathetically. She knew it wasn't what he'd hoped to find.

"What's that?" He started cleaning if off with his fingers.

"Ladies hold their hair in place with them," Anne said.

"Oh." He let it drop on the grass beside the hole and bent over to replace the clump of dirt.

"What are you going to do with it?" she asked.

"Nothing." He stomped on the repaired spot.

"Wrong. You have two choices. I know Mr. Spinner told you that."

"Put it in my treasure bag or bury it in the same spot for someone else to find."

He picked it up and shuffled over to the large brown paper grocery bag that he'd brought outside to hold his finds.

"You've picked a good place," Anne said to cheer him up. "There could be neat things just waiting to be found."

Fortunately, he got over his disappointment quickly and made several more finds. By the time the summer sun was low in the sky, he'd found a dime so old it was made of real silver, and the buckle on a dog collar.

After Ben rinsed his finds off under the outside faucet, he was tired enough to get into his bath without protest. Anne was comfortable with her decision to let him have the metal detector. Maybe she could keep him happy right in their own yard until school started.

So far things seemed to be falling into place for the rest of the month of August. Now if only she didn't have the nagging doubt about the damage on Alex's truck. How many names would be on his list of who borrowed it? Who could operate a lift to remove the statue?

The bronze likeness of the famous architect hadn't walked off on her own.

CHAPTER ELEVEN

Thursday morning Anne was deep in conversation with Remi Miller when she looked up to see an unlikely duo headed her way.

"Alex, Mr. Buchanan, what's in those boxes?" she asked. Both men were laden down with heavy-looking cardboard cartons.

"Books," the two said in unison.

"Well, this is a library," Anne said, smiling even though she was puzzled about why they were together.

"Do you remember when you stopped by to see me the other day?" Harold Buchanan asked rhetorically as he put down the large box he'd been holding. Without waiting for an answer he continued, "I'm taking some boxes of old junk to George Franklin at Franklin's Antiques, but I thought you might like these books for the library."

"I appreciate that," Anne said as Alex put an even larger box on the floor.

"Harold and I just happened to run into each other outside," Alex said.

"I sure appreciate your help," Harold said, wiping sweat off his brow. "It's already toasty out there."

Anne was happy to see Alex but wondered what he was doing at the library on a workday morning.

As though he could read her thoughts, Alex answered her unspoken question. "I came to tell you I talked to the police about the scratch on my truck. Unfortunately, I can't remember everyone who may have borrowed it during the time they think the theft took place. Given that they're not exactly sure which night it was, it's pretty open."

"I wish I could be of more assistance," Harold said. "But once I was done with the cleaning and restoration, I didn't go back to look at the statue."

"That makes perfect sense," Anne said to encourage him.

"I have some boxes in my truck to deliver to Franklin's Antiques. I'd better get at it," Harold said. "Thanks for the help, Alex."

After thanking him for the donation of books, Anne bent down to look through the boxes.

"Do you think there's anything you can use for the library?" Alex asked as she quickly sorted through the boxes.

"Not really," Anne said, straightening up. "But it was nice of him to think of us while sorting through his stuff."

"Do you want me to put the boxes somewhere out of the way?" he asked.

"Yes, please," she said.

Alex came back to the front desk after depositing the heavy boxes in a work area where she could go through them more carefully later. He didn't seem in a big hurry to leave, considering it was Thursday morning and a workday for him. She didn't want to press him, instead waiting for him to say more about his talk with the local police.

Anne knew how difficult this had to be for him. There didn't seem to be any doubt that his truck was used to commit a felony.

"I'd hoped to talk with Michael when I stopped by the police station, but he's off today, so I just spoke with another officer on duty. Basically, I gave them a list of everyone who might have been using my truck in the past week or so. But the police can't pinpoint the time when the statue was carted off, and I can't be sure who might have used my truck about that time. I've been too busy to keep track of everything."

Anne knew how hectic life was for Alex. He ran a thriving business and still spent lots of time with Ryan. She admired him and valued their renewed relationship. She only wished the two of them could figure out who'd scratched his truck. Until then he was living under a shadow.

"I'd better get back to work," he said, "I just wanted to stop by and let you know about my talk with the police. They were cordial, and I don't seem to be on their list of prime suspects."

"I'm glad you told me," Anne said. "Thanks for hauling in the books."

Alex grinned, and Anne liked the way his smile extended all the way to his eyes.

"I hope you find some you can add to the library's collection," he said. "If not, just give me a call. I'll take them to Franklin's Antiques for you if any look collectible."

"Thanks, I appreciate your offer," she said.

After he left, she debated whether to go through the donated books or take care of some paperwork. She opted for the paperwork.

When she unlocked the library door that morning, she'd found three bulging grocery bags and a long box that had originally contained bananas. All were full of books, although the box also had a living passenger: a big black spider.

Anne had managed to shoo it away, but she'd felt compelled to look through the entire box and the accompanying bags of books for other undesirable wildlife before she brought the items inside. Apparently, the treasure-hunting fever had inspired people to weed out their books, and she felt swamped by older titles. Most were just reprints of older books, but people kept hoping they would find something hiding in their grandparents' basement like a first edition of the Lewis and Clark journals that Anne had seen at a book show several years ago. The memory of the excitement Anne had felt seeing that rare book could almost help her understand the mania her neighbors seemed to have for finding hidden treasures.

What would Aunt Edie think of the avalanche of old books being donated to the library? Her aunt had always been game for anything. Anne fondly imagined her sitting on the floor surrounded by stacks of books, giving a brief history of ones that caught her fancy. She was such a book lover, it was surprising she'd never become a librarian herself.

On the other hand, Edie had been much too busy traveling the world and writing her articles to settle down in Blue Hill before her retirement. It had been Anne's good fortune she got to know her lovable relative. Maybe someday she'd write a book about her. Or maybe not. It would be almost impossible to capture Edie's spirit and love of life with paper and ink.

The memorial service for Lois Stover would, in Anne's heart, also honor Aunt Edie. She only wished her adored late great-aunt could see how the library was progressing. More people were using it all the time, and Anne rarely heard negative comments.

"You look miles away." Wendy had come in without Anne noticing.

"Sorry. I was thinking about my aunt Edie. I think she would approve of what we've done with the library."

"What you've done," Wendy said. "You get all the credit."

"You forget about Alex's brilliant job of renovating. Not to mention you and the other volunteers. I never could've done it alone."

"You're too modest, but I didn't come here to trade compliments. Chad is in such a good mood since his team was cleared of grand-theft-statue, he offered to make lunch for the kids so I could have a meal out — with my favorite friend, if that's possible."

"Possible and a pleasure. I have a volunteer coming to give me a lunch break. Where do you want to go?"

"We could go to Coffee Joe's," Wendy said, suggesting a small shop between the sporting goods store and a health food market.

"His ice cream is too tempting," Anne said. "Since we don't get to do lunch together very often, let's go to the Keystone Café — my treat."

"You don't need to do that," Wendy protested. "But I do love that place."

"We'll have to get there a little before noon if we want to get a table."

"No problem. Call me when you're ready to leave. I'll drive by for you," Wendy said.

The library's noontime volunteer got there early, so by 11:45 Anne was seated across from Wendy at a small table with a faux granite top.

After they ordered spinach salads and a grilled cheese sandwich to split, they settled down to exchange family news.

"For a while I was really worried," Wendy said. "Chad loves his coaching job. If his boys were guilty, he feared he might be accused of being unable to handle his team members and be removed from his coaching position. He could still teach, of course, but football is the center of his universe."

"I'm sure that's not exactly true," Anne said. "He adores you and the kids."

"Well, yes, but it would still be a devastating blow if he had to give up coaching." Wendy nibbled on one of the homemade potato chips in a basket on the table. "I probably gained five pounds stress eating."

Anne made a sympathetic sound, then her attention was diverted.

"The two Umsted boys just came in," she said.

To her credit, Wendy didn't turn around and look at them. Instead she lowered her voice, hardly a necessity since the restaurant was full of people talking in moderately loud tones.

"Are they finding a table?" she asked.

"No, they're going to the counter," Anne reported. "They seem to be looking at the take-out menu."

"It figures Derek would be hungry. He had football camp this morning."

"Camp?"

"High school teams aren't allowed to start practices yet, so most squads get around it by having football camps. Chad's not crazy about it, but he can't afford to let the other teams in the conference get more practice time than Blue Hill." Wendy sipped a glass of iced tea just delivered to their table.

"I have a lot to learn about how things work in the schools — and the town," Anne said, laughing, although she was quite serious about needing to know more.

"Ah, the Umsted boys got their takeout before we got what we ordered," Wendy said.

"They probably called ahead," Anne said. "Eric and I always did that when we wanted takeout."

"You're probably right," Wendy said. "Anyway, it's nice to be able to see team members without thinking thief."

"They showed good planning," Anne mused, thinking of how the theft of the statue had required a master plan to avoid being seen.

"What are you thinking?" Wendy asked.

"Oh, nothing. I have to stop looking at everyone in town as suspects."

Somewhat to Anne's surprise, the two young men headed directly to their table.

"Hi, Mrs. Pyle, Mrs. Gibson," the younger Umsted said. "I don't know whether you know my brother, Mitch. Mitch, Mrs. Pyle is the coach's wife."

"My claim to fame," Wendy joked. "I certainly saw you play, Mitch. I rarely miss a game my husband coaches. In fact, my son Christian came close to being born in the bleachers. That was the season you had that fabulous kicker. What was his name?"

"Remington Carlson. We figured his mother watched too much TV."

"He went to the pros, didn't he?" Anne asked.

"He washed out," Mitch said. "Last I heard, he owned a car wash somewhere."

"We have to go," the younger brother Derek said. "Nice talking to you."

"Same here," Wendy said, while Anne nodded agreement.

"They seem like nice young men," Anne said.

Wendy shrugged her shoulders. "When Mitch was on the team, he gave Chad some trouble. He didn't like to be told what to do, not even by his coach. But no doubt he's matured since then."

"I have a lot to learn about teenage rebellion before Ben gets there. He's already shown a stubborn streak," Anne said.

"What's the story about Ben and his metal detector?" Anne's friend asked after their server unloaded a tray with their lunch. Wendy added her favorite blue cheese dressing to the fresh spinach and pushed the plate that held the sandwich to the middle of the table so they could share it.

"I still have a little regret about letting him have it, but fortunately for Ben, Mr. Spinner wanted to find a good home for his metal detector. His arthritis is too bad for him to keep using it."

"Has Ben found anything of interest?"

"An old bobby pin, a dog collar buckle, and some coins. So far I've only let him use it in the yard around the library."

"How long will he be satisfied with that?"

"He isn't," Anne admitted. "He really wants to go to the park."

"To hunt for hidden treasure, like everyone else in town." Wendy grinned.

"Something like that. But if people see him hunting in the park, they might think to start looking there for old, lost valuables like jewelry."

"From what I hear, people are especially buzzing about the missing time capsule and its contents almost as much as the missing statue. Some even think that Lois Stover hid the jewels she brought back from Europe in it, given that no one knows what she did with them."

"It would be exciting to see what Lois put in the time capsule. What does it look like—do you know?"

"It's my understanding that it was in the architectural plans tube that her statue's depiction is holding in her left hand," Wendy said. "Though I'm not certain about that."

"That would mean that the historical objects inside would have to be fairly small." It wouldn't have to contain jewelry to spark Anne's interest. She was intrigued by the very idea of the time capsule.

"I guess," Wendy said, adding more blue cheese dressing to her salad. "This is such a treat. I haven't heard the word *Mom* once since we got here. I adore each and every one of my brood, but not when they're all trying to get my attention at once."

"Time goes so fast when we're together," Anne said when both women had finished eating and declined to order dessert. "Afraid I have to get back to the library. I have a whole bunch of donated books to sort through while I still have a volunteer to help patrons."

"Anything exciting?" Wendy asked as she stood to leave.

"Not that I spotted right away, but most seem to be pretty old."

"If you'd like help going through them, I have a couple of hours before I have to serve hot dogs at the ball park."

"I'd love help," Anne said. "Two pairs of eyes are much better than one."

CHAPTER TWELVE

"Mommy, I can't find my pink socks," Liddie called out from her bedroom.

"That's because they haven't been washed yet," Anne said, leaving the kitchen to solve her daughter's dilemma.

Liddie had dressed herself in a favorite garment, a sunsuit her grandma had made for her. It had a cheerful pattern of bright circles on a white background, but it was getting a little small.

"You probably shouldn't wear pink socks with all those red, yellow, and purple circles," Anne said. "White looks much nicer."

Liddie took more time to be convinced, and the oatmeal on the stove boiled over, making a mess for Anne to clean up.

"Can I use my metal detector today?" Ben asked, trying to pick the raisins out of his toast.

"When I get home from work," his mother said. "I don't think you've searched the front side of the house."

"There's nothing good in our yard. Can't we go to the park?"

"You know the answer to that." Anne switched cold cereal for the overcooked oatmeal and filled bowls for both children.

"After the memory thing," Ben said, not trying to hide his disappointment.

"Memorial," Anne automatically corrected him. "Let's not have this conversation again. If you get your chores done before dinner, we can go to the school playground."

"They take too long," Ben protested.

"That's because you play with your toys instead of putting them away," Liddie said, although she was more likely to dawdle than Ben.

"Enough," Anne said to both, and they quit arguing.

Somehow Anne managed to open the library on time. Although time went fast when she was busy, she hoped things would be a little calmer today. A day-care group had visited yesterday, and one little boy had thrown up in the Children's Room, thankfully not on any of the books. There had been a steady stream of patrons, and an unusually large number needing her help.

As curious as she'd been to go through the donated books, she couldn't get to them. She'd had to call Wendy and postpone the time when they would sort through them together.

Hopefully, that would be today. Bella was coming in the early afternoon, and Wendy had a couple of hours free then. Anne knew they might not find anything of value, but looking at old books was always fun.

The morning was busy, but the traffic slowed by early afternoon. It was a pleasant, sunny day but not scorching hot. Perhaps people were leaving for long weekends or visits to nearby friends or relatives. Anne checked out a lot of books she called light reading, perfect for lounging and not doing much of anything.

"I'm excited you asked me to help. I love old books," Wendy said when she showed up to help sort the donations.

"And new ones," Anne teased. Wendy was one of the few people she knew whose enthusiasm for books matched her own.

"I love them all! New, used, old, fiction, nonfiction, even the books I read to my children."

"We'll be sorting donations in the work room," Anne told Bella. "Call me on my cell phone if you need anything."

"Sure thing, Mrs. G." Bella was already processing the day's returns, being careful not to get her silky white shirt dirty. The twins' wardrobes never failed to entertain Anne—and make her feel like a dowdy middle-aged woman.

Today she'd dressed for what could be a dirty job going through the donations. Her tan shorts were practically dirt proof, and her green knit shirt was saved from looking like a T-shirt by the addition of a pert little collar.

"Shall we get on with it?" Anne asked.

"Lead on!" Wendy was so enthusiastic some of it rubbed off on Anne.

This was Anne's idea of a treasure hunt. Even if she couldn't put any of the donations on one of the library's shelves, it was an adventure to explore what people were willing to give to the library. Anne would try to raise money on any rejected books. Maybe there were some collectible older books.

"Bless Alex!" She stepped into the work area and was pleased to see that he'd put all the boxes and bags on the long table that served for sorting and processing. They wouldn't have to lift them up from the floor.

"I wasn't expecting this many," Wendy said.

"We'll get through them," Anne assured her. "Remember to check for things people put inside."

Once she'd found an unused postage stamp issued to commemorate the Columbian Exhibition in 1893. Anne offered to give it back, but the donor insisted she sell it and use the proceeds for the library. Anne sold it online, and it brought a nice donation to the book fund.

"I'm most curious about what Harold Buchanan brought," Wendy said.

"Then we'll check those first." Anne opened a box that had once contained canned corn.

With Wendy's good help, Anne unloaded both of the corrugated cardboard boxes Harold had given to the library.

"Look at the paintings in this one," Wendy said, paging through what Anne called a coffee table book: heavy on illustrations and light on information.

"They're beautiful," Anne said, "but not exactly what I'd hoped to find."

"Should I start a pile of rejects?" Wendy asked.

"Please do. Put aside the better ones. I'll take them to the antiques shop."

"Here's one you may like to add to the library's collection," Wendy said, carefully handing over a green cover with gold embossing.

"A trip through Canada in 1842," Anne read. "You're right. We don't have much on our neighbor to the north. I'll add it to the history collection."

"Here's another that seems to be in the same set." Wendy handed her a second green and gold title.

"Mexico," Anne said. "This is a keeper too."

She took others out of Harold's box, but they were mostly art texts and others he would have used in his teaching days. The banana box held a number of old series books for girls. She didn't include any in the library collection, but she thought they would sell well as collectibles. By the time she added them to the pile for the antiques shop, she thought they'd done a good job of sorting.

"This bag is all outdated fiction from the fifties and sixties. There are a few Western novels. Do you want them?" Wendy asked.

"Yes, we have a few regulars who can't get enough of them," Anne said as she dusted the few books she'd decided to keep.

"I've been thinking," Wendy said, loading the books to go to the antiques shop into one of the empty boxes. "Seeing the Umsted brothers at lunch made me wonder if Chad was too quick to dismiss all his team members as potential thieves."

"I guess he knows them pretty well," Anne said, trying to be tactful.

"Usually I'd agree," her friend said. "But don't you think it's odd that the police haven't located the statue yet? There's only a week and a day until the ceremony. You'd think they'd be able to find something as large as the Lois Stover statue by now."

"If it hasn't turned up anywhere on the secondary market, it could be hidden in any one of a number of places. Professional thieves are probably easier to catch than ones who are just up to mischief."

Anne thoughtfully finished putting books for recycling into the banana box. She was sorry there were so many, but mold had started to attack the ones that had been on the bottom. Most likely they'd been stored on a basement floor where dampness had gotten to them.

"If it shows up at a football game anywhere in the conference, we'll have our answer," Wendy said.

"It may have been melted for scrap," Anne said, suggesting the possibility to her friend for the first time.

"That would be terrible! Imagine all the work that went into it. I'd almost rather hear that one of the Blue Hill football players is behind stealing it."

"One or more," Anne said.

What bothered her the most was the unsettling feeling that she didn't know who in Blue Hill she could trust…and who she couldn't.

Chapter Thirteen

Anne was pleased that Wendy had helped her sort through the donated books. George Franklin, the owner of Franklin's Antiques, had agreed to look over the ones the library couldn't use.

"You ready?" Alex asked her as he came into the library Friday morning.

"Yes, thanks so much," she said. Anne was relieved when Alex made good on his offer to take her to Franklin's Antiques with the load of books.

"It's not a problem," he said. "I have some errands to run before I get back to the job site."

Remi came up to Anne to ask a question, temporarily getting Anne's attention. Alex signaled he'd start loading the boxes into his truck. Anne had made the task easier by labeling the bags and boxes that were to go.

A few minutes later Anne was scrambling into the passenger seat beside Alex in his truck. Anne couldn't help noticing the scratch still hadn't been repaired, but she didn't want to mention it.

As though reading her mind, Alex said, "I have some touch-up paint," he said. "The damage doesn't meet the deductible on my insurance, so I'm going to do what I can myself."

"But you haven't tested the color match yet?" She asked for the sole reason of keeping the conversation going. In her heart she believed Alex hadn't had anything to do with the theft, but her pragmatic side still wanted confirmation.

"Not yet," he said with an ironic smile. "There's never enough time in the day to do everything I'd like to accomplish."

Anne sighed. "Sorry, I didn't mean to pressure you. It's just that the anniversary celebration is coming up fast. I haven't given up hope that Lois Stover's statue will be returned by then, but no one seems close to knowing what happened to it. I wonder if the thieves will borrow your truck again to put it back in the park."

Alex frowned, and Anne knew he wanted the statue found as badly as she did. The fact that his truck had almost certainly been used in the theft weighed heavily on him.

"It will turn up somewhere," he said.

When they got to Franklin's Antiques, Anne gasped. Boxes and boxes of items were piled outside the store. A harried looking clerk was trying to keep the door open and shove one box in with his foot while balancing another in his arms.

"What's going on?" Anne asked as she and Alex walked up to him.

"Here let me help you," Alex said, taking the box out of the young man's arms.

"I'll tell you what's going on," Mr. Franklin said, appearing just inside the doorway.

Anne followed Alex into the store and looked around in amazement. Usually, Franklin's Antiques was extremely well organized with sections for best sellers like glass, pottery, books, and furniture. Today it was chaos. Boxes of stuff were everywhere, making it a challenge to walk through the store. She narrowly missed falling over a plastic grocery bag that had fallen off one of the piles.

"Careful," Alex said, putting the box on a pile and reaching out to steady her.

With his hand on her arm, she slowly made her way to the rear of the store where the floor wasn't quite as cluttered

"Everyone in Blue Hill is going through their attics, basements, and garages," Mr. Franklin said. "Not that I mind getting first chance at so much fresh stock, but it's more than I can handle right now. People have gone treasure-happy since Lois Stover's so-called lost jewelry became the main topic of discussion around here. Everyone seems to have decided to see if their shabby heirlooms will make them rich."

His comment made Anne smile. "Even my ten-year-old son isn't immune," she said. "He just bought a metal detector."

"Good for him. If I were on my A game, I'd be out checking the trash piles still on the curbs. As it is, I don't have nearly enough help to process all this stuff people have dumped on me."

"I feel guilty bringing you books," Anne said. "Would you prefer I keep them until you have time to sort through them?"

"No, no. If you're not in a hurry for my offer, I'll put them in the workroom. I sell a lot of books in the store and online, so I always need fresh stock."

"There's no hurry," Anne assured him.

"I'll write your name on the boxes. It's the only way I can keep track of who brought what. I already have several stacks that people left before I could determine whom they belonged to."

"How can you buy them if you don't know who owns them?" Alex asked.

"I'll have to rely on the owners checking up on their stuff," Mr. Franklin said in a disgruntled voice. "This isn't the way I like to do business."

"I imagine not," Anne said.

Alex was engrossed in looking at a display of duck decoys, leaning over a stack of boxes for a closer look.

"There's some real workmanship in some of these," he said.

"I only carry hand-carved ones. There were some master carvers in the county back in the 1930s. The Great Depression put a lot of folks out of work, and they made some sweet decoys."

"I have to get back to the library," Anne said, ducking as the shop helper squeezed past her with a child's rocking chair. It looked like wicker, but Anne knew enough about the painted furniture in the thirties to know it was woven with tight strips of paper.

She could happily spend hours looking at the antiques and collectibles on display, just because the stock in Mr. Franklin's shop was so appealing to anyone who appreciated beautiful objects. But there was a limit to how long she could leave a volunteer in charge of the library. And, of course, Alex had to get back to his job site.

"I'll get to your books as soon as I can," Mr. Franklin said, picking up another box to make a path in front of them.

"No hurry," Anne reassured him. "There may not be any you can use. The only thing going for most is that they're old, but there is a Dick and Jane reader and some series books that may be collectible."

"Sounds good," Mr. Franklin said without enthusiasm.

On the way out, Anne gave a lingering look at the piles of boxes and odd pieces of furniture. She would love to go through them all, if only to satisfy her curiosity, but obviously it was a job only Mr. Franklin could do.

On the way back to the library, Alex was unusually quiet. She tried to draw him out by asking about Ryan, but even questions about his nephew only brought brief responses.

"I really appreciate your help with the books," she said when they were close to the library.

"Glad to help. I hate to see books go to recycling if there's any other interest in them."

It was the most he'd said on the way home, but Anne could understand his gloomy mood. His truck had been used in a felony. Either a stranger had stolen it or one of his friends or employees had gone behind his back to use it. Alex valued his friendships and put a lot of trust in the men who worked on his jobs. Even if he was 100 percent innocent—and she wholeheartedly believed he was—his reputation was at stake.

Alex helped her out of the high seat of his truck but didn't walk her to the library entrance. She thanked him again, reluctant to leave him in such a gloomy mood. She'd seen a range of his moods, but he'd never been down like this since she had returned to Blue Hill.

In her eyes, he couldn't possibly be guilty of anything, but the success of his contracting business depended on the trust people had in him. He had good reason to be worried if the real culprits weren't discovered soon.

A friend was waiting to see her when she went inside the library.

"I thought you'd like to know the status of Art-in-the-Park," Maggie said. She didn't have any books to check out, but she'd been chatting with Bella at the counter.

"What do people think of the idea?" Anne asked as she put her purse out of sight under the counter. Once she'd assumed no one in Blue Hill would touch it if she left it lying out, but her faith in the honesty of the townspeople had been shaken. Even if teenagers were behind the theft of Lois Stover's statue, they had to have a place to hide it. That meant some adult may have helped conceal it.

"Everyone thinks it's a great idea to have an art show in conjunction with the ceremony. The big problem is the shortness of time. We can borrow tables from the church," Maggie said. "And it's so great that Harold Buchanan agreed to jury a show. That will give us a bigger show without all the crafts that these things usually attract."

"At least there won't be velvet Elvis paintings or pictures made of uncooked macaroni." Anne laughed. "My only worry is that Harold was clear that he didn't want to be judging too many potential exhibitors. I don't know what we'll do if we get more than about twenty applicants."

"We have a problem," Bella said approaching the amused women.

"The volunteer schedule is wrong."

"That's okay," Anne said. "I can manage alone this afternoon."

"The problem is too many volunteers, not too few," her young assistant said, brushing back a strand of hair that had fallen over her face.

"Who's coming this afternoon?" Anne asked, wondering if she should call and cancel one. She hated to do it. People didn't like their schedules changed at the last minute, and she certainly didn't want to lose a volunteer by telling her she wasn't needed that day.

"Mrs. Pyle and a woman I don't know, Agnes Green."

"We're okay then," Anne said. Wendy would do a great job showing the new volunteer the ropes.

Maggie left looking very pleased with herself, and Anne didn't blame her. The Art-in-the-Park could've become Disaster-in-the-Park if the committee members had had to make decisions about whom to refuse. She was surprised Harold was willing to take on so much work, but then, she didn't know him all that well.

When Wendy came, Anne had a sudden inspiration.

"Since there will be two of you this afternoon, would you mind terribly if I took a few hours off?" Anne asked.

"Not at all. You need some time to yourself," Wendy said.

"It's not exactly for myself," Anne said. "I promised to let Ben use his metal detector after dinner, but it would be so much nicer if I could pick him up early. He loves to go out to lunch with me, and then we could do a little treasure hunting. Liddie won't have to go with us. She likes talking about treasure hunting, but she's mostly trying to copy her brother. The reality is that she always wanders off with Hershey when Ben's using his metal detector."

"It wouldn't be my idea of fun," Wendy agreed. "Why don't you take the whole afternoon off? You deserve it."

"Thanks so much," Anne said. "It will be great not to squeeze the metal detector in between dinner and bedtime."

For a few minutes she'd been distracted, but as she prepared to pick up her son for lunch, her anxiety returned. What motive did people have to steal? Profit came to mind first, but realistically, how much could anyone make on the statue? It was so well known, it was practically impossible to sell, even for scrap.

Revenge came to mind, but it was a risky prank—if that's what it was. Did someone have a long-standing grudge against Lois Stover? Or the sculptor who made the statue?

Her mind spun while she drove to pick up Ben from the babysitter. Every possible motive was easy to dismiss, but without a motive the theft was senseless.

CHAPTER FOURTEEN

O w!"

Anne jumped up from the playground swing she was sitting on and raced over to her son. He was howling, whether from pain or shock she couldn't immediately tell. Blood was welling up from the index finger on his right hand. It only took her a moment to realize he'd cut himself on something he'd found with his metal detector.

Ben was wearing a bandana as a pirate headpiece. She quickly pulled it off and wrapped it tightly around his wounded finger.

Unfortunately, they'd walked to the playground, so they would have to go home on foot to get her car. Anne was no nurse, but she suspected Ben would need stitches and a tetanus shot.

First she wanted to know what had caused the cut. She leaned over the small hole and saw a glint of metal. Cautiously, so she wouldn't cut herself, she pulled out the sharp object, a corroded razor blade.

"What on earth is this doing on school property?" she asked, not expecting an answer from her son. He was clutching his wounded hand, watching blood seep through her makeshift bandage.

"I'll bring this along," she said, dropping the razor blade into the sack she carried to hold Ben's finds. "I don't want someone else digging it up and getting cut."

She replaced the divot and stomped to flatten it. Ben had already started home, and she hurried to catch up.

While Ben gingerly buckled his seat belt in the backseat of her vehicle, she speed-dialed her doctor's office.

"Sorry," his nurse said. "The doctor left this morning to do volunteer work in Guatemala for a week. Would you like to make an appointment when he's back?"

Anne explained the situation and received advice to go to the hospital emergency room. She headed in that direction immediately.

Ben was being a trouper, but his biggest fear wasn't stitches or a shot.

"Mom, can I still use my metal detector?" he asked as they waited for their turn in the half-full waiting area.

Anne wanted to say he could never touch it again, but it wouldn't be fair to Ben. After all, no one would expect to find an old-fashioned razor blade on a school playground. Maybe someone had dumped trash there when it was only a vacant lot.

"Yes," Anne said, gratified by the look of sheer relief on her son's face. "But first we'd better find a pair of tough leather gloves you can wear while you're using it."

Perhaps buoyed up by her assurance, Ben tolerated his stitches and shot with a minimum of fuss. He was released with instructions to keep his wound clean and take it easy the rest of the day. So back at home Anne helped him get comfortable and set him up to watch a movie on the couch until it was time for her to close the library.

When Anne made her way back downstairs, a familiar figure was standing by the checkout desk. Mildred looked dressed for dinner out in a new heather-colored pantsuit with an attractive blouse that reminded Anne of an impressionist painting with its swirls of vivid color. Her pretty white hair looked freshly curled, and she was wearing more makeup than she usually did.

"My, don't you look nice, Mildred," Anne said as she approached the counter.

"Thank you, but I'm a little upset right now. Remember that book you ordered for me, the one about making miniature gardens? I thought they would make lovely little gifts to take when friends are in the hospital. Sometimes the rooms are so crowded, it hardly pays to bring cut flowers or full-size plants."

"Yes, that's a great idea. I glanced through it. Some of the projects used coat buttons as a base. I thought they were charming."

"Yes, yes," Mildred said with unusual impatience.

"Didn't a volunteer call you to say it was here?"

"Yes, Bella did. Or maybe it was Remi. Either way, the book was supposed to be here waiting for me to pick it up."

"Isn't it?" Anne asked, turning to look at the shelf of reserved books.

She hated to see her late aunt's close friend so distressed.

"It is not," Mildred said. "I've had the girl looking in every nook and cranny. There's no sign of my book."

Things seemed to be disappearing all over Blue Hill. "I'll look for it," Anne said. "Would you like to have a seat in the reading area?"

"No thank you," the elderly woman said. "I'm going to dinner with some friends. I wanted to show them the book and suggest we make miniature gardens as a group project."

"It has to be somewhere," Anne said. "I remember processing it. Maybe it never left the workroom."

"I'll have to leave in a few minutes. One of the girls is picking me up at my home to go to supper, and I need to be there when she arrives."

Anne always smiled when Mildred called her friends "the girls."

Racewalking through the library, she found her volunteer, Miss Hayes, but no book for Mildred.

Miss Hayes was the most elderly of the library volunteers, but her vision and mental agility were good. As a retired third-grade teacher and elementary school librarian, she shouldn't have had any trouble locating a reserved book.

Anne's frustration grew as she went over places that Miss Hayes had already searched. Her last hope was the area where books were processed and put into the online catalog.

There were a few unfinished projects on the long worktable but no book on miniature gardens. Anne even crawled under the table to be sure no books were hidden there. Then another possibility struck her: Maybe Mildred's book had been scooped up with the books going to the antiques shop. There had been so many books that day. Perhaps Alex had grabbed some of the wrong boxes by mistake to take to Mr. Franklin.

It was improbable but not impossible. She hurried to phone the antiques dealer but didn't get any satisfaction from him.

"I haven't touched the books since you dropped them off," he said sounding a bit harried. "If you want to come to the shop and go through them, you're welcome to do so. It's going to take me weeks to appraise all the stuff people have dropped on me."

"Thank you," Anne said. "I'll do that as soon as I have a chance."

Meanwhile, she had to give Mildred the bad news.

Her elderly friend was pacing the front of the library, taking small, measured steps and frowning in a way that wasn't at all like her usually cheerful disposition.

"I have bad news and good news," Anne said. "The book isn't in the library, but I have a strong hunch where it is."

"Someone else checked it out?" She sounded betrayed.

"No, absolutely not." Anne quickly explained about the books she'd taken to the antiques dealer. "I'll go there and look for yours."

"If I know that Mr. Franklin, he's probably already sold it. He likes to turn a quick profit."

"He hasn't even opened the boxes," Anne said. "His shop is overrun with stuff people want to sell."

"Well, I'll have to save my idea for next time. My friends and I often get together for dinner. I have to rush home. The restaurant fills up quickly on Friday nights, so we go early."

It wasn't quite four o'clock, but apparently this was the best time to beat the dinner crowd.

"The first ten dinner customers get a free choice from the dessert tray. I'm partial to carrot cake if they have it this week."

For a person in a hurry, Mildred seemed more interested in chatting than leaving. Before she could tell Anne about her favorite restaurant dishes, she paused for a moment to get her breath. Anne was quick to interrupt.

"I'll look for the book," she promised. "If it's permanently lost, I'll reorder it. But I want you to do something for me."

"That's sweet of you," Mildred said, beaming. "What could I possibly do for you?"

"Listen carefully at dinner. See if you hear any rumors about the missing statue."

"Do you really think it will be found?" Mildred asked.

"We can hope."

And pray, Anne said to herself. She certainly didn't want any residents of Blue Hill to be guilty.

CHAPTER FIFTEEN

Anne was glad it was time to close the library. As soon as the door was locked she made two phone calls.

The first was to Mr. Franklin.

"I'll stay in the shop until you get here," he said, not sounding at all happy about it. "Are you leaving now?"

"In about two minutes. Thank you so much."

Next, Anne got permission to be late picking Liddie up at the sitter's. That done, she raced upstairs and hurried Ben down to her vehicle. He wasn't keen to go to the antiques shop, but he cooperated when he heard it was for Mildred. He'd become fond of her since they'd moved back to Blue Hill; no wonder, since she was always willing to play a board game with him or bake a batch of chocolate chip cookies.

When they got there, Anne was able to park directly in front of the shop. She hurried Ben up to the door and found it locked.

"They're closed," he said. "We can go home. Maybe I can do a little metal detecting."

"Not today," Anne said. "You need to let your finger heal a bit first."

"You said..."

Those were some of Anne's least favorite words.

"I said you can still use your metal detector but not today."

She knocked on the glass pane in the door, gently at first but more vigorously when Mr. Franklin didn't appear to open it. Had he changed his mind and gone home?

She couldn't believe she'd dragged Ben to the store for no reason.

"Look, Mom." He pointed to a small bell beside the door. "I think you're supposed to push that."

"You're absolutely right. Why don't you push it for me?"

Ben pushed the doorbell with one of his uninjured fingers. Anne could hear it resounding in the store but still no Mr. Franklin.

She was ready to leave when the door swung open.

"Come on in," the shop owner said. "Watch your step. I didn't have time to do any sorting today."

He sounded the opposite of cordial, but Anne wasn't going to be put off by his grumpiness. Although she was naturally rather shy and retiring, she rose to the occasion when it involved a friend.

"The one I'm looking for is the size of a coffee table book. It still has the dust jacket, and I haven't had time to process it for the library's collection."

"Sounds like a couple hundred other books I have around here."

"I'll recognize my boxes if you wouldn't mind turning on more lights."

"I can't have people thinking I'm open. I'd never get home for supper."

He grudgingly turned on the overhead lights and stood with his arms crossed as she searched for her boxes. They were nowhere in sight, which probably meant other boxes had been piled on top of them.

"Have you moved anything?" Anne asked, as eager to find the book and leave as he was to have them go.

"That's all I've done all day. My back is killing me. I have to get home and put on a hot patch."

In other words, she was on her own in the search.

One of her boxes had come from an online publisher. In fact, the book about miniature gardens had probably been delivered to the library in it. She saw another banana box, not surprising since the supermarket was the main source of empty containers. Hopefully, it didn't harbor any scary spiders.

"Here it is, Mom," Ben said, pointing at a box that was half-concealed under a shelf.

"Good work!" Anne said. Ben was spot-on right that the box was from the library. How could she have forgotten how good he was at finding things? He really was a natural treasure hunter.

He wandered off, followed by Mr. Franklin who didn't seem keen on young boys looking through his boxes.

The book she wanted wasn't in the box Ben found, but the other one was only a few feet away under an old-fashioned spool box with two drawers. It had once held thread for sale in a store, but some misguided person had painted it an ugly battleship gray over the original red. It was partially restored, leaving a mishmash of the two paint colors.

Much to Anne's relief, she found the book she wanted near the top of the box.

"Mom, what's this for?" Ben called out, scampering toward her holding a metallic object.

"You really shouldn't poke around in the boxes," Mr. Franklin said. "If the contents get mixed, I'll never know who brought what."

"Mr. Franklin is right," Anne said taking the object from him. "He's been nice enough to wait here for us after closing time. Please don't touch any other boxes."

"But what is it?" Ben tended to be single-minded when his curiosity was aroused.

"Not our concern," Anne said, looking at the object with puzzlement.

It was like a cylindrical tube used for mailing large paper objects that could be rolled up, but this one had nothing to do with the postal service. Instead it was made of copper with a screw-on lid at one end.

"I've never seen anything quite like this," Anne said, handing it to Mr. Franklin when he reached for it.

"I've been meaning to have a look at it," the antiques dealer said. "I guess now is as good a time as any."

Looking inside wasn't easy. The cap was corroded just enough to make unscrewing it difficult. Mr. Franklin tried several times before he could remove it. Then he carefully turned it upside down so the contents slid out easily on the counter that held his cash register.

"Drawings. Architectural drawings," Anne said as Mr. Franklin carefully unrolled them.

She bent forward to study them.

"That seems to be Lois Stover's name on the corner," Mr. Franklin said. "You know what I think we have here?"

"The time capsule?" Anne asked.

"Bingo! What better way for a thief to get rid of it than to add it to the mountain of stuff people have brought here. Where did you find it, sonny?"

"My name is Ben, sir."

"Ben, where did you find it?"

"In a box."

"Yes, yes, of course, but which box? Can you show me?"

Anne could see her son was getting rattled.

"Just take a deep breath," Anne said as much to Mr. Franklin as to her son. "Then you can show us where you think you found it."

Ben led them up and down the length of the store, stopping to look into several boxes.

"It had a lot of other stuff in with it," her son said.

Since that applied to dozens of boxes waiting to be searched, Anne knew it wasn't much help.

"Were you at the back of the store or the front when you spotted it?" Mr. Franklin asked.

Ben bit his lower lip, a sure sign he was agitated. "Maybe in the middle."

"About here?" The antiques shop owner inched along, but it only seemed to confuse Ben.

"He's only nine," Anne said. "Maybe it will come to him in a minute."

"I know I saw that tube somewhere," Mr. Franklin said, softening his tone. "I was going to investigate, but a good customer came looking for a gift. Then it slipped my mind."

"I guess we agree this was very likely the time capsule or part of it," Anne said.

She looked through the numbered pages of drawings and noticed something missing: pages three and four. Could Mr. Franklin only be pretending to see the time capsule for the first time? Could he have removed the missing pages hoping they might hold clues to where the missing jewelry was? Was she starting to believe all the hidden treasures stories?

Ben was hovering near the front door, obviously eager to get away from the questions.

"I have a request," Anne said. "The rededication ceremony is going on as planned, but with the statue missing, we have very little to display for the public. This is almost certainly the time capsule from the missing statue. Will you go with me to see the police and convince them to let us display the capsule and the drawings at the art show and memorial? Afterwards we can figure out what should happen to the time capsule and its contents."

"Actually, I would rather you take it there. I'm swamped with all these new items, and I'd rather not have to deal with the police," Mr. Franklin said. "We're not going to figure out which box it came out of, and it would be a shame if the police insisted on making the time capsule sit in an evidence locker. We can be pretty certain that the tube hadn't been previously opened, given how hard it was to get the cover off."

Anne wasn't nearly so certain about the tube having been unopened. Though she hated to think it, Mr. Franklin could have made it look harder than it really was to open.

She had the book for Mildred and the time capsule. Ben had had a rough day, but he was her hero of the day. Without his curiosity, she wouldn't have known the capsule had turned up in a box of odds and ends. That told her someone wanted to return it anonymously, but where was the rest of the original contents?

Liddie was antsy by the time Anne picked her up, but she was immediately fascinated by Ben's bandaged finger. On the way home she managed to find a scrape on her knee that had healed days ago.

"I need a bandage," she said as soon as they were home.

"No, you don't," Ben said, apparently eager to preserve his status as the walking wounded.

Anne made Liddie happy by putting a cartoon bandage on her knee. If only she could solve adult problems so easily!

At least she couldn't wait to tell Wendy and Maggie about the tube Ben had found. Maybe Harold Buchanan's sculptor father had shared with his son what Lois Stover had stowed in the time capsule.

CHAPTER SIXTEEN

W rap it around your fork the way I showed you," Anne told her son as he sucked in a strand of spaghetti.

Across from him at the kitchen table, Liddie was smashing each individual green pea on her plate.

"Liddie, please eat your dinner. Don't play with it."

Spaghetti had seemed like a quick and easy Friday evening dinner, especially since the whole family liked the sauce that came ready-to-use in a glass jar. Her kids weren't crazy about peas, but they usually ate them with a minimum of fuss.

"I don't want to get sauce on my bandage," Ben said holding up his injured finger.

"If you do, I'll change it," Anne assured him.

"Do you know how to do it like the nurse did?"

He sounded genuinely concerned so she took his question seriously.

"Probably not, but I have gauze pads and tape. We'll manage, but it would be nice if you don't get your finger in the sauce."

Even though her workday was officially over, Anne still had lots to do that evening. First of all, she needed to tell Wendy and Maggie about the time capsule. Unfortunately, they couldn't track down the rest of the contents until they knew what had been in it.

The phone startled her, mostly because she hadn't expected anyone to call her now. She smiled broadly when she heard the voice on the other end.

"Hi." One word was enough for Anne to recognize Alex's voice.

"Hi, yourself," she responded.

"Ryan wants to invite Ben to spend the night. He has a new video game he'd like to try out with him. I wanted to make sure it's all right with you before he asks Ben."

"I think that's just the thing to cheer Ben up." She explained about her son's injured finger, then passed the phone to him.

"Can I go, Mom?"

"Yes, but first finish your dinner and change your shirt. You have tomato sauce on the front."

This was just what Ben needed. He had been complaining that his finger was still throbbing, and he might have a hard time getting to sleep at home. Alex was good about getting the boys to bed at a reasonable time, and Ben wouldn't want Ryan to think he was acting babyish about his finger.

Anne put sleepwear and a clean outfit for tomorrow into Ben's backpack while he hurriedly finished his dinner. Hershey was in attendance by Liddie's chair, but tonight he turned up his nose at the crushed peas she dropped beside him.

By the time she walked down the stairs to watch Ben leave with Alex and Ryan, Anne realized how weary she was. The food left on her plate was cold and unappetizing, so she put it in the garbage after Liddie went to her room to play. Anne cleared the table, wiped up the smashed peas on the floor, and wondered whether she could get Liddie to bed early. Since she was learning to tell time, it was getting more difficult.

Just as Anne was heading toward her daughter's bedroom to tell her it was bath time, the phone sounded again. Hopefully, it wasn't Ben wanting to come home because his finger hurt.

"Hello, Mrs. Gibson."

"Please call me Anne," she told Harold Buchanan. She couldn't imagine why he was calling at this time of day, but he soon enlightened her.

"Hope I'm not calling too late," he said.

"No, not at all. Is there something I can do for you?"

"Not exactly, but maybe I can do something for you. The head nurse at Blue Hill Retirement Center called me. My father had an exceptionally good day. He remembered an old friend who visited him and even called an LPN by her correct name. The nurse suggested this evening would be a good time for me to visit him."

"That's encouraging," Anne said, not knowing where this conversation was going.

"I thought you might like to go with me. I know you have questions about the statue that only Dad can answer. Anyway, he can be pretty entertaining when he's alert."

"I'd love to, but I will have to bring Liddie. It's too last-minute to get a babysitter on a Friday night."

"That's fine. Bring her along."

Liddie wouldn't like going to the retirement home, but Anne didn't have much choice about taking her. Liddie's shirt showed a hard day of playing, including finger-painting in a particularly gross shade of green, so she changed her into a favorite bright pink top with a big rabbit head on the front.

Anne had agreed to meet Harold at the Blue Hill Retirement Center. It was too much of a hassle to let him pick her up. She'd have to move Liddie's car seat to his car, which could sometimes be a lot of work. On a last-minute impulse, she grabbed the empty capsule and put it in a bag to take along. Maybe it would help jog the elder Mr. Buchanan's memory if he saw it. When Anne had gotten home with the tube, she had taken the plans out of the capsule and put them in an acid-free library document folder to help them flatten out.

Harold arrived just after Anne and Liddie. He pulled up behind them and got out of his vehicle.

"I'll show you where my dad's room is," he said. "The corridors are confusing when you first see them."

He led them through the twists and turns of the retirement home. A few residents were having an evening stroll, and others clustered in pairs or small groups to visit. The nursing staff wore colorful cotton tops, many with cartoon characters on them. All in all, it was a cheerful place.

Arlen Buchanan's door was half open, but his son still knocked so they wouldn't startle him.

"Hello, Dad," Harold said. "I brought you some visitors."

"Is that Gavin?" a rasping male voice asked when the three of them stepped into his room.

"No, Dad. It's Harold. Gavin has gone to a better place, remember?"

He whispered an aside to Anne, "My father was so devastated when my younger brother died in a car crash years ago that sometimes he refuses to accept it."

"I understand," Anne said, although her hope of getting information from the elderly man was fading.

"This is Anne, our librarian," Harold said. "And her daughter. Did you have a good dinner, Dad?"

"Shepherd's pie again," he said. "Three inches of mashed potatoes and a few carrots. This place needs a new cook."

Anne could tell Harold didn't want to talk about the quality of the food but patiently listened until his father exhausted the topic.

"Anne loves your statue of Lois Stover in Rosehill Park," Harold said, giving her a strong clue his father didn't know about the theft.

"Do you have candy?" Liddie asked.

"No candy, but how would you like an American flag?" Arlen reached over to his nightstand and gave her a small one. "They passed them out to everyone here for the Fourth of July. Just one more thing to clutter my space."

Anne could see where that was a problem. Arlen Buchanan had a room to himself, but the space was anything but generous. He'd settled in with a number of art magazines and books, not to mention colored pencils and a thick stack of drawing paper. A number of well-executed drawings were spread out on every available surface. Apparently, the urge to make art survived beyond other memories.

"The whole town loves your statue," Anne said.

"When was it I made the first sketches?" Arlen asked his son.

"In the early fifties, Dad. Lois Stover was still alive and modeled for you."

"She was a spunky one," Arlen said with a chuckle. "I was glad she didn't live to see all the delays. It's always about the money."

"Well, they finally installed it in 1990," Harold said to Anne and his father.

"I had blueberry muffins for breakfast," Arlen said.

"That's nice," Anne said. "It's been a good year for blueberries."

"About the time capsule," Harold said, trying to keep his father on message. "Do you remember what it looks like?"

"My watch has the wrong time," his father said. "Have we gone on daylight saving time yet?"

"I'll check that you have the right time," Harold said, although Arlen didn't seem inclined to take it off.

Liddie was waving the flag in the doorway, and Anne was afraid her good behavior wouldn't last much longer.

"I have something to show you, Mr. Buchanan," Anne said taking the capsule out of the bag she'd used to bring it there. "Do you recognize this?"

He reached out and took it. The lid was too tight for him to unscrew it, but he shook it to see if anything was inside.

"Where did you get that?" Harold said to Anne, his eyes wide. "Is this the time capsule you remember, Dad?" Harold took it and removed the lid, showing his father the inside.

"Where's all the stuff?" Arlen asked.

"Good question," Anne said. "We found it mostly empty in an antiques shop. All that was in it was an incomplete set of architectural drawings."

"Empty?" Arlen got a faraway look, and Anne was afraid his memory had lapsed again.

"Do you remember what was in it?" she asked, noticing that Liddie had ducked into the corridor.

"Plans," he whispered.

"Drawings by Lois Stover?" Anne asked.

"Yes, she was a spunky woman. Spunky." He seemed to like the sound of the word.

"What else was in it?" Harold asked.

"We had tacos for lunch. They were too spicy. Old people don't like too much spice. Did you bring me a candy bar?"

"Right here," Harold said handing him a wrapped granola bar. "Do you remember what else was in the capsule? The tube could hold many small items."

Arlen reached his hand into the tube. "It's empty," he said. "Where's the rest of it?"

"That's what we're trying to determine," Harold said. "Can you remember anything else that was in it?"

"I like chocolate better," Arlen said as he unwrapped the granola bar.

"They're not good for you, Dad. You know that."

Arlen held the granola bar but didn't bite into it. His eyes drooped shut, and Anne knew the visit was over. She had other questions about the time capsule and Lois Stover, but the window of opportunity had slammed shut.

"Mommy, look what a lady gave me!" Liddie said, running down the corridor to her mother as she left the room. "It's a pot holder for when I make cookies. She knits them all the time."

Anne had seen a woman knitting in the activity room on the way in, so she went there to thank her on the way out.

"Sorry my father couldn't remember more," Harold said as he caught up with her out by their cars. "He wasn't at his worst— but he wasn't at his best either."

"Thanks so much for asking me to come," Anne said.

It had been a long day, but the best thing to come out of it was that Liddie learned older people weren't scary. That alone was worth coming for.

Anne wished her own fears could be put aside that easily. Why had the time capsule been in Mr. Franklin's shop? Who put it there? Did the thief who stole the statue have an attack of conscience?

If so, why?

CHAPTER SEVENTEEN

A s they sat around the table at the Sloans' house Saturday morning, Anne brought Maggie and Wendy up-to-date. Over steaming cups of coffee, she showed them the time capsule and the architectural drawings.

Wendy was dressed casually in jeans and a sweatshirt that read *Go Blue Hill*. Maggie was wearing a flowery patterned dress in shades of turquoise and white. Anne was somewhere in between with navy slacks and a favorite top because she had other plans after the informal committee meeting.

"I can't believe the capsule was found in Franklin's Antiques," Wendy said. "I wonder how long it was there."

"It's hard to believe he hadn't discovered it sooner—if he's telling the truth," Maggie said, topping off their coffees without asking.

"He had noticed it was in one of the boxes people had dropped off, but he hadn't had any time to give it any thought," Anne said, always willing to believe the best of people as long as she could although the same thought had occurred to her.

"Aren't you curious to know what else was originally in it?" Wendy asked.

"That's the other thing I wanted to tell you," Anne said, relating to them the visit to Arlen Buchanan. "I really hoped Harold's father could shed some light on the contents, but his memory is sketchy."

"That's sad," Maggie said. "My husband stops in to see him when he visits the retirement home, but he never knows what to expect. Sometimes Mr. Buchanan talks a blue streak, and other times he just seems confused."

"I wonder what the significance of those missing pages of architectural drawings could be?" Wendy said.

Anne had asked herself the same thing over and over as she'd tried to fall asleep the night before. She'd thought of one possibility and wanted to run it past her fellow committee members, but she didn't want to make unfounded accusations against anyone.

"I have an idea . . . ." Anne started slowly, choosing her words carefully. She hesitated.

"What is it?" Maggie prodded her. "If it's going to cause more problems with the anniversary celebration next Saturday, please tell us."

Anne sighed. "Ben found the time capsule in a box of junk dropped at Mr. Franklin's store . . ."

"But you think maybe he might have information he's not sharing about the theft of the statue?" Wendy finished for her.

"Maybe," Anne said, with nothing but a hunch to go on. "I just don't know what his motivation might be to keep quiet about it, unless he expected to find the hoard of jewelry or some other priceless treasure inside the tube or the statue."

Maybe she shouldn't have said anything to the other women. As hard as Anne tried, she couldn't see a direct connection between Mr. Franklin and the missing statue. And she couldn't see him "borrowing" Alex's truck. He had a huge van he used to haul antiques. And his name wasn't on the list Alex had made of people who might have driven his truck.

Wendy thought for a minute then said, "Even if he has some reason to keep information about the statue to himself, I don't see a reputable businessman like Mr. Franklin engaging in any sort of criminal activity. But what about those missing pages you just told us about? He could have concealed them before you got to his shop because they contained clues to Lois Stover's missing jewels!"

"She's got a point," Maggie said.

Wendy looked so triumphant, Anne hated to burst her friend's bubble, but she had to say something.

"We don't have any idea what the status of the jewels is," she said. "We don't even know whether the jewels are still in their original settings," she said. "Lois could've mailed them back to her aunt — after all, they belonged to her. Or even more likely, she could've sold them to a jeweler in some place like New York City where no one would see her doing it. She was successful as an architect, but that doesn't mean she didn't run short of cash from time to time."

"Maybe," Wendy said dubiously. "But rumors about a hidden cache of jewelry have circulated for years. There must be a grain of truth in them to keep people speculating."

Maggie nodded her head in agreement. "Now we really need to finalize the details for next Saturday's ceremony. I wish that statue would show up!"

"So do I," Anne said. "But at least we have the empty time capsule to show people. I stopped by the police station this morning, and talked to Michael about it. He is okay with letting us take care of it until it's needed for the investigation. He took pictures of it, but given all the people who had handled it and the fact that we didn't know which box it came out of, he didn't think it was feasible to collect fingerprints or other evidence from it. What ideas do you have to display it?"

Maggie suggested a case the church used to display historical artifacts related to the first building on the site. Wendy thought they could borrow one from the entryway of the high school building.

"All we'd have to do is take out the trophies," she said.

"One hitch," Anne pointed out. "They both weigh a ton. I hate to ask our helpers to move them outside to the park."

"Maybe we could put the capsule and the pages we have in the lobby of the town hall. They have display cases already in place. Then we can direct people to see them there. It's not too far from the park," Maggie suggested.

"Good idea!" Anne said. "We could leave them on display for a longer time than just the one day of the celebration. More people would get to see them."

"I just wish we knew what's supposed to be inside the capsule," Wendy said, idly turning it around in her hands. "An empty container isn't very exciting."

"It's big enough to hold quite a few small items," Maggie said, taking it from Wendy and attempting to unscrew the cap. "It takes some muscle to get it open, doesn't it? I'd sort of like to see the inside even if it's empty."

"Let me try," Anne said. "I've had it open a couple of times."

"Had what open?" Reverend Tom came into the kitchen looking casual in a red and blue plaid shirt. He quickly volunteered to unscrew the lid.

"Well done," his wife said when he managed to open the tube in one strong-armed twist.

The women passed it around until it came to Anne. She ran her finger around the opening, speculating on how to make the cover turn more easily.

"Maybe a little petroleum jelly around the edge would make it easier to open," she said.

"I don't have that, but I do have cooking oil," Maggie said, jumping up to get a bottle from a cupboard.

Anne watched with some trepidation while her friend lubricated the opening of the tube. Maggie's method did work, as she proved by replacing the lid, then opening it again. The trouble was the tube was now slippery with cooking oil.

"Do you have a paper towel?" Anne asked when it was handed to her.

"Sure thing," Maggie said. "That stuff really does spread around."

Anne held the tube at arms' length hoping to avoid getting oil on her clothes. She really didn't want to go home to change before meeting Alex and the boys for lunch at their favorite pizza restaurant. Liddie had been invited for a playdate at a friend's, and Anne had several hours before she was supposed to pick her up.

The oil on the outside of the tube quickly soaked into a paper towel, but some had spread to the inside. Anne rolled up one sleeve of her shirt and used a clean paper towel to start cleaning the inside.

She was nearly done when she paused. The inside of the tube was mostly smooth, but she ran the towel over a rougher spot. Investigating with her fingers, she detected a tiny envelope with something in it stuck to the inside of the tube. With a little fiddling, the envelope came free, thanks to the cooking oil.

"What is it?" Wendy asked when Anne pulled it out and laid it on a clean paper towel to absorb the coating of oil.

"It's a little envelope," Maggie said, opening it up excitedly. "There's a small key inside, and there's some faint writing on the front of it. I think it's the number 236."

Reverend Tom picked it up and looked at both sides.

"I've seen a key like this before," he said. "Just a minute." He put the key down and left the room, returning shortly with something in his hand. "This is the key to our safe-deposit box," he said, putting it beside the one from the tube.

"It's practically a match," Anne said.

"Of course they are cut slightly different," Maggie said. "But they're enough alike to belong to boxes in the same bank. And the number on the envelope could be the number of the box."

"If you like, I'll get it checked out," Anne said, holding a key in both hands. "You'd better take yours back before I get them mixed up."

When her friends agreed, she wrapped the found key in another section of towel and put it in her billfold.

Only the bank's drive-through window was open on Saturday, so Anne knew she couldn't get access to the mystery box until Monday. It was a long time to contain her curiosity, but at least she had lunch with Alex and the boys to look forward to.

"We have one more problem," Maggie said in a hesitant voice. "The Art-in-the-Park."

"We've borrowed enough tables, haven't we?" Anne asked.

"If not, we may be able to locate some card tables. Most people have one or two," Wendy said.

"That's not the problem," Maggie said. "For a last-minute plan, it's attracted the attention of everyone in town who's ever held a paintbrush. My phone has been swamped by people wanting to sell their art there."

"I'm sorry you're having to deal with it," Anne said. "I'm getting nervous about the numbers. I promised Harold Buchanan that he wouldn't have to deal with judging too many entries. It never occurred to me we would get so many entries."

"I think it might help if the committee published some rules I can cite," Maggie said.

"We've already agreed on no used merchandise, even if it's antique," Wendy said.

"That's not the problem," Maggie said. "It's cats."

"Cats?" Anne echoed while Wendy just looked puzzled.

"Anita Ferris is crazy about them," Maggie said. "She also thinks she's an artist. I wouldn't be surprised if she has hundreds of cats captured in oils and water paints. They look like they were painted with pudding."

"Well, maybe if we put out some guidelines we can get the numbers down to what Harold is willing to deal with," Anne replied

"If you need any help, let me know," Reverend Tom said after quietly listening to their problem and possible solution.

Anne stood to leave as Maggie carefully gave the capsule another quick wipe to be sure the oil was off. Anne put the tube and the key in the bag she'd used to bring them there, thanked her friend for the coffee, and left.

As she drove to the pizza place, easily her least favorite place to eat even though young people seemed to love the newly opened eatery, she went over what she knew about the disappearance of the statue. By the time she reached the strip just outside town, she'd exhausted all the possibilities in her mind.

Her friends had trusted her with the capsule and the drawings. Before she went into the restaurant, she put the bag on the floor of the backseat and covered it with Liddie's car toys. Then she locked the car, something she rarely did. She wasn't going to let this important Blue Hill artifact disappear again.

How much should she tell Alex about the time capsule?

She'd love to get his opinion on the find, but she didn't want to worry him with information about the capsule. After all, he'd had an opportunity to put the tube in one of the boxes when he carried in the books from the library into the shop. He might take anything she said about it as an accusation.

For now she wouldn't say anything, although it made her sad to be a keeper of secrets.

CHAPTER EIGHTEEN

S ound came out through the door like the blast of a jet engine when Anne opened it.

No way would she step foot into this new pizza place if Ben didn't enjoy it so much. They served chicken wings and a few other kid favorites besides pizza, but it wasn't necessarily the food Ben and Ryan liked about the place. Usually, they made a beeline for the video games in a side room, and today was no exception.

She looked around the crowded room where a birthday party was obviously in progress. The guests had been rounded up for cake and singing, so Ben and Ryan had a chance to play with their favorite games.

At first she didn't see Alex, but when he stood up and waved at her, she hurried to the side booth where he was. A supersize pizza was on the table with plates and utensils for the boys, but no one had started eating.

"Sorry about this," he said as she slid into the booth across from him. "Ryan has been asking to come here for weeks."

"That's okay," Anne said as he sat down. "This is Ben's idea of a perfect place to eat — or not eat. We usually end up taking the pizza home to reheat."

"We've done that a time or two," Alex said. "It's nice to have an adult to shout at while they play."

He wasn't kidding about shouting. The din in the room made it necessary to raise their voices.

"The pizza is half pepperoni and half everything," Alex said, waiting to pull off a piece for her. "I'll get something else if you prefer."

"The half everything is fine," Anne said, guessing the pepperoni was the boys' choice.

The first bite was so hot it burned her tongue. She quickly cooled her mouth with the soda, then smiled to show Alex she was okay.

"Did you work this morning?" he asked. He looked ruggedly handsome in a forest green polo shirt and jeans, reminding Anne of the boy she knew and liked in high school.

"No, I take off on Saturdays when I have good volunteer help. I was overdue for a weekend day off."

"I know how hard you work." He lowered his voice but Anne still heard his words.

In a roomful of noisy people, one table could be heard over the rest. Anne looked across the room and saw four boys in the process of consuming a supersize pizza. One she knew for sure was Derek Umsted, but the others were unknown to her—high school kids in jeans, T-shirts, and fluorescent running shoes.

"That was the best camping trip we've ever had," a freckle-faced boy said, taking off his baseball cap to stuff some of his wild blond hair back under it.

"Did you see Smith run from that tiny little garter snake?" Derek asked. "You'd think it was a Burmese python. Now *that* I would run from."

"Hey, when can we do it again? Borrowing that truck was a stroke of genius," a beefy boy with a head of dark curls said.

He was immediately shushed, and Derek looked around to see who might have heard. His face paled when he saw Alex.

To his credit, he got up and walked toward the booth where Alex and Anne were waiting for the pizza to cool a bit.

"I guess you heard," Derek said, looking shamefaced.

"Were you talking about my truck, the one that was supposed to sit in your driveway at home after you got back late from delivering a load of lumber?" It was a rhetorical question. Alex knew perfectly well it was.

"Yes, sir."

Would Alex fire him? Anne suspected that might not be a big deal to Derek because school was starting soon.

"So where did you take my truck for the night?"

"To the campgrounds. We needed something big to carry our tents and stuff."

"Will the guys confirm it was there all night?"

"I guess. I slept most of the night." He shifted from one foot to the other, no longer the happy teen when he was confronted with borrowing the truck without permission.

"Tell me, how did the damage get on the door?" Alex asked.

"What damage?" Derek looked even more distressed. Either he was giving an Academy Award performance, or he really didn't know about the dent.

"On the passenger side door. The paint scraped off matches paint on one of the concrete posts surrounding the statue of Lois Stover. You wouldn't know how it happened to get there, would you?"

Even though Alex was angry about his truck, he also sounded relieved to Anne. Now he had a possible explanation for where his truck had been when the theft occurred. It would be better if they knew exactly which night the statue had been taken, but this was a start. The bigger question was, did Derek and his friends steal the statue?

And though Anne could barely allow herself to think it, it would be convenient for Alex if there was a possible explanation for someone else having his truck at the time surrounding the theft.

Where could they possibly hide it so even the police couldn't find it? Wendy's husband, the football coach, was convinced none of his boys were involved—but he didn't know a group had had access to Alex's truck.

Derek's confession, delivered over the din in the restaurant, explained who had the truck overnight, but they still didn't know exactly when the statue was stolen. She didn't see any way to prove the truck was at the campground when the crime was committed.

Anne had a hard time believing boys still in high school would risk college scholarships and job offers to commit a felony. If they were found guilty, their future would be pretty murky. What could they possibly gain from it?

"I'm sorry," Derek said genuinely. "I won't take it again without asking you."

"It's partly my fault," Alex said. "I've been careless about letting people drive it. From now on, the keys come back to me after someone else uses it."

"Thanks for being such a good sport," Derek said, sounding as though the world had been lifted from his shoulders.

When he went back to his friends, Anne asked the question on both their minds, "Do you think he was involved in the theft?"

"I doubt it. He's always been a pretty good kid, and he sounded genuinely shocked about the scratch." Alex looked more puzzled than angry. "Even so, I'll fill Michael Banks in on this new information."

"Hey, Uncle Alex," Ryan said racing over to their table followed by Ben. "We have a great idea."

"Ryan wants to see how my metal detector works. I thought we could go home and get it. Maybe this would be a good time to check out the park," Ben said.

"You're not going to dig around in the park until after the celebration," Anne reminded him. "But I guess Ryan could come to our house. You could demonstrate it for him in our yard."

"Mom, there's nothing left to find there."

"I think that's a good idea," Alex said, quick to support her decision. "I'll hang out and watch the boys. I've been curious about the metal detector myself. But first, you guys need to eat some of this pizza."

They groaned in unison but quickly helped themselves to a big slice of pizza. Anne finished hers while they took seconds, but in a surprisingly short time, they were ready to go.

After making a big dent in the pizza, they all agreed Anne should take the rest home with her.

Ben rode with Ryan and Alex, and she followed them home. When they got to the library, it was past the Saturday closing time. She checked to see that the door the public used was locked, then went out to the yard to watch the treasure hunting.

"I have to admit it's fun to play with," Alex said, walking toward her when she went outside. "Ryan found a 1952 copper penny. You'd think it was a chest of gold. That's how excited he was. Maybe I'll have to check online to see if I can find an inexpensive used one."

Anne explained how Ben had gotten his and wished Alex good luck in finding an affordable metal detector.

"They make child sizes," she said. "But Ryan might think they're too babyish."

"How are things going with you?" Alex asked after the excitement of Ben finding a much-corroded compact, the kind a woman would carry in the 1940s or '50s.

"I can't get it open," Ben called out as he repaired the ground where he'd found it.

"Let me see," Alex said.

He managed to open it without knocking off any of the mother-of-pearl on the top. Inside, some pancake makeup was rock hard.

"Nice," Alex said. "Now you've both found something, so we'll be going home."

"Uncle Alex!" Ryan protested. "All I found was a dinky little penny."

"I'm sure Ben will let you use his metal detector again sometime soon," Alex said.

"Can Ryan sleep over at my house tonight?" Ben asked.

"Not tonight," Alex said before Anne could answer.

They'd agreed some time ago that two nights in a row were too much. Growing boys needed sleep—and adults needed a quiet evening.

* * *

Anne put a clean bandage on Ben's finger and loaded him into the car to get Liddie. She was waiting just inside a picket fence with Cindy and Becca Jacobs and their mother, Yvette, but she scampered out as soon as Anne stopped by the curb.

"We played in the sandbox," Liddie said, climbing into her seat with sand falling off her blue-and-white striped shirt and yellow shorts.

"You certainly did," Anne said, walking to the backseat door and trying to brush some of the sand off her daughter.

It was embedded in her scalp and leaking out of her tennis shoes, so Anne gave up. The car and her daughter would need cleaning after this playdate.

"Sorry about the sand," Yvette said. "My girls just love playing in their sandbox."

Liddie did not love having the sand washed out of her hair and scalp when they returned home. It took Anne several washes and rinses before her daughter was sand free.

Meanwhile, Ben tried to heat the leftover pizza in the oven and managed to burn his finger. Now he was a two-bandage casualty. He used them as an excuse not to take a bath, but Anne found a plastic bag to keep both injuries dry.

Neither child protested an early bedtime.

Anne put on her nightgown shortly after they were tucked in. Her plan was to read in bed until it was closer to her usual time to settle down for the night.

Sometime between pulling a light cover over her legs and opening the book, Anne felt too drowsy to do anything but turn off the bedside lamp and give in to sleep.

Something woke her, and she bolted out of bed to check on her children. They were still asleep, and she recognized the familiar sound of her cell phone. She usually kept it on the table beside her, but she'd been so weary she'd left it on the kitchen counter.

She grabbed it just as the rings were about to end.

"Hello." She glanced at the kitchen clock and saw it was nearly two in the morning.

"Anne, it's Wendy. Sorry to wake you up, but something has happened."

Anne's first thought was that something had happened to one of Wendy's children.

"They're fine," her friend assured her when Anne asked. "Someone broke into Franklin's Antiques."

CHAPTER NINETEEN

N ow that she was fully awake, Anne tried to make sense of what Wendy had just told her. Her friend sounded breathless with excitement.

"Someone broke into Mr. Franklin's shop?" Anne repeated.

"Yes, but this wasn't a well-planned break-in," Wendy said. "They didn't know about the alarm or the camera up by the ceiling. Franklin's has enough security to guard Fort Knox."

"How did you hear about it?" Anne asked, still a little confused. She didn't quite understand why Wendy was calling her about an antiques store break-in.

"The police called Chad to come over and identify the kids who did it. They were only a few blocks away when the police caught up with them."

"Does Chad know them?"

"Oh yes, but not because they're on his team. They're Deshler players. Chad recognized them because Blue Hill plays them every season."

"So tell me what happened," Anne said, hoping her friend's late-night call meant the statue was found.

"Oh dear, Chad's trying to call me. I'll get right back to you," Wendy said.

Anne knew her chances of sleeping were nil until she heard back from Wendy. If the statue had been left in the antiques shop, it changed everything. There was still time to reinstall it before the big day. That would really be cause for celebration.

"Mommy, are you okay?" A sleepy-eyed Ben came into the kitchen, padding on bare feet with his hair tousled.

"I'm fine, honey. I was just about to make some tea. Would you like a glass of milk?"

"Do you have cookies?" Ben wasn't so sleepy he forgot about a sweet treat.

Anne took out a package of butter cookies, the kind with a hole in the middle. As a kid she loved to put one on her finger and eat around it until it was narrow enough to be a ring. Ben was all business as he ate several with a glass of milk. He wasn't one to play with his food.

By the time Ben was through, he was wide awake and in no mood to go back to bed.

"Can we play Monopoly?" he asked. "Just one game."

He was just learning the game and couldn't get enough of it.

"Not tonight, honey. It's time for you to go back to bed."

Although she didn't encourage late night forays into the kitchen, she was grateful to him for passing the time while she waited for Wendy's call. She walked him back to his room and tucked him in a second time, carrying her phone so she wouldn't miss hearing it ring.

Her tea was tepid, so she reheated it in the microwave. When the phone finally rang, she burned her tongue on the too-hot beverage.

"Sorry to keep you waiting," Wendy said.

"Was it the..."

Anne's question was cut off when Wendy started talking to someone in the background.

"Sorry again," Wendy said. "What were you asking me?"

"Why did the boys break into the antiques shop?"

"It's strange," Wendy said, sounding dejected. "They were looking for the time capsule tube that Ben found in Mr. Franklin's store. They apparently had heard a rumor about it, and thought it was still there."

"What on earth did they want that for?" Anne asked. "It doesn't have any real value other than historical significance."

"I'll tell you, but there's more to it than just the tube. They apparently put up a dressmaker's dummy wrapped in a tarp on the pedestal where the Lois Stover statue should be. The jokers put a battered old football helmet where the face would've been and dressed it in a Blue Hill jersey. They weighed the whole thing down with lots of rocks. Then it sounds like they were going to have the dummy carrying the tube like a football."

"Where did they get a dummy from?" Anne asked.

"They found it beside a trash pile when everyone was putting unwanted items out by the curb," Wendy said. "It seemed like a good joke to dress it up and put it on the pedestal."

"But why break into the store? Why the tube?"

"According to the boys—who confessed to breaking into the store once they were caught—they didn't think a guy who sold old junk would bother with an alarm or a camera. They said even if they couldn't find the time capsule, it seemed like a safe place to look for something fun to add to the stunt. What they really wanted was to have their creation shown in the newspaper."

"And to be able to brag about it to other teammates," Anne said.

"Did the police arrest them?"

"They took them to the police station until their parents could go get them. But Chad thinks they'll have to face charges for breaking and entering."

"I guess one good thing comes out of it," Anne said. "The Deshler boys were caught so easily that it's highly unlikely they were involved in taking the statue. Whoever did that planned very carefully to get away with it and not have witnesses."

"I agree," Wendy said. "But I guess the Deshler players were never serious suspects. A prank is no fun unless you can show it to other people. Lois Stover's statue has vanished into thin air."

Anne didn't debate that. Almost anyone could be under suspicion when it was such an odd crime, but any motive the rival team members had was pretty flimsy.

"Do the police have any other suspects?"

"Chad didn't say, but he usually is pretty discreet around home. We have lots of little ears — and a few that are getting pretty big."

"I'm reaching that point myself," Anne said, telling her friend about Ben's late night foray into the kitchen. "Leaving the dress dummy seems like such a pointless prank."

"At least the police had an opportunity to question the Deshler boys about the statue, but I'm not optimistic about their involvement."

Anne could hear the frustration in her friend's voice.

"If we eliminate the Deshler football players, what suspects do we have left?" Wendy asked. "Chad is convinced his team isn't behind it."

"Oh, Wendy, I must be sleepier than I thought. I totally forgot to tell you what I learned at dinner tonight..." She hurried to explain how Derek Umsted and his buddies had borrowed Alex's truck for an overnight camping expedition around the time of the statue's disappearance.

And Anne thought it so strange that the tube from the time capsule had shown up in Mr. Franklin's store. Could Derek have been involved?

Maybe when she had a chance to look in the safe-deposit box, she'd have more answers.

* * *

When Anne woke up on Sunday morning, she only had a half hour to get ready for church. Although she didn't remember doing it, she must have turned off her alarm clock.

Much to her delight, she found her kids had dressed themselves for Sunday school. Ben had put on old jeans that were a little too short with a bright purple T-shirt. She was too pleased with him to criticize his choices.

Liddie came through with flying colors. She was wearing a vivid pink chiffon dress, one she'd worn as a flower girl in a wedding. All Anne had to do for her was fasten a hook at the back of the neckline and brush some snarls out of her hair.

While both children ate toaster pastries Ben had found in the cupboard, Anne rushed to get herself ready for church.

By the time Anne ushered her children into the church, the organist was already playing. She didn't want to be conspicuous walking down the aisle to her usual pew close to the front, so she slipped into a vacant spot in the last row.

It wasn't until the opening prayer that she realized how tired she was. She clenched her hands and forced her eyes to stay open, not wanting the embarrassment of falling asleep during the service.

Fortunately, Reverend Tom's sermon was a lively one based on the calling of the disciples. He vividly described the rocky shore of the lake where Peter and others fished, and Anne could see it in her mind's eye.

Although it was hard to be sure from where she sat at the back, she didn't think Maggie was sitting in her usual place. Almost every Sunday she sat in the pew directly in front of the pulpit.

Of all the people Anne wanted to see that morning, Maggie was on the top of her list. No doubt her friend would be mingling with the congregation where coffee and donuts were served in the fellowship hall.

After the service Reverend Tom was greeting people as they left the church, but Maggie was nowhere in sight. Anne led her children to the front door, where Reverend Tom was still talking to members of the congregation.

"Can we go home now?" Ben asked as they waited their turns to greet the pastor.

"In a minute," Anne said, although she hoped the woman in front of her wasn't in a chatty mood this morning. She had a reputation for talking nonstop whenever she could corner a listener.

Reverend Tom patted the woman's shoulder and sent her on her way in his usual kind way. Liddie was the next to greet him, shyly offering her hand as the grown-ups did. Ben didn't hesitate to reach out for his version of a manly handshake.

Anne felt a bit misty eyed when she thought about how her little boy was becoming a man. Eric would've been proud of him—and of Liddie.

"Good morning, Anne," Reverend Tom said when it was her turn.

"Good morning. I've been looking for Maggie but haven't found her," Anne said.

"Unfortunately, she's home with a bad summer cold. When I left she could hardly speak."

"That's a shame," Anne said, wondering what the committee would do without a chairperson. "Please give her my best wishes."

"Thanks, I will. She did give me a message for you. She wants to know if you'll chair the Stover committee," Reverend Tom said.

"Me?" Anne felt as though a rug had been pulled out from under her. "Wendy is the best organizer I know. Shouldn't she be offered the job?"

"Wendy had an unexpected family emergency this morning. The Pyles left early to drive to Chad's grandparents' house. There was a severe storm in their area. They don't have flood insurance, so Chad is going to see what he can do to drain the basement."

"Are the grandparents okay?" Anne asked.

"As far as I know. Maggie just had a quick call from Wendy to tell her she'd be gone today. You can call her if you have any questions."

Several times a year, Wendy's family went to the farm where Chad's grandparents had gradually retired from working their land themselves. As sorry as Anne felt for the elderly couple, the timing couldn't be worse. She needed Wendy to be on her A game.

"Chad has to be back for football camp Monday morning, so Wendy was pretty sure they'll be home late this evening," Reverend Tom said. "And there's a folder on the desk in my office with all Maggie's notes about the event if you'd like to pick it up before you leave."

"That's good," Anne said as Liddie tugged on the skirt of her pink chiffon dress. She thanked Reverend Tom for the message from his wife and wished him well.

Ben slipped out the door to wait for his mother outside while Anne hurried to pick up the folder of information.

Liddie skipped out to the parking lot beside her once Anne had collected the folder. Ben rushed up to her.

"Can Ryan spend the day with us?" he asked.

"Not today," Anne said, wondering when she'd find time to go over all the notes from Maggie.

"He wants to help with my metal detector," Ben insisted.

"I'm afraid it will have to be another time," Anne said, hurrying her children to the car. How could she explain to a nine-year-old that a world of work had just been given to her?

Driving away from the church, Anne couldn't get over the bombshell Reverend Tom had just dropped on her. As soon as she got home, she began making a list of everything she'd have to do, using Maggie's information and her own memory.

After she took a break to put a pasta casserole in the oven for their Sunday supper, her phone rang.

"Hope I'm not interrupting anything," Wendy said.

"Are you home?" It was wishful thinking on Anne's part.

"No, we'll probably be back late tonight. Chad rounded up the equipment and the help he needs to pump out the floodwater, but he'll want to stay until it's done. Are you okay heading the committee? When I talked to Maggie this morning, her voice was like a fog horn."

"I guess she's really sick," Anne said. "I mean stay-in-bed ill. It's not like Maggie to give up on anything she's started."

"I'll help you all I can when I get back," Wendy said. "It's not just the food and the program that Maggie was in charge of."

"Yes, I see that from the folder Reverend Tom passed on to me. I'll have to contact the mayor right away to see if we can display the time capsule in the town hall."

"And the architectural drawings," Wendy unnecessarily reminded her. "That's not the real problem though."

"Art-in-the-Park," Anne said, beginning to wish she'd never thought of the idea to get Harold Buchanan to participate.

"Last I heard, applications had come in from as far away as Erie. Since it's such short notice, you'll probably have to interview all the applicants by phone."

"The band I lined up is good, but they're a little shaky when it comes to getting places on time," Anne said. "I'll have to check what they plan to play too. I told them it was a community event with lots of older folks, so hard rock music is out."

"Then there's the big question," Wendy said after telling one of her children to be quiet.

"Big question?" Anne didn't know if she had room in her brain for one more problem.

"What will we do in case of rain?"

"Oh." Anne remembered talking about it, but they'd left it open. Both the church and the high school had space enough to hold the event, but she didn't have official permission for either one. She wrote it at the top of her priority list.

"You're still in charge of games for the children, aren't you?" Anne asked. "What about some for the adults?"

"Horseshoes would be good," Wendy said. "Maybe Bingo, but then we'd have to get some prizes donated."

The simple ceremony honoring Lois Stover had turned into a massive undertaking, and it was Anne's responsibility to make sure every task was accomplished.

After Wendy hung up, Anne tried to organize everything in her mind. She had one big distraction: Had the police learned anything from the Deshler football players? Even if they didn't steal the statue themselves, they might have heard rumors about who did. With the charge of breaking and entering hanging over their heads, this might be the ideal time to learn anything they knew. And what about Derek Umsted and his friends? Were they questioned as well?

What other surprises lay in store for Blue Hill before the big day? If as many artists participated as they expected now, they'd have art worth hundreds or even thousands of dollars sitting out in the open.

They'd need security. She scribbled it on her list. The Blue Hill police force was small, and she doubted if her police-officer friend Michael Banks would be interested in the assignment, even if he was off duty that day. But maybe they had a list of retired officers who would accept the job.

And where would the money come from? She was afraid they'd already gone beyond the budget the town had given them. Was she going to have to solicit donations on top of everything else she had to do?

The whole event had snowballed into much more than anyone had anticipated.

CHAPTER TWENTY

Anne's plan was to get to the Blue Hill Bank and Trust first thing Monday morning.

Unfortunately, her volunteer was home sick with the same kind of summer cold Maggie had. She reminded herself that "the best laid plans of mice and men often go awry."

It was nearly noon when she was finally able to leave the library in Bella's capable hands.

Once she got outside, the heat from the sidewalk assailed her. She was instantly sorry she'd worn her navy pinstripe pantsuit. It was much too warm, but she wanted to look as professional as possible. Anyway, it was too late to change.

Ignoring another source of discomfort, the rumbling in her stomach, she headed straight to the bank. Even going to a fast food drive-through would delay her visit to the bank too long.

When she got to the downtown financial institution, she parked on the street and sat in the car a moment. She went over in her mind what she was going to say. Nothing seemed persuasive enough, but she headed to the bank's entrance determined to do her best.

"Can I help you?" the receptionist at the front desk asked when Anne approached her.

She was a slender young woman with black hair cut like a helmet. She'd colored the part that fell over her face a bright red.

Anne didn't recognize her, but there seemed to be a lot of turnover among the bank's junior employees.

"Yes, thank you," she said. "I have a problem, and the solution might be complicated."

The receptionist tried to look helpful and interested, but Anne saw her glance pointedly at the large round clock dominating one of the bank's walls.

She was sure the woman was eager to go on her lunch break, but Anne was determined to persevere. Time was running out to discover anything that could lead to the whereabouts of Lois Stover's statue. She knew the police were baffled. Questions about what happened to it were still the main topic of conversation among the patrons who came into the library.

"I'd be happy to help you any way I can," the receptionist said. She had the grace to look away from the clock and meet Anne's gaze.

Anne took a deep breath. "I'm chairperson of the committee working on the big event to honor Lois Stover next weekend."

The receptionist's face was blank. Anne suspected she didn't have the authority to let her get into a safe-deposit box.

"I have a key we found hidden in a time capsule that was enclosed in the document tube on the Lois Stover statue that was stolen from the park. My fellow committee members and I think it's a key to a safe-deposit box here."

The young woman followed Anne's words, but her face didn't show any reaction. Her eyes were focused on her long black fingernails. Anne almost expected her to take a touch-up kit out of her desk drawer.

"We were hoping to check out the contents of the box this key opens." Anne held it out for emphasis. "According to the envelope the key was in, it should be box number 236."

The receptionist straightened up in her chair, seemingly happy she could give a negative answer to Anne.

"I'm sorry, but unless your signature matches the signature card on file, I can't allow you access to the box."

No matter how bad she—or the young woman staring resolutely at her—wanted lunch, Anne couldn't leave the bank until she had done everything within her power to examine the contents of the safe-deposit box. She had to know if the missing pages from the set of drawings were in the box. If they weren't, it could mean that they had been stolen from the time capsule.

"I know you generally need a signature from the person on the key card, but this key was placed in the time capsule more than sixty years ago, most likely by the person who rented the box," Anne explained. "Whoever he or she was must certainly be deceased by now."

"I'll see what we have," the receptionist said. "If the owner is dead, we need a court order to open the lock."

Anne followed as the bank employee race-walked to the rear of the lobby.

"Oh," she said, stopping abruptly halfway down. "I forgot to ask if you preferred to use the elevator."

"No, thank you," Anne said, wondering how old this young woman thought she was.

She felt decidedly dowdy in her pinstripe suit.

The receptionist went behind a long counter and busied herself pulling out a yellow card.

"This is strange," she said.

"What?" Anne's stomach rumbled, but the other woman didn't seem to notice.

"The rental fee has been paid up-to-date by direct withdrawal from the client's account. That means the contents are probably still intact."

"Great," Anne said. "I don't want to remove anything. I only need to see what's in the box."

"Nevertheless," the woman said, "your signature has to be on file as the person who rented the box in order to look at the contents. I'm sorry, but the bank has a very strict policy about that."

Anne tried another approach. "May I please see a manager to discuss this?"

"Certainly, I'll see if Mr. Royer is available," the receptionist said. Her heels clicked on the tiled floor as she headed for the stairs.

It was only a few minutes, but it seemed longer until the young woman returned followed by a middle-aged man. Anne recognized him as a frequent patron of the library. He especially liked action thrillers, maybe to compensate for his placid occupation at the bank.

"Thank you, Miss Dawes," he said to the receptionist, who hurried back up the stairs. "Hello, Mrs. Gibson. How can I help you?"

"I didn't know you were the manager here," she said.

"I recently transferred from another branch," he said. "I grew up here, so it's nice to be back in Blue Hill. Now, you want to get into your safe-deposit box?"

"No, not mine," she said producing the key and the envelope it came in and showing it to the bank manager.

He examined it and handed it back to her. "It looks old. Where did you say you found it?"

Briefly, Anne explained to Mr. Royer how she and the other committee members discovered the key hidden in the time capsule. Fortunately, everyone in town knew about the missing statue and the reputed mystery contents of the time capsule, so she didn't have to explain that.

"This is an unusual situation," he said. "As you know, the bank has one key for a safe-deposit box and the owner of the box has the other. Under normal circumstances the handwriting on the signature card must match that of the person requesting access to the box."

"Is there any chance that the person who rented the box left any instructions for letting someone in the future open the box? It was likely Lois Stover who had rented the box, and she had been dying of cancer at the time she would have put the key in the time capsule."

"Let me have someone go down to our inactive file archives to see what she can find." He brushed a speck of nonexistent dust off the sleeve of his light gray jacket and didn't meet her eyes. "We'll call you later this afternoon, once we've had a chance to check."

"I'll go get some lunch and then come back to check," Anne said. "It really is urgent."

Anne was nervous as she walked over to Coffee Joe's for lunch, and when she got there, her stomach was churning so much she wasn't sure she could eat. Instead of getting a sandwich, she had a bowl of strawberry frozen yogurt topped with granola.

Anne rationalized that the treat was a reasonable lunch, given that it was really more health food than dessert—an argument she would never accept from her children.

When Anne got back to the bank, she was greeted by the same grumpy receptionist. Apparently the "someone" who was going to go look for the old file from the archives was the receptionist, who now looked like she had not gotten even a morsel of food for lunch.

Without a word, the receptionist took Anne back to Mr. Royer, who greeted her with a friendly smile.

"There was a letter of understanding in the archives, along with the original contract for the box," Mr. Royer said. "The box belongs to the late Lois Stover. That letter established the account that pays for the box in perpetuity. It goes on to say that we are to grant access to whoever brings in the box's key in its official envelope. I'm not comfortable letting you take the contents of the box without further advice from our attorneys, but based on this letter, I'm happy to let you look in the box. However, I'll have to watch while you open it and go through it."

"That won't be a problem. Thank you so much!"

He left her standing by the counter for a few minutes, which seemed much longer. When he returned, he had the bank's key in hand.

What if the key she handed to him didn't open the box? Her palms were damp, and she felt claustrophobic in the confines of the chilly room lined with lockboxes.

Anne held her breath, watching as Mr. Royer first inserted the bank's key into one of the keyholes, then tried to turn her key in the other slot.

Nothing happened. The door didn't pop open. Her key wouldn't turn the lock.

"Oh dear," Mr. Royer said. "It seems your key isn't the right one for this box."

"Please try again."

He did, trying as hard as he could to turn the key.

"I don't want to break off the key in the lock," he said. "It's expensive to have a box cut open."

"I understand," Anne said. "Would it be all right it I try?"

"Have at it," he said, not sounding at all optimistic.

Anne tried but wasn't any more successful than the bank manager. She did notice one thing about the key.

"Look how the metal on the tip of the key is bent," she said, holding it up for him. "That may have happened when I was getting the envelope out of the tube. It didn't really want to come out."

Mr. Royer took the key, held it up, and grinned.

"I think I have something in my office that will flatten it out the way it should be. Wait here."

She wandered back to the counter and leaned her elbows on it. The high heels she'd put on before leaving for the bank were starting to pinch, and her stomach reminded her that she should have had more than just a small dish of frozen yogurt for lunch.

Trying to stay patient, she thought of all the things she still needed to accomplish today. Perhaps most important, Maggie had scheduled a meeting for all the artists who wanted to exhibit in the park. She'd gotten permission to hold it in the church fellowship hall, so Anne needed to be sure the custodian would leave the back entrance unlocked.

"I think this will make a significant difference," Mr. Royer said when he returned. "I looked at it under a magnifying glass before I tried to flatten it, and sure enough, there was a significant bend in the tip."

Anne held her breath as he inserted her key once again.

"Would you like to do the honors?" he asked.

She wiped her moist palms on the sides of her slacks and gingerly turned the stubborn key. Expecting failure, she was delighted when it turned all the way and released the door of the compartment holding a metal box with a lid.

"We'll go over here for privacy," he said, although the bank vault was empty except for them.

Carrying the metal box, he led the way to a small room. After putting it on a table, he pulled a curtain shut behind them and turned on the light.

"Now comes the moment of truth," Anne said under her breath.

Mr. Royer lifted the lid and revealed the contents.

"Would you like me to spread them out so you can see what they are?" he asked.

"Yes, please." Anne caught herself wringing her hands and made an effort to appear calmer than she felt.

"They're architectural plans," Mr. Royer said.

Anne could see that for herself. The big question was whether they'd been drawn by Lois Stover. She leaned over the first one and got confirmation. The architect's signature was easy to spot.

Next she checked the page numbers. They were the missing plans from the time capsule.

"I know the plans have to go back into the box, but would it be possible to take a picture of them with my phone?"

Mr. Royer's frown told her she'd already pushed him too hard. She expected him to turn her down.

"Tell me one thing: Are these plans going to help find the stolen statue?"

"Until I have the chance to go through them, I really don't know what they will lead to," she said. "But I certainly hope so. At the very least they might give us a motive for whoever stole the statue."

"Well, I don't see any harm with taking a picture here in the room. But once you've taken those pictures, we really need to close up the box, and I need to get back to my desk."

Anne spread the drawing out on the table and took several images of each of the pages. She then thanked Mr. Royer profusely for all of his help.

"It was my pleasure," the banker said, wiping his brow. "Now let's close up the box and I will show you out. I'll call you once I've had more time to check out the legal status of the box's letter of understanding."

After leaving the bank, Anne sat down on a bench. She took out her cell phone to check for messages received while it was turned off.

Ben asked when he could go out with his metal detector. No surprise there. She would wait on answering that one until later.

Wendy wanted to know what she'd learned. She would love to talk with her friend, but with everything going on, that one would have to wait as well.

Walking back to the library, Anne alternated between feeling elated and downcast. She was glad Mr. Franklin didn't have the missing pages hidden away, making it highly unlikely he was guilty of any crime, including the theft of the statue. And while she was excited that she got the chance to see the plans, she really wished she could have taken the originals with her. Now she was excited to see what secrets they contained.

Chapter Twenty-One

Anne was delighted when Wendy came into the library shortly before closing time Monday. She had much to tell her, and she badly wanted her friend's input about the art meeting that evening.

"I'm so sorry I can't be there," Wendy said. "Chad has a meeting with his football staff, and three of my kids have the summer cold that's going around."

"I understand. My biggest problem is how to limit the number of artists who participate," Anne said. "I have a whole stack of requests for space, but I don't want it to turn into a free-for-all."

"Do you think they'll all show up for the meeting?"

"That's up to them. I spent most of the afternoon on my cell phone contacting everyone who applied."

"Maybe you can appeal to their community spirit. The park will take a beating with all the spectators overflowing the walkways and trampling the grass," Wendy said, frowning at the prospect. "Most of the people in Blue Hill want the park to remain pristine."

"The number of participants has to be limited, but where do we draw the line?" Anne wished she'd never made the offer to Harold Buchanan.

"There's a nice wide walkway just north of the spot where the statue was. If I remember right, there are several trash cans and a nice drinking fountain along the way."

"That would be a good place to set up art tables," Anne said. "How many could we fit along that path?"

"Not nearly enough for all the people who applied," Wendy said. "I hope people remember that Harold is scheduled to be judging who gets to have the display places."

Anne walked over to lock the front door, knowing she had to hurry to get her kids fed before the meeting. Fortunately, Mildred had agreed to watch them at her house during the meeting.

"The big question is, how many we can accommodate?" Anne said.

"I can help you there. When the soccer mothers had a baked goods/rummage sale in the park a few years ago, we used twelve tables, six on each side of the path."

"That helps a lot," Anne said. "Now all I have to do is tell Harold to select eleven lucky artists to display at the show along with him. The problem is that he really didn't want to deal with a large number of entrants. I'm not sure we can get him to cut this many artists."

"Well, good luck. I have to get to the drugstore for cough medicine." Wendy let herself out, and Anne locked the door again after her.

Dinner didn't go well. Anne was too nervous to do more than nibble at a chicken potpie. Ben ate with a good appetite, but Liddie played with her food and knocked over her milk, soaking herself and the floor around her.

The spilled milk was beyond a quick wipe with a paper towel. Anne had to get her mop and pail. Even when she was finished, the floor still felt a little sticky. It would require a good scrubbing in the near future, but there wasn't time now.

The doorbell sounded while she was finding a clean outfit for Liddie. Ben raced to answer it, expecting Mildred had come to pick them up to take them to her house. He had his Monopoly game under his arm in anticipation of playing a game with Aunt Edie's closest friend.

"Mom, it's Ryan's uncle," he called up the stairs.

"Ask him to come in." Anne was trying to find something in her closet appropriate for chairing a meeting. She settled on clean jeans and a turquoise pullover but still needed time to change into them.

"We're going to Mildred's house," Ben told him. "She likes to play games. Can Ryan come too? Monopoly is more fun with more people."

"Sorry," Alex said as Anne came into the room. "Ryan is at his grandparents' house."

"Hi," Anne said, wondering why Alex had come. "We're in something of a panic around here. I have to be at a meeting by seven to finish planning on the art show."

She tied a dish towel around Liddie so she could finish eating without another outfit change.

"I thought we could hang out, maybe watch a movie on TV," Alex said. "I'm not used to being home alone anymore."

"I'd love to," Anne said, "but there's no way I can get out of this meeting. We must have fifty applications, and I really don't want to have to ask Harold Buchanan to judge that many. We can't take more than eleven."

"Draw names. Let chance decide," Alex suggested.

"I'd like to, but that might exclude some of the best artists. Harold may just have to do a lot of judging."

It was hard to turn Alex down and shuffle her kids off to Mildred's, but there wasn't any other option. Maggie's voice on the phone still sounded like she was talking through a towel. And Anne couldn't ask Wendy to leave her sick kids to take over the meeting.

When Anne got to the church, she was surprised by the number of vehicles already parked in the lot. She hoped some of them were here for some other reason, but she was afraid they were all waiting for her.

Before she could go inside, she saw Harold walking toward her.

"Mr. Buchanan—Harold—I was hoping you'd come. We have to cut the number from over fifty to eleven—plus you, of course. You had promised to judge, but I really hate to ask you to view that many. I would offer to help if I knew more about art..."

"No," he said before she could finish her sentence. "I'm sorry. It's just I judged students' art for longer than it took to paint the ceiling of the Sistine Chapel. I hate the thought of turning this many people away. I said I would look at twenty or so, but this is way more than that."

"Will you just take a look at what they've brought?"

"I don't mind doing that, but I'm not really up to telling this many people they can't be in the show, not that I don't appreciate all your planning committee is doing."

He held the door open for her and waved her through with a flourish. Chivalry wasn't what she needed from him, but it seemed she was on her own.

The first thing she saw when she got to the fellowship hall was a huge stag head—or maybe a moose head—painted on velvet. Whatever it was supposed to be, it wasn't something she'd want hanging in her home.

As she looked around for familiar faces, she had a *eureka* moment. Everyone in the room probably knew more about art than she did. Her new idea could solve her problem.

Every artist had been invited to bring one drawing or painting. It looked like they all had complied. Now she had to get them judged with more than just a former art teacher's expertise.

When she got everyone's attention, Anne explained how they were limiting the show to twelve tables, eleven to be decided tonight. First she gave the rules: Every artist was responsible for watching their display, bringing their own chairs and tables, and shutting down during the speeches.

Fortunately, she'd brought a spiral notebook with lots of unused pages. She started tearing out pages. Next she gave a number on a slip of paper to all the people there. She directed them to spread their art out on the tables and lay their numbers on it.

"I'm not an expert on art," she said, "but like you, I know what I want hanging in my home. Tonight I'll give you twenty minutes to look carefully at all the lovely art displayed here. Take one of these sheets of paper and write your number at the top, then circle it."

"I don't have a pencil." Anne recognized Blanche Underwood, an acquaintance who lived in Deshler.

Anne knew quite a few people in the room, either from church or the library, but there were enough strangers to make her wonder how they'd found out about Art-in-the-Park.

"I can help," Marta Henshaw said. She was a local photographer, tall and thin with arresting green eyes. Anne thought she was slender enough to be a fashion model, but she already had a great business taking portraits of the town's children.

Marta walked over to the closet where Sunday school supplies were stored.

"No pencils," she said, "but crayons will work, won't they? Or felt markers."

While Marta passed them out, several people came up to Anne with their art, hoping to win her approval.

"I've only been painting for a year," Marianne Cummings said. She was a widow with two young children she was supporting by working as the mayor's personal assistant.

Holding up her oil painting, Marianne explained how she'd been inspired by the county fair. Anne thought it was more likely Grandma Moses was her role model.

"I'm not going to choose who shows in the park," Anne explained for the third or fourth time. "Be sure to put your numbers on the tops of the papers."

"Like school," a man Anne recognized as Mr. Diggers said. He worked for the water and sewer department and seemed an unlikely artist. It turned out he only painted pictures of manhole covers. Whenever he went on vacation, he searched for unusual examples. He probably would win her vote for originality, but it wasn't her call.

"Now," Anne said, "you're going to pick three pieces of art you'd like to hang in your home. You can't vote for yourself, but that's the only restriction. Write down the numbers of your favorite three, then give me your selections."

"What if something of historical value is overlooked?" asked Garrett Jones from the Blue Hill Historical Society.

He was standing by a smudgy battle scene. He'd gotten carried away showing wounded men, liberally applying red paint. Anne smiled weakly.

"The winners will be the artists with the most votes," she repeated. "No exceptions."

Mr. Diggers hurried up and down the rows of paintings spread out on tables. He kept changing his mind, crossing out so many numbers he had to start over on the back of his paper.

Anne wouldn't have been so indecisive. She was immediately charmed by an acrylic portrait of a little red-haired girl playing in the sand on the beach. An artist might call it calendar art, but she thought it was adorable. She also liked a watercolor of garden flowers and a black-and-white sketch of the church.

Although she wasn't voting herself, she was fascinated by the way Harold studied each entry and chewed on his lower lip as he made his selections. Somewhat to her surprise, he picked the unappealing battle scene. He apparently didn't mind judging when he wasn't the person who was solely responsible for cutting people from the show.

When the time was up, she collected all the ballots and was faced with another problem: counting them.

"Would you like some help?"

The offer came from Mr. Willet, a church deacon and Sunday school teacher. His entry was a portrait made of different kinds of pasta. Anne was afraid he wouldn't get many votes, but she gratefully accepted his offer.

Apparently, Mr. Willet had some bookkeeping experience. With his help they finished in a reasonable amount of time while the room buzzed with speculation.

Mr. Willet returned to his macaroni man to await the results, although he already knew he'd only gotten two votes.

No one was going to help her out. She had to read the winners' names. Hopefully, there wouldn't be tears or anger, but there was no way she could get out of dashing artists' hopes.

"I'll read the names of the eleven people whose art you liked best. They won't be in any particular order, so the first name didn't necessarily have the most votes. These people are invited to display their art in the park on Saturday. Please be there by eight a.m. at the latest."

"Let's hear them," an impatient artist called out. "I'm going to miss a good show on TV." He was the creator of the horned animal on velvet. It had gotten one vote.

Anne started reading the names, interrupted by cheers from those selected. She was happy her choice of a little girl on the beach was a favorite, but sorry the grim battle scene was chosen as the number two favorite.

Afterward she hurried out of the church as quickly as possible. Several artists seemed disgruntled that they weren't selected. She was so grateful it hadn't been her decision.

The whole event was shaping up nicely except for the missing statue. Would the thieves choose to bring it back in time for the ceremony? If they wanted a dramatic return that would make the newspaper, Saturday was the day to pull it off.

CHAPTER TWENTY-TWO

In the library Tuesday morning, Anne spread out prints she'd made of the photos of the documents from Lois Stover's safe-deposit box across the table she used to process new books. From her vantage point at the rear, she could hear if any patrons came in. For now, only the newspaper readers were in the building. She knew from experience they only wanted to be left in peace to go through the papers subscribed to by the library.

"Is that all of them?" Wendy asked, standing beside Anne.

"Yes, these are photos of everything I found in the safe-deposit box," she said, squinting at the faint drawings and small letters on the different pages.

Wendy peered at the pages over Anne's shoulder. "Any maps or directions to a fortune in family jewels?" she asked hopefully.

Anne straightened up. "Not that I've seen so far," she said, sighing as she moved the pages around hoping something significant would jump out at her.

"What's that?" Wendy pointed to a blueprint for the Stover statue and its base that Anne had skimmed past previously.

"That's the diagram for that bronze four-paneled statue base. Do you remember each panel depicts a different scene from the architect's life?" Anne said.

"I guess I've never paid that much attention to the base of the statue," Wendy said.

"Me neither," Anne said.

"I do remember from one of our committee meetings that Harold Buchanan said Lois did the drawings for the statue base herself when she was ill," Wendy said.

"He did." Anne shuffled the papers again hoping for inspiration but none came. "I wonder why Lois Stover omitted some of the drawings from that group in the time capsule and secreted them in the safe-deposit box."

"It doesn't make sense at all." Wendy slumped down, elbows on the table, looking as dejected as Anne felt.

"Unless..."

"Unless what?" Wendy asked, perking up.

"Well...we learned Lois Stover loved puzzles and mysteries. What if she removed the pages from the time capsule so whoever opened it would keep looking and hopefully discover the key to the safe-deposit box and its contents."

"But why?"

Anne sighed deeply. "No idea. I guess if we knew maybe we might also discover a clue to the location of the missing jewelry, assuming there is one. As it is, we couldn't be more in the dark. I was stunned to learn Lois Stover set up a special account to keep the rent on the box paid. Who does that?"

"Our eccentric architect," Wendy said.

Together she and Wendy spent a few more minutes poring over the pages.

"I've been so preoccupied, I didn't even ask how your children are doing," Anne said.

"Now I have four with runny noses and hacking coughs. Since one of them is my husband, I'm delighted to take my turn as a library volunteer."

Anne smiled to herself as she remembered when her adult husband had his tonsils out. He'd kept her running for three days getting him popsicles and giving him sympathy. How she wished she could relive those days when he was the center of her universe.

Aunt Edie liked to say she'd picked a winner in Eric, and Anne never had reason to disagree.

"This one is different," Wendy said, pushing one of the copies forward.

"Yes, it's a map," Anne said. "I think it's Blue Hill, but there aren't any street names on it."

"I guess Lois Stover would know them by heart since she grew up here."

"Aunt Edie told me a good story about the architect," Anne said. "She loved puzzles so much she made one to send as her Christmas card one year. Those who could find the solution found an invitation to Lois's New Year's Eve party."

"Did your aunt say whether everyone could figure it out?"

"According to her, several people were left out because they tossed away the Christmas card without bothering to work the puzzle."

"I'm betting your aunt wasn't one of them," Wendy said, leaning over for a closer look at the copy of the map.

"No, she certainly wasn't. She knew about Lois's mania for all kinds of puzzles even if she was too young for a New Year's Eve party."

"I wonder...," Wendy said.

"Are you thinking what I am?" Anne asked. "That the map may be one of Stover's famous puzzles?"

"It's not impossible." Wendy turned the map to study it from different directions.

"Blue Hill was laid out on a grid, so most of the streets run north and south or east and west." Anne tapped the eraser end of a pencil on the map.

"Except for Euclid Drive," Wendy said, running her finger along a curvy line.

"Where Lois lived when she was still a toddler. Look, there's one of the little houses drawn in right in the middle," Anne said.

"When she started school, the family was a little more prosperous. They bought a house in a more upscale neighborhood."

"Look, there's another house symbol here," Anne said. "It's common knowledge she was influenced by the big Victorian houses in Blue Hill. She didn't use the fancy gingerbread trim in her house designs, but she did seem to love towers and irregular roof slopes."

"She seemed to love the big front porches too," Wendy said. "When I read about her online, she was praised for putting decks on the backs of houses long before it was fashionable."

"I can see why she got along so well with my great-aunt," Anne said. "Aunt Edie had more friends than she knew what to do with, but she was always her own person."

"You know what we need to do, don't you?" Wendy asked.

"Go look at all the homes marked on this map." Anne was troubled by the prospect, and Wendy picked up on her doubt.

"It may just be a waste of time," Wendy admitted. "But it looks like Lois used the time capsule as one big, big puzzle to lead to some kind of treasure. It certainly could be the mysterious jewels...."

"Yes," Anne agreed. "If Lois went to this much trouble, she must have something she wants us to find. I'd bet she left some instructions to go with whatever she's hidden."

"So we need to get to it!" Wendy said excitedly. "Can you work on it after supper this evening?"

Anne sighed. "I hate to leave the kids with a sitter again tonight. Ben dearly wants to go hunting with his metal detector. Liddie needs to get to bed earlier than she has been. She isn't taking naps in the afternoon anymore."

"Bring them along. I'll see if I have any games they can play in the car without making too much of a mess," Wendy said.

"I guess that would work," Anne agreed, giving Wendy a time when her family would be done with their evening meal.

She thought of Alex's offer to watch a movie together yesterday. She'd even thought of calling him to come over if he still wanted to, but she'd given her word to go with Wendy. Anne didn't know what they could possibly learn by looking at the outsides of houses, but at this point they didn't have a clue to where the missing statue was. Or the jewelry or whatever else it was that Lois might have hidden.

As soon as the library closed, Anne did something she almost never did: She hustled the kids into the car and drove to a fast food place on the edge of town.

They were thrilled with their kids' meals of chicken nuggets and French fries, especially since it was a rare thing to be allowed to eat in the car. Anne nibbled at one of Liddie's chicken pieces since she knew there were more than her daughter could possibly eat. It was a bit greasy for her taste, so she was glad she'd decided to postpone her supper until after she looked at houses with Wendy.

While the kids finished their meals, she stepped out of the car to stretch her legs. Much to her surprise, a tall, dark-haired man came around the corner of the yellow tiled wall of the restaurant.

"I guess you know my guilty secret now," Alex said walking up to her with a large sack in his hands. "I'd rather eat fast-food chicken than cook just for myself while Ryan is gone."

"I won't hold it against you," Anne said with a chuckle, "if you'll forget that I'm feeding my kids fast food in the backseat of the car."

Alex leaned in the car to gaze at Liddie and Ben.

"Hi, guys," he said, sticking his head through the open window. "What's up with you this evening?"

"We have to go look at houses," Ben said, his mouth full of fries.

Anne explained Wendy's plan to look at all the places marked on the map.

"There are no street names, so it may take a while," Anne said.

"Can I see the map? I know this town like the back of my hand."

She took it from the canvas bag lying on the front seat. "We've figured out this is Euclid Avenue because there aren't many curving streets in town."

"Actually, this is Baylor Road," he said, spreading the map on the hood of the car and pointing to a faint line she'd overlooked. "Euclid runs out of town on the north. If you like, I'll pencil in some street names for you."

"Wonderful!" Anne said. "Since the kids are coming along, I want to spend as little time as possible searching for the places we want to see."

"Here," he said, "is the library." He made a mark with the stub of a carpenter's pencil he had in his jacket pocket.

Watching as he quickly wrote the names of familiar streets, Anne couldn't have been more grateful. Her take on the map had been wrong on several points. Alex was saving her as much as an hour to find all the houses marked on the map.

"You guys ready to go house hunting?" Alex asked, again sticking his head through the open window.

"No," Ben said. "I want to go treasure hunting with my metal detector."

"I have an idea. I'll run it past your mom," Alex said.

Anne was still holding the map on the hood, studying it with a new perspective.

"Ryan has been wanting a trampoline for a long time. I finally found one I could afford, but no one has tested it yet. How about I take your kids home with me and let them be my test pilots?"

"Right now?" Anne worried it might be dangerous. "They've never been on one. Are you sure it's safe?"

"I promise it is. And just to be doubly safe, I'll keep a good grip on Liddie if she wants to give it a try."

"Well, okay." Anne trusted Alex, but she also knew how easily children could get hurt.

184 | *Secrets of the Blue Hill Library*

"We'll just have a quick practice since they've just eaten, then I have a fresh carton of rocky road ice cream," he said to Ben who hadn't missed a word of the exchange with his mother.

"I couldn't be more grateful," Anne said. "Wendy and I will breeze through this. I'll come collect the kids as soon as we're done."

"No hurry," Alex said. "We'll have fun."

"Well, thanks. Thanks a lot," Anne said.

With her kids happily on their way to Alex's, Anne still had over forty-five minutes until she had to meet Wendy. She knew exactly how she wanted to spend that time.

Maggie was home alone when Anne got to her house. She still had watery red eyes and a cough, but her voice had improved.

"I made a list of things I should be doing," Maggie said wearing a pretty flowered housecoat and fuzzy pink slippers. "I know I can't expect you to do everything, but I am so grateful for all you've done so far."

"It's going well. I let the artists decide whose art they would want hanging in their homes. It's narrowed down to eleven plus Mr. Buchanan displaying their art in the park. The meeting was a great idea of yours."

"It wasn't mine alone," Maggie said modestly. "There's one thing preying on my mind—I'm almost afraid to ask. The statue hasn't turned up, has it?"

"Regretfully, no." Anne told her about the contents of the safe-deposit box and their plan to look at the houses marked on the map.

"I guess we'll have to be resigned to an anniversary celebration without the 'guest of honor,'" Maggie said in a depressed voice. "I've done nothing but think about where it could possibly be, but I've come up empty."

"Well, don't worry. You need to get well fast," Anne said, wanting to leave on a cheerful note. "The event won't be a success if you're not there."

"It's sweet of you to say so," Maggie said. "I'll do my best."

As Anne drove away to meet Wendy, she thought about how much the stolen statue had affected the town. It was hard to be enthusiastic about Saturday when they'd have to look at an empty base and whatever covering was left over it.

At this moment, the chance of recovering Lois Stover's missing statue was too slight to consider. What possible value could it have to the thieves? Certainly, the felony theft was far too serious to be called a prank.

As far as she knew, the police didn't have any solid leads other than scratched paint that pointed right at Alex's truck. That left Alex and the students who borrowed his truck as suspects, but Anne didn't really consider either of those options. There was also the strange connection to George Franklin's shop with the mysterious appearance of the time capsule there. Could the antiques dealer have taken the statue?

Was there anything she could do to shed light on the theft? She went over the known facts in her mind again and again, but it was futile.

Blue Hill was harboring a very clever thief.

CHAPTER TWENTY-THREE

"W ell that wasn't very productive," Anne said as Wendy pulled up in front of the library to drop her off.

Wendy shook her head. "No, it sure wasn't. I was hoping Lois Stover had left some kind of clue inspired by the houses she lived in. Maybe something in the designs made her think of a puzzle."

She and Wendy had discovered a vacant lot on the street Lois Stover first lived on as a small child, so any clue from the house on Euclid would have been razed when the house was torn down back in the 1960s.

The house the architect had lived in as a schoolgirl was not only standing, it was one of Blue Hill's nicest old Victorians. The couple that had resided there for years painted the exterior in shades of mauve and ivory. The landscaping added to the attractiveness of the house. It included some blooms Anne couldn't identify.

"You could definitely see the influence of that house on Lois Stover's style," Wendy said.

"Yes," Anne agreed. The sloping roof of the second house was similar in design to the small Pittsburgh museum the architect was particularly well known for.

"I'm sorry it was such a bust," Wendy said, sighing.

"Me too," Anne agreed. They hadn't found any clues pointing to hidden secrets, much less jewels, but they did get insight into how Blue Hill shaped Stover and made her the architect she was. Anne wondered if any information could be gleaned from Lois Stover's design philosophy?

"A penny for your thoughts," Wendy joked as Anne hesitated getting out of the vehicle.

Anne shook her head. "Sorry. I was just wishing something would provide a clue to the missing statue."

"You don't suppose," Wendy said, "that there is some kind of treasure hidden in the statue itself and that's why it was stolen?"

"Sadly, no. The most obvious hiding place would have been in the tube holding the time capsule. And why the thieves let that go, I don't understand. Probably because they had trouble getting into it, or thought it was empty except for all those papers."

"And the key," Wendy reminded her.

Anne got out of the car. "I'd offer you a soft drink, but I know you want to get home to your sick kids."

Wendy laughed. "Maybe 'want to' is the wrong way to put it, but yes, I need to get home."

Dusk was rapidly approaching, and Anne knew it was past Liddie's bedtime. She was good about going to sleep while it was still light on long summer days, but tonight was going to be a late night for her.

Her cell phone rang as she ran upstairs to get her car keys.

"I have a sleepy girl here," Alex said. "She conked out on a patio lounge chair. If you're home, I'll carry her to the car and bring her home."

"Ask my mom if I can stay overnight," Ben coached beside him.

"Tell him it's a definite no," Anne said, smiling because her son never missed an opportunity to have fun.

When the kids were safely delivered and tucked into bed, Anne took one more look at the map. She experimented with drawing a line between the house symbols, but they didn't form a meaningful pattern. If Lois Stover had left behind a clue to the jewelry's location, they had yet to find the puzzle, let alone decipher it.

What would Aunt Edie do in a situation like this? One thing was certain, she'd make sure Saturday was a day to remember in Blue Hill history. Anne fell asleep trying to remember if there was anything she'd forgotten to do.

* * *

"Who's calling please," Anne asked when she answered the library phone Wednesday morning.

"I'm with the band you scheduled for your event," a man's deep voice said. "The thing is, we got a gig in the Catskills this weekend."

"You agreed to play for the Stover anniversary celebration," Anne reminded him.

"Sorry, but we need the money. The resort is paying us triple what the town offered, plus expenses."

"Could I speak to the band's manager, please?" Anne asked.

"You're talking to him," the man said none too politely.

"Can we schedule a meeting with the town's attorney?" She was grasping at straws and knew it. "There may be legal issues."

"No legal eagle can stop us from playing the Catskill gig. If you want, I can recommend a band that plays bluegrass on washboards and stuff like that."

"No thank you," Anne said, slumping down on a stool beside the checkout counter as the phone went dead in her ear.

Now she had to find another band with only a few days' notice. Her first impulse was to call Maggie, but she didn't want to distress her friend before she tried to find a substitute group on her own.

By noon, she knew she was in trouble. She'd found a barbershop quartet that would have been totally willing to perform on Saturday but they had a wedding to attend. An elderly man was willing to play his cello if his arthritis wasn't bothering him that day, but there was only a fifty-fifty chance he'd show up.

Bella came in at noon to give Anne a lunch break.

"You wouldn't know a band that could play in the park on Saturday, would you?" Anne asked.

Bella was looking especially cute in white denim shorts and a green striped tank top, not her usual library outfit.

"No, but I'll ask my boyfriend. We're going bike riding after you get back from lunch," Bella said.

Anne had little appetite with all she had to do, but she wanted some exercise to relax her muscles. She put the cheese and tomato sandwich she'd made for lunch into her shoulder bag and set off at a brisk pace.

Without consciously picking her route, she found herself close enough to the high school to hear the marching band practicing for the first football halftime show. She'd always admired the dedication of the teenage musicians. Today they inspired her to think of a possible solution to her band problem.

She jogged toward the field where the drum line was tapping out a fast beat. The man she needed was the teacher in charge. He called for a rest just as she approached.

"What can I do for you?" he asked. He was a redhead with his face flushed from the hot August sun. "We're almost done here."

Did he think she was a parent coming to complain that it was too warm for the rehearsal?

After quickly introducing herself, she learned his name was Brian Nichols, new to Blue Hill and in charge of the music program at the high school.

"Your marching band looks good. Sounds good too," she said to break the ice. "Can I run something past you?"

"Sure. You're not one of the band parents trying to raise money for new uniforms, are you? I think the old wool ones are older than the kids who will be wearing them."

"Sorry, no."

His question gave her an idea, but could she trust herself after Art-in-the-Park snowballed into a big deal?

She took a deep breath and explained how the band they'd hired had let them down. "This would be a great opportunity to collect pledges to help pay for new uniforms. You could set up a table near the musicians."

Mr. Nichols was a bright young man. He understood what she had in mind before she fully laid it out for him.

"Some band members are out of town on vacation," he said. "We don't have a full marching band yet, but we do have plenty of players to send over who are in the jazz band. They've been meeting regularly for several weeks. They're ready and eager to play."

"That would be perfect," Anne said, relief washing over her. "They can set up to the left of the temporary platform. I'll leave it to you to decide what they'll play."

"Will you have electrical outlets for the amplifiers for the bass and guitar?"

"Fortunately, yes, since you're taking the place of a rock band. Thanks so much for saving the day," she said, sincerely meaning it.

What had started as a simple ceremony to honor Blue Hill's famous citizen was quickly becoming a big community event. Fortunately, Wendy was planning activities to keep the younger children involved. Anne couldn't wait to see what the lady who painted faces would do for Liddie and Ben.

A dark cloud had blocked the sun while she talked to the band director. Now that she studied the sky, she knew it was likely to rain at any moment. As she race-walked back to the library, several big drops hit the pavement just ahead of her. She broke into a run when she felt rain on her face. It was a warm summer downpour, not at all unpleasant, but what would happen if the weather didn't cooperate Saturday? She knew there was a plan to move the event to the church fellowship hall, but participation had swelled beyond the capacity of any indoor venue.

By the time she got inside, her top was clinging damply to her shoulders and back. She dashed upstairs to change, still worrying about rain ruining the special day for Blue Hill.

Chapter Twenty-Four

Anne was lying in bed unable to get to sleep when Liddie appeared in her doorway, shivering in her summer pajamas.

"Sweetheart, it's the middle of the night. Why are you out of bed?"

"I want to sleep with you," her daughter said, clutching her blanket to her chest.

Just then a huge bolt of lightning illuminated the room, and Hershey let out a long howl from his pen to go with the thunderclap. Anne didn't need to ask what had roused her little girl.

"Crawl in," she said, moving over and patting the space beside her.

She couldn't blame Liddie for being afraid. This was a monster storm that showed no sign of abating.

As cuddly as Liddie could be, she wasn't a restful bed partner. She dozed off curled up with her knees firmly planted against her mother's back. It was impossible for Anne to get comfortable without disturbing Liddie.

The thunderstorm gradually moved away, but the rain came down even harder. By three Anne was still awake listening to the pounding rhythm of the downpour on the roof. Fortunately,

Alex had made sure the roof was waterproof when he first did the renovations for the library.

It wasn't the safety of her home or the library that kept Anne awake. She couldn't help but worry about the big event on Saturday. Would it be washed out after all their hard work? Even if they moved it into the church fellowship hall, it was unlikely a big crowd would come out in a deluge.

Anne crept silently out of bed and padded to the living room area on bare feet. After muting the sound on the TV, she turned to the weather channel.

There was bad news and good news: The rain was predicted to fall through much of Thursday with sunny skies predicted for Friday and Saturday. Residents of the county were warned to watch for flash floods. In no circumstances was it safe to drive a vehicle on a water-covered road.

Anne turned off the rest of the weather report. At least Saturday promised to be sunny and reasonably warm.

As soon as she got back to her bedroom, she had another little visitor when Ben wandered into the room and saw his little sister curled up on the bed.

"What's wrong with Liddie?" he asked, rubbing his eyes to wake up all the way.

"She was afraid of the storm. I know a big boy like you wouldn't let a little thunder and lightning bother you."

Her explanation sent Ben back to his room. Anne knew she had to get up soon, but she still hoped to get a little sleep before her alarm rang. Her cozy bed was inviting while rain still hammered the roof.

When her clock did ring, she didn't have the option of going back to sleep. She dragged herself out of bed, being careful not to wake Liddie yet. Pushing aside the window curtains for a look outside, she wasn't surprised to see a gray sky and rain splashing on the ground below. Puddles were growing on the ground where the earth couldn't absorb the rain quickly enough.

"Can I sail my boat in the gutter?" Ben asked, appearing in her doorway fully dressed.

"Not the way the rain is coming down now," she said. "I'm afraid you'll have to be content with inside games."

"I'll never get to use my metal detector," he said unhappily. "It's almost time for school to start up again."

"As soon as the sun comes out and the ground dries, you can hunt to your heart's delight."

It occurred to her that this was a rash promise, given Ben's long memory, but she understood how hard it was for him not being able to use his new prized possession.

"While you wait for me to make breakfast, why don't you get your puzzle box and see how long it takes you to open it?"

"My fastest time is nine minutes and twelve seconds," he said proudly. "Maybe I can do it even faster now."

Anne smiled at her son. He might forget to bring his homework home or need reminding to feed his dog, but when he was interested in something, his memory was phenomenal.

She gathered a change of clothes as quietly as possible and went to the bathroom to shower and dress. It was going to be a long, hard day, especially if the rain didn't let up. Mentally she tried to make a list of everything she had to do that day and

Friday, but before she got halfway through, a soft little knock on the door told her Liddie was up.

* * *

When she got to work, she found some mats to spread in front of the door. They helped absorb the rain clinging to clothes and feet, but the entryway was going to need a serious mop job before the day was over.

Few people came to the library the first hour or so, only the diehard newspaper readers braving the inclement weather. Anne had more than her usual number of volunteers lined up because the memorial event would require her to be gone most of today and Friday. Even with Maggie feeling well enough to help, she had a mountain of details to check out.

Saturday the library would be closed in honor of the special day. She walked to the door and stared out through the streaks of steamy water clouding the glass panel. Across the street Bella was headed for the library, struggling with a huge umbrella that only partially kept her dry. The bottoms of her pants legs looked soaked as she ran toward the door. Anne was filled with gratitude that the young woman had come to help out in such nasty weather.

Before she could open the door for her volunteer, she heard the library phone ring. She hustled over to pick it up, expecting a patron to ask whether they were open. Anne might opt to close the library for a snow day, but she'd never considered closing for a rain day.

"Anne, I have bad news." It was Maggie, sounding more like herself but with an undertone of panic.

What possible crisis could there be now? Anne imagined the high school band taking off for the Catskills too or the main speaker, the mayor, backing out.

"The park is flooded," Maggie said.

"Surely not!" Anne didn't want to believe it.

"Tom drove by on his way to visit the hospital. Actually, I asked him to make sure the platform for the speeches had been assembled. The street on the north side of the park is under water. It's spilled over on the park."

"How bad is it?" Anne was almost afraid to hear her answer.

"Very bad." Maggie sounded a bit weepy. She, of all people, had labored long and hard to make the event a reality.

"What caused it? I don't remember that area flooding before." Anne was struggling to take in the bad news.

"The storm sewers are blocked. Water spilled over into the park. The area where we were going to put the artists' tables is totally flooded. Can you come see for yourself?"

"Are you there now?" Anne asked.

"Yes, I'll wait for you to get here."

Fortunately, Bella arrived just as Anne tried to digest Maggie's bad news. She explained the crisis to her volunteer and left her in charge of the library.

Anne put on a transparent plastic raincoat with a hood and headed out into the deluge. When she drove close to the park, she saw barriers erected across one road that was obviously under fairly deep water. She circled around and found a parking place a block or so away, going on foot over wet pavement with unavoidable puddles quickly soaking her feet to the ankles.

Maggie was true to her word. She was waiting near the speakers' platform engulfed in an oversized yellow rain slicker and a hat to match.

"See," she said, pointing beyond the place where the statue used to stand.

Anne rubbed the rainwater off her face with her fingers the way swimmers did and saw a pond where no pond had been. The back part of the park was under water, completely flooding the area where the artists were supposed to set up.

"Even where it's not flooded, the ground is mushy," Maggie said. "What are we going to do?"

Anne felt close to panic herself. It wasn't like her friend to despair, but no one could've imagined this watery crisis. In the distance she saw two figures with long-handled tools poking at what must be a storm drain along the side of the street.

With her glasses speckled by the continuing rain, Anne couldn't identify the people trying to clean the drain.

"Who are those men poking at the drain?" Anne asked. "They look familiar, but I can't be sure from here."

As she spoke, a huge yellowish orange truck stopped by the barricade. One of the men got out to move it, then replace it when the truck slowly moved through the water flooding the street.

"It's a town maintenance crew," Maggie said.

"They have enough equipment to drain Niagara Falls," Anne said with relief.

"Not quite," Maggie said laughing with relief. "If we get a full day of sun tomorrow, maybe the park will dry enough to use it. Or maybe not."

Anne didn't have a clue how long it would take, assuming the town crew cleared the blocked storm drain. At least she felt a ray of hope.

The two men who'd ambitiously tackled the blocked drain on their own stood back to watch the professionals take over. Anne walked closer, curious about how they'd proceed.

She stopped when she was close enough to identify the two would-be drain cleaners. Harold Buchanan was gesturing with the arm that wasn't holding the shovel. Of course, he'd want the park dried out so he could set up his art. But who was his helper?

The younger man had his back to her, but he still looked somewhat familiar. Of course, it wasn't surprising that a retired high school teacher would know quite a few young men who'd taken his class. His helper was husky compared to most high school students.

He turned, and Anne was surprised. It was Derek Umsted's older brother. Was Mitch a former art student, or had he just wandered by out of curiosity and been drafted? He and Harold looked deep in serious conversation from where she was standing.

Maggie said something to her, but Anne was so lost in thought she missed the gist of it.

"Sorry, what did you say?" she asked.

"Alex just pulled up behind the barricade in his big truck," Maggie repeated.

Anne watched as he got out and walked toward them.

"Everyone in town is talking about the flood in the park," he said after greeting them. "I thought I'd see if I could help, but it looks like the town has things under control."

"Harold Buchanan was trying to unplug the storm drain when we got here. Mitch Umsted was helping him," Anne said.

"Mitch? I doubt that kid ever took an art class," Alex said. "The little work he did for me, he was all thumbs."

"Maybe he just happened by while Harold was working on the drain," Maggie suggested.

Anne was pretty sure people who 'happened by' didn't bring shovels with them.

"I got my truck fixed," Alex said, looking pleased with himself. "Want to see if you can tell where it was scratched?"

"I'll pass," Maggie said. "There's nothing I can do here until we know if the town can drain all that water."

As Maggie splashed off to where she'd parked her car, Anne followed Alex to his truck, happy for a few moments alone with him.

Down the street, still out of hearing, Harold and his would-be helper were still deep in conversation.

"I had it done," Alex said. "I have too much work to do to take care of it myself I decided."

"I'd never know it was damaged," Anne said. "I wonder what Harold and Mitch Umsted are talking about. They seem like an unlikely pair to have much in common."

"Football, baseball, you know, manly topics," Alex said in a teasing voice.

"You're probably right," Anne said, looking up at his smile. He had a knack for bringing sunshine into her life, even in the continuing deluge.

"Need a ride back to the library?" he asked.

"I have my car," she said regretfully. A little time with Alex was just what she needed to brighten her day.

As she started back to her vehicle, her legs soaked halfway up her slacks, she looked behind her and saw the two still deep in conversation. What could they be so serious about?

Chapter Twenty-Five

Anne arrived at the park early Friday morning with Ben in tow. Fortunately, Liddie was spending the day with a sitter while she took care of the countless details of the Stover event.

"Do you remember what we talked about?" she asked her son.

He'd begged to go to the park with her to hunt for treasure with his metal detector. Naturally, he remembered her promise to let him use it as soon as the sun was shining.

"Yes, I have to stay out of the way of people getting the park ready for Saturday." He recited her warning word for word, a good sign that he was paying attention.

"And don't go over to the area where it was flooded. The water is gone, but the ground is still mushy."

Anne looked around the park at volunteers busy preparing for the big event. The weather forecast predicted sunny skies through the weekend, relieving her mind of one serious problem.

She wasn't the only one with an eye on the weather report. In fact, everyone involved had to be keeping a wary eye on the prediction. Several participants of Art-in-the-Park had requested they be allowed to set up their tables today.

Some had brought lattice backdrops or painted canvas murals to draw attention to their art. When artists showed them to Anne, she suggested they not put them up until Saturday morning.

"We can never be certain about weather reports," she said to several different artists. "There's always the wind too. You don't want to chase your backdrop into the next county."

Fortunately, no one complained about having the art tables moved to a different part of the park. The town workers had put up barricades and a plastic streamer to keep people off the wet ground. Too many footprints could ruin the grass and leave unsightly indentations.

When she thought of holes in the ground, she immediately thought of Ben. He hadn't raced over to her to show off a find in some time.

"Ben!" She looked in all directions for the familiar red T-shirt he was wearing but didn't see him.

Relief flooded over her when he answered her call and hurried over to her. She knew Ben wouldn't wander far without her permission, but it was a big park. She didn't relish the idea of looking for him.

"Stay where I can see you," she said.

"I was by the place where the statue was. I found this."

He held out a metal button with the design of an anchor crushed almost beyond recognition.

"Nice," Anne said automatically, wondering if they had enough grills to do hot dogs for everyone who came.

"What are those pictures around the statue thing?" Ben asked.

"I can tell you what they are," Maggie said, coming up to Anne and her son. She was wearing jeans, something she rarely did, and a long sleeved knit shirt with the sleeves rolled up.

"I'm glad to see you," Anne said. "It feels like I should be doing something, but I don't know what."

"You have everything so well organized there isn't much left to do," Maggie said. "Sorry I'm late, but the mayor had me on the phone for ages. He wanted to run his speech by me."

"Is it good?" Anne asked.

"It could be—if he cuts it by at least a third. I don't think he liked hearing that, but his audience will be eager to get to the hot dogs and all the pies we have lined up."

Anne followed Maggie and Ben to the base where the statue had stood.

"There are four sides," Maggie said stooping down to Ben's level. "Each one shows a scene from Lois Stover's life. I believe she had a lot to do with planning the theme."

"I'd never paid that much attention to the base," Anne admitted.

"The one on this side depicts her birth and early years." Maggie reached down to rub away a coat of dust. "The motto reads 'The possibilities are endless when we're born.'"

"This one shows her graduating," Anne said. "It reads, 'Education is the greatest treasure.'"

"My father designed and executed the base, but Lois gave him the ideas and the mottos."

"Goodness, Harold," Maggie said. "You scared me out of a year's growth, sneaking up on us like that."

"Sorry," he said. "But you've given me an idea. Maybe I'll call attention to the scenes on the base in my little talk."

"What's this?" Ben called out from the back of the base where he was studying a third scene.

"That's the museum Lois Stover designed," Harold said. "And around the other corner she's shown with the governor giving her an award."

Ben's curiosity was quickly satisfied. He started to point his metal detector at the ground behind the statue base.

"We have a problem," Maggie said when Harold had drifted away to check out the platform where he would speak. "You know a service club is donating and grilling the hot dogs?"

"Yes. Don't tell me they've backed out."

"No, nothing like that. But they want estimates from us of how many they'll need."

"A whole lot—but that's not a very good answer." Anne frowned. She'd been wrestling with the head count all week, but there was no way to predict how many people would come.

"I've heard from a friend in Deshler," Maggie said. "She intends to come and bring the members of her book club with her. I wonder how many out-of-town people will show up."

"Oh my," Anne said. "That could really swell our numbers."

"We'll be ready for them," Maggie said with an optimism Anne didn't fully share. "One of the men grilling hot dogs can run to the market if necessary."

"The caterer is bringing huge pans of baked beans, potato salad, and macaroni salad. That will help," Anne said.

"And we have promises of enough home-baked pies to feed the whole town," Maggie said. "I know Alice Covell is busy making dozens and dozens of her famous lemon bars, but I expect they'll disappear fast."

"Should we try to provide coffee?" Anne asked. It was good to have Maggie healthy again. Anne appreciated being able to bounce ideas off of her and get helpful feedback.

"No, it's too late. I think lemonade and iced tea will suffice."

"Yes, I agree," Anne said. "When I first said I'd help, the event was just a quiet ceremony to rededicate the statue. Now we're planning to feed the whole town. What other food do we have lined up?"

"I'm bringing a car load of chips and other nibbles," Maggie said. "I expect the congregation to turn up in large numbers, many bringing a dish to share. Can you think of anything we've overlooked?"

"Do we know whether Arlen Buchanan will come? He might need help with his wheelchair."

"I've asked Harold, but he only said it depends on whether he's having a good day," Maggie said.

"If he does come, we should treat him like an honored guest," Anne said. "I thought he should have a place on the speakers' platform so it's easy to introduce him."

"Good idea," Maggie said, surveying the park with a practiced eye.

"Is there anything else I can do today?" Anne asked, happy that Maggie was there to take charge.

"Wendy is picking up the buns at the bakery. That pretty much takes care of my list for now." Maggie studied a paper on her clipboard.

"Then I'll check on the library. What time do you need me in the morning?"

"If you can be here by nine, that would be great," Maggie said. "Wendy may need a little help with the children's games."

Anne nodded agreement. Her eyes scanned the park looking for Ben. He ran up to her before she could call him.

"Look what I found!" he said, clutching something shiny in his hand.

"What do you have there?" Harold asked, walking over to where Anne and Maggie stood.

Ben proudly held out the object on the palm of his hand. It was one of the bolts that had held the statue in place.

"I didn't know there were more to find," Harold said.

"It was pushed all the way down into the ground," Ben said, explaining how he'd found it with his metal detector.

"Good work," Harold said. "You deserve a reward."

Ben looked at his mother, but she wasn't sure what Harold had in mind.

"Tell you what," Harold said, reaching into the wallet in his back pocket. "I'll give you a finder's fee. Do you know what this is?"

"Five dollars," Ben said, his eyes wide.

"I'll give you this for the bolt," Harold said.

"I think I'd rather keep it." Ben looked up at Harold as if asking permission.

"I thought I'd give it to the police in case they want it for their investigation," Harold said.

Anne doubted the police could tell much from one more bolt, but she knew having the statue missing must be very hard on the former art teacher.

"I have a better idea," Harold said, stooping to talk to Ben on his level. "You drive a hard bargain, but I just happen to have one of these."

He held out a twenty-dollar bill.

Ben looked from the money to his mother.

"It's your decision," Anne told him even though she had some misgivings.

He thought about it for several long moments.

"Thank you, sir," Ben said, taking the bill and handing over the bolt.

For a few moments her son looked so unhappy she thought he'd change his mind, but Ben stuck to his decision. He was always saving up for something, and no doubt this would buy an item on his wish list.

It was a lot to pay for a useless bolt. Anne couldn't understand Harold's eagerness to have it, but it was a done deal.

* * *

On the way home, fatigue hit Anne hard. Fortunately, everything was quiet in the library when she got there. She was tempted to slip upstairs for a short nap, but she didn't want to take unfair advantage of her volunteer. Bella was hoping she could go biking with her new boyfriend, and the day was perfect for it.

Ben was still conflicted about the bolt, but he went to the Children's Room and entertained himself until it was time to close the library.

The last person through the door was also the most welcome to Anne. Alex was beaming with his hair newly cut and a pair of new jeans to go with the sky-blue sweater she especially liked.

"You look done in," he said. "I thought maybe we could order take-out Chinese and watch a movie once the kids go to bed."

Anne perked up with the prospect of an evening with Alex.

"I'd love to," she said, checking the clock to see it was nearly closing time.

She found the neatly lettered sign Remi had made for the door to let people know the library would be closed for the Stover event.

Alex left to pick up a Chinese dinner, first asking her what she would like.

"Surprise Ben and me," she said. "And I think they have a child-size entrée that would be perfect for Liddie. She loves chicken in almost every form."

As Anne checked all the rooms and the restroom for patrons who might still be there, she felt her fatigue slipping away. An evening with Alex was just what she needed to put aside thoughts of the missing statue and worries that they couldn't feed a huge crowd.

By the time she picked up Liddie and sent both kids to wash for dinner, Alex was back with their takeout dinner.

When her kids saw the nice meal they were having, they were especially cooperative. They even went through their bedtime routine with a minimum of fuss.

It wasn't late when she settled down on the couch to watch the movie Alex had brought. To his credit, he'd picked a rather touching love story and had it set up to play.

Anne doubted she could stay awake through any movie, but she wanted to tell Alex about the bolt.

"Strange," Alex said when he heard about Harold's twenty-dollar offer. "That's a lot of money to give a kid for something that's basically useless.

"It is," Anne said. "For a little while I didn't think Ben would accept any amount of money."

"I'm sure Ben will find something even better with his metal detector," Alex said.

"Eventually," Anne agreed. She was still confused, though. Harold had paid far too much to buy the bolt from Ben. What good were bolts if the statue was gone forever?

Chapter Twenty-Six

I have a secret," Ben said, perched on the edge of his chair as he made his scrambled eggs disappear as fast as possible.

"Right now I need you to finish your breakfast and brush your teeth," Anne said, scarcely noticing what he'd said.

Mildred had invited Liddie to spend the day with her and attend the events at the park together. Liddie couldn't have been more excited if she'd been invited to a circus.

Anne was extremely grateful that she wouldn't have to keep track of a five-year-old in a crowd since she was partly responsible for things going smoothly.

When she heard Mildred's soft knock on the door she didn't need to ask if Liddie was ready to go. She had her backpack full to capacity and was wearing her little red tennis shoes with a favorite lime-green outfit.

"Ben, are you ready?" Anne called out.

He emerged from the bathroom, his toothbrush foamy with paste.

"You told me to brush my teeth," he said. "Do you want to hear my secret now?"

"In the car," Anne said. "We have to leave."

It was past nine on Saturday morning. Anne had done her best to be on time, but every two minutes her children had some small problem for her to solve. Her stomach was so jumpy she couldn't wait to get to the park. Hopefully, every bad thing that was going to happen had already happened, but a lot of people had to do their jobs well for everything to go smoothly.

Ben chatted about puzzle boxes and statue bases as Anne drove. She tried to give him her full attention, but it was soon obvious that parking was going to be a problem. She circled the block adjacent to the park and finally found a spot close enough to carry the boxes of paper napkins she was contributing to the lunch.

"Can I show you now?" Ben asked as he carried one of her boxes for her.

"As soon as I can, honey," Anne said, knowing she should have paid more attention to what he was trying to tell her. "These napkins have to go on the table."

The wind was brisk, and the first pile of napkins fluttered with the top ones flying away. Ben ran after them without being asked, but the ones he caught were too soiled to put out for the public. In hindsight Anne knew she should've brought something to weigh down the paper napkins.

"Can I help you?" a tall slender man with a bushy white mustache asked.

Anne didn't remember his name, but he was wearing an apron with a badge to show he belonged to a noontime service club.

"Can you maybe stop the wind?" she asked, an attempt at a joke.

"I'll do that if I see Dorothy and her little dog Toto flying by," he said with a chuckle. "But for now, leave the napkins in the boxes. I'll weigh them down with stones."

"Thank you so much," Anne said.

She was about to introduce herself when Ben tugged on the long blue-and-yellow flowered shirt she was wearing for the occasion.

"Now will you come look?" he asked with an urgency she couldn't ignore.

The park was filling up with people, many of them with their own lawn chairs. It took Anne a few minutes to get past all the volunteers who had questions for her. Ben scampered ahead and turned back several times in his urgency to have her follow.

It wasn't like Ben to be this impatient. She hoped he wouldn't show her where another bolt was buried. She'd let him bring his metal detector but only if he agreed not to use it where there were people. That pretty much limited him to poking around the empty base where the statue had been.

"It's here," he said, falling to his knees beside the scene of Lois Stover in a cap and gown. "See, Mom?"

Anne wasn't sure what she was looking at other than a metal casting of one phase of the architect's life. She stooped beside her son, holding her long skirt so it wouldn't drag in the dirt.

"Tell me," Anne said in a gentle voice, not wanting to challenge Ben no matter what he'd imagined about the scene.

"It's like my puzzle box, Mom. Here's the key." He pointed at an object in the architect's hand. "It moves."

Much to her surprise, there was a subtle change in the scene when Ben pushed at the round object. She didn't immediately pick up on it, but once she saw the difference it was unmistakable.

"I guess Lois Stover left one final puzzle," she said as Ben continued to push and prod parts of the scene.

Anne was distracted by the arrival of a large white van from the retirement home. Instead of a bevy of elderly women, it was only carrying one resident.

The man being lowered to the ground in a wheelchair looked tiny compared to the burly man in scrubs who was helping him. Harold Buchanan was hovering, silently supervising as the attendant pushed his father's chair up a temporary ramp to the speakers' platform.

In front of the platform, the high school jazz band was playing a vigorous tune. It sounded more like a Civil War era marching song than a twenty-first-century pop number, but she trusted their leader to provide more contemporary music after the serious part of the program was over.

"Mom, you're not paying attention," Ben said, sounding a bit disappointed. "I'm trying to solve the rest of the puzzle, and I need your help."

"Maybe we should work on it when there aren't so many people in the park," Anne suggested. "We don't want to attract a crowd."

Ben stood and looked at the multitude gathering in front of the speakers' platform. He blinked as if noticing them for the first time.

"Can we do it when the people go home?" he asked in a whisper.

"We sure can," Anne said, patting his shoulder. She was almost as curious as Ben about the possibility of the panel opening.

Hauling chairs to the park had seemed like one too many things to do, so she and Ben found a place to stand at the back of the rows of chairs.

"Anne, over here." A familiar voice called out to her. She was happy to see Alex.

"I brought some extra chairs," he said gesturing at two beside him.

"How did you know I wouldn't bother to bring ours?" She asked, slipping into his row and sitting beside him.

"Just a guess. Here's a chair for you too, Ben."

Anne saw her son hesitate and knew exactly what he had in mind. He was looking for a way to go back to the statue base and work on what he saw as a puzzle. Maybe he was right, but she'd already told him to wait.

Her son slumped down in the chair and leaned his elbows on his knees.

"Folks, we have a celebrity guest this morning."

A woman in dark-rimmed glasses and a mop of fashionable brunette curls tied back in a ponytail stood at the microphone. Anne thought she worked in the mayor's office, although she didn't know her name.

"I'd like to introduce Arlen Buchanan, the man who sculpted our beloved statue of Lois Stover."

The elderly man stood up on shaky legs, and his son was quick to move to his side and take his arm. The crowd applauded, and Arlen responded by making his way to the microphone.

"Where's Gavin?" he asked in a surprisingly strong voice.

Harold whispered something to him, possibly reminding him that his other son had passed away some years ago. He was obviously urging him to go back to his wheelchair but not having any success.

"Is this Lois's hundredth birthday?" Arlen asked. "She's older than me, but not by much."

"No, Dad," Harold said, his words caught by the microphone. "Remember, there was a problem funding the statue. It wasn't installed until 1990, so the community decided to wait with opening the time capsule until twenty-five years after the original dedication. This is the anniversary."

Harold gently tugged on his father's arm, but the older man refused to budge.

"Where's my statue?" His voice boomed out with surprising volume.

"It's being cleaned, Dad."

Anne didn't blame Harold for concealing the truth from his father. The retired art teacher's face was flushed, and the starched white collar under his navy suit seemed to wilt in front of her eyes. She could only imagine the stress he was under as he tried to get his father away from the microphone.

"It's time to sit down, Dad."

The mayor's helper took one arm, and Harold took the other. The young woman seemed to have more success than his son in talking the elderly man into sitting back down in his wheelchair.

At least the sculptor had gotten the crowd's attention. There was none of the restless stirring that usually preceded a program.

After Reverend Tom gave an invocation, the mayor was next on the program.

The mayor began with a brief history of Blue Hill. Anne caught Maggie's eye and wondered if this was the part of his speech she'd wanted him to delete.

Half an hour later, Ben was squirming and Anne was having a hard time keeping her eyes open. When the mayor was finally through with his speech, a soprano from church sang a familiar hymn. Then Harold had his turn at the podium.

Years of teaching must have given him confidence as a speaker. Anne found herself enjoying his stories about growing up with a renowned sculptor—his father—and meeting Lois Stover when he was still very young.

His talk perked up the large crowd, and soon afterward the aroma of grilled hot dogs encouraged people to form lines for the early luncheon.

"Now, Mom?" Ben asked after Alex said good-bye to pick up some supplies he needed.

"We'll have a little lunch first," Anne said. "You didn't eat much for breakfast, and all I had was coffee."

The lines were long, but the wait was worth it—at least to Anne. Ben fidgeted but didn't say anything else about the graduation scene.

They ate standing up, and to his credit, Ben managed to eat potato salad and baked beans without dribbling anything on his shirt.

"Anne, I need you," Wendy said, dashing up as they were finishing slices of apple pie. "There are twice as many kids here as I expected."

Anne remembered her promise to help with children's games. She looked at Ben. He shrugged his shoulders in a very adult way.

"I guess if you promised to help, you should," he said. Lowering his voice, he assured her no one else would discover his secret.

Fortunately, Ben enjoyed the games as much as anyone. As one of the older children, he got a turn to toss horseshoes. He came in second in a potato sack race and helped his mother organize musical chairs.

Gradually, parents called to their children and started drifting away from the park. Anne worried when one little girl went unclaimed, but her parents came for her when they finished policing the area for carelessly disposed trash.

As much as Anne appreciated the praise for a splendid event that came her way, she kept thinking of a long nap on her couch at home. The Art-in-the-Park portion had seemed a rousing success too.

"Now, Mom?" Ben asked as only the volunteers dismantling the speakers' platform and folding up tables were left.

"Thanks for waiting so patiently," Anne said. "Let's go check out the panel."

When they got there, she sat down in front of the graduation scene, heedless of her skirt. Ben joined her and started trying to manipulate all the raised parts. Nothing happened until he tried to move the tassel on the engraved architect's cap.

"It moved, Mom!"

Anne scooted closer and peered at the tassel. "Try again," she said, although Ben didn't need any urging.

It took him a minute to realize the tassel had to be pulled outward, not slid sideways. When he did it right, he revealed a small knob under it.

"It's a lot like my puzzle box," he said in awe, stabbing at the knob with his finger. "Now we just need to find the key."

"Key?" Anne asked.

"Not like a key that opens a lock," Ben explained as he prodded with his fingers. "The key is the one mechanism that releases the secret panel."

"Mechanism," Anne repeated, impressed by her son's use of the word.

"Press here, Mom. I don't have enough fingers."

She followed his directions while he investigated all the other parts of the scene. Just when her eyes wandered to the few people still cleaning up, Ben yelped in pleasure.

"This is it, Mom! I knew it would open."

Anne bent almost double to bring her eye to the opening. It was dark inside, and her first thought was that spiders liked small cavities.

"Let me put my hand in first," Anne said, not to deprive him of the pleasure but to make sure no undesirable bugs or snakes were lurking inside.

The space they'd found was relatively small. All Anne could find inside was an envelope with a bit of black mold on the flap. She held it for a minute, wondering whether to open it.

"What is it, Mom?" Ben stood over her, literally dancing with excitement.

"I guess it's okay if I look," she said.

The envelope looked unsavory with damp spots on the address side. It only took a slight pressure with her thumbnail to open it.

She gasped as she read with Ben looking over her shoulder. This changed everything.

Chapter Twenty-Seven

I t's just a piece of paper," Ben said, sounding disappointed as only a nine-year-old boy could.

"But what a piece of paper," his mother said, reading the legal document for the second time. "You'll be a hero to the whole town for discovering how to find the secret hiding place."

"I will?" Ben cheered up a little. "I thought we'd find jewels."

"This is better," Anne said. "It tells us what Lois Stover wanted done with her real-life treasure after she was gone. We only found the solution because you love puzzles the way she did."

Anne stood and brushed off her skirt, hardly realizing it was soiled by the dirt at the statue's base. What she'd found had shaken her world, and she couldn't wait to share it with her friends.

"Can I go look for real treasure now?" Ben asked.

"Yes, but stay where I can see you," Anne said. "I just want to show this to the other committee members."

Ben scampered off, going to the opening behind the graduation scene. Not surprisingly, he put his hand in the hidden compartment to make sure there was nothing else in it.

There wasn't, so he closed the hidden compartment and waved at her when it was done.

Anne didn't blame him for wanting to keep his find a secret, but sooner or later she had to reveal it to her friends and other interested parties.

Wendy was in the process of hauling the things she'd brought for the children's games to her SUV. Two of her own kids were helping her, so Anne didn't offer to carry anything. Instead she waved at her friend to join her out of the hearing of everyone still there.

Behind Anne the volunteers were taking apart the speakers' platform to store it in a town garage until it was needed again. They were making so much noise she had to gesture to Wendy to meet her closer to the statue base.

"What's up?" Wendy asked, her cheeks pink from exertion or the sun.

"Show Mrs. Pyle what you discovered," Anne called to her son who was running his metal detector over the ground just beyond the statue base.

He galloped up to them, leaving his precious metal detector behind. This was his moment to shine, and he took full advantage of it. He explained about his puzzle box and the way he found the first moving part in the graduation scene. Anne resisted an urge to tell the story faster.

When Ben had it open again, Wendy knelt down and put her hand inside.

"There's nothing in it," she said.

"I took it out," Anne said, holding the envelope in front of her friend. "You need to read it for yourself."

"It's a legal paper," Wendy said as she took the paper out of the envelope. "See, there's a notary seal on it. It looks authentic."

"Read on," Anne urged her, enjoying the look of surprise and delight when her friend realized what it was.

"It sets up a scholarship fund for women who want to go into architecture or engineering," Wendy said.

"Go into what?" Maggie asked, coming up to them still wearing a big white apron from serving food. A hairnet contained her hair, and her face was flushed by the sun beating down.

"Read this," Anne said, retrieving it from Wendy. "Ben found a way to open the panel with the graduation scene. This was inside."

"Wow!" Maggie broke the silence around her and expressed the way all three of them felt. "There's a note on the back too, but the ink is so faded I can hardly make it out."

"Oh dear, I was so dumbfounded by the bequest I never thought to turn the paper over. What does it say?" Anne asked.

"See for yourself," Maggie said handing it over.

Squinting in the bright sun, Anne read the two sentences faded to faint brown swirls:

I bet you thought this secret compartment had jewels hidden in it, but as I've always said, 'Education is the greatest treasure.' I've used my aunt's jewels and the rest of my estate to finance a scholarship fund so that more girls can follow in my footsteps.

"The missing jewelry isn't a mystery anymore," she said. "Lois sold it long ago to help finance her scholarship fund. Now all we need to do is go to the bank and see what's to be done with it."

"And how much money is available," Wendy added. "College is so expensive these days. This may just be a drop in the bucket to those who are awarded a Stover scholarship."

"Or not," Maggie said. "If it's been collecting interest all these years, it could be substantial."

"Until we can talk to the bank and whoever was left in charge of Lois's estate, let's keep it between the three of us," Anne said.

"And our husbands," Maggie said. "Mine always seems to know when I have something on my mind."

Anne wanted to confide in someone too, and her first thought was telling Alex.

"I think Bella is my volunteer Monday morning," Anne said. "If she is, I'll feel completely comfortable leaving her in charge and running to the bank then. Do you two want to come along?"

"I'd love to," Wendy said, "but I promised to take my kids to the shore one more time before school starts. We'll be leaving early Monday morning and staying overnight at one of Chad's aunt's. She should get a medal of honor for putting up my whole gang, so I don't want to change plans on her."

"It shouldn't take too long at the bank," Anne said. "Do you want to come along, Maggie?"

"I'd love to, but I have an appointment with my eye doctor. If I cancel, it could be months before she has another opening. I think my reading glasses should be a bit stronger."

Her friends left, eager to get home after a long day at the park. Anne didn't notice her own fatigue until she was in the car with Ben. Much to her surprise, her legs felt shaky and she had to take several deep breaths before she started the car. Of all the things that could've happened that day, finding a scholarship bequest from Lois Stover was the most unlikely.

"Can I tell Ryan what I found?"

"Yes, but let's wait until after I go to the bank Monday. Then we'll know for sure what's involved."

It was hard to ask her son to keep quiet for a while, but she knew how easy it was to start a rumor. And after all the excitement the Lois Stover statue and time capsule had generated, the last thing Blue Hill needed was another round of rumors and speculation. Anne wanted the good news of the bequest to go out clearly and accurately. Her other concern, which she did not voice to her son, was what might be the implications of Ben's discovery on the mysterious someones who had taken the statue.

Chapter Twenty-Eight

"C an I go too?" Ben was waiting for the blueberry pancake still sizzling in the skillet Monday morning. Hershey sat expectantly at his feet, waiting for the bits of pancake that were sure to come. Sometimes Anne thought that all that dog did was wait for table scraps.

"Me too," Liddie said, holding a bite of pancake in her cheek.

"Sorry," Anne said. "I have no idea when I'll be able to get away from the library, Ben. I'm as eager as you are to learn more about the scholarship bequest, but a trip to the bank is pretty dull compared to what you're up to today."

"Oh yeah, I forgot."

Both he and Liddie had fun days planned with their caregivers. Anne knew his exciting find overshadowed everything.

After breakfast and before she left to go down to the library, Anne checked for the third time the hiding place where she'd put the document. It seemed secure enough in her bottom dresser drawer under some flannel nightgowns she only wore in the winter. But now that she thought of it, the first place a burglar would look was in bedroom drawers.

It would be safer in the library, but she still felt as if she had to guard it like precious treasure. At the last minute she decided to take it to work with her.

Maybe the bank had a duplicate, but Anne decided to be doubly safe. She made several copies on the library copy machine and put them in her desk. The original she left in her purse, hoping to get to the bank soon.

Unfortunately, Bella called in sick, afflicted with the summer cold that was going around town. It was after eleven before Anne found a substitute volunteer and could leave for the bank.

The last time she'd been there, she persuaded the bank manager to find the letter that let her into the safe-deposit box. She asked to speak to him as soon as she entered the lobby, only to learn he was on vacation for a week.

"I need to speak to someone who knows about bequests," she told the unhelpful receptionist who'd been on duty last time.

"I can take a look," she said, snapping her gum as she stood to reach for whatever Anne had.

"Thank you, but I'll wait for a senior staff member."

"Oh, you'll want Mr. Sanders. He's been here since before I was born."

She led the way to an office at the rear, rapped loudly on the door and waited until a low-pitched voice told her to come in.

The receptionist immediately left Anne alone with a small man behind a large desk. He had an elfin face with wisps of pure white hair covering his scalp, but his smartly tailored navy suit and brilliant white shirt assured Anne that he was a respected senior member of the bank staff.

"I'm Albert Sanders. What can I do for you?" he asked, standing to offer his hand.

Anne took it, impressed by his firm grasp. She introduced herself, pleased that he'd seen her once or twice in the library.

"I'd like to show you a document," Anne said, sitting when he gestured toward a leather-upholstered chair in front of his desk.

She debated with herself whether to tell him the whole story of Ben finding the secret hiding place. Maybe it would be better to show him the document before revealing the hiding place.

"Here it is," she said, handing it to him in the envelope they'd found with it.

Either he was a slow reader, or he was reading it twice. Or maybe Anne was so eager for his reaction that time seemed to stop.

"Where did you find it?" he asked in a mild voice.

"My son gets the credit," she said, explaining how Ben had discovered the secret hiding place.

"So that's where she hid it," Mr. Sanders said. "I thought it might be in the time capsule, but that was too simple for our Lois."

"You knew about this?" Anne felt as if she were on the edge of discovering all there was to know about Lois Stover, but she wasn't quite there.

"Yes, I was just getting my start as a bank officer twenty-five years ago when the statue was dedicated. Mr. Powers, the manager back then, thought it would be good experience for me to work on the Stover bequest. She'd left elaborate instructions before she died back in 1955. Mr. Powers, who had known Lois personally, said that it was essential that I meet the requirements she laid out as perfectly as possible."

"I know she loved puzzles," Anne said, still trying to take it all in.

"She was obsessed with them. Apparently her years as a spy in World War I were the most exciting time in her life. She tried to re-create them in her mania for puzzles and mysteries," the older gentleman said.

"Then this document is genuine?"

"If it matches the bank's copy, it is. I'll have to compare them to be certain, but I don't have any doubts. No one could forge it because no one knew it existed. If you don't mind waiting, I'll find our copy now."

"No, I'm happy to wait," Anne said, trying to take in everything the bank officer had told her.

"Please help yourself to coffee if you like," he said, gesturing at a cart with a hot plate to keep a pot of the brew warm.

The last thing Anne needed was caffeine to make her more hyper than she already was.

"Oh, by the way," he said, poking his head into the room a moment after he'd left. "It's caffeine-free almond roast. Quite refreshing, really."

Anne poured some of the aromatic beverage into a delicate white china cup and sat down again. It was too hot to sip at first, but just holding it gave her something to keep her hands occupied. What if the documents didn't match? Would this be another puzzle inside a puzzle dreamed up by Lois Stover?

Anne drank the coffee and returned the cup to the cart, but Mr. Sanders still hadn't returned. Didn't the bank keep all their documents and records on computers? What could possibly be taking him so long?

She paced and fretted, worried something was wrong with the document. Maybe Mr. Sanders didn't have the authority to validate the endowment. He might be trying to reach the bank manager by phone wherever he was on vacation.

Or worse, he was working on a gentle way to tell her it was a fraud, a joke played by Lois Stover.

When she heard the doorknob she raced back to the chair and tried to look casual and relaxed.

"Sorry to keep you waiting," he said without giving an explanation.

The elderly bank officer was carrying a manila envelope in his hand, but he didn't immediately show her the contents.

"You understand there are legal issues to be resolved," he said, returning to the chair behind the desk that seemed too large for him.

Anne's spirits nosedived. Did that mean lawyers and court hearings and who knew what else? She sagged in the chair and waited to hear the rest.

"Of course," she said to encourage him to tell her more.

"Lois Stover left it to the bank to manage her bequest, but that could change now that her copy of the document has surfaced," he said, still hanging onto the envelope without opening it.

"Then it's genuine?" She couldn't stand the suspense any longer.

"Oh my, yes. The bank has an exact copy right here." He tapped his fingers on the envelope but still didn't show it to her. "You can't imagine the thrilling story she told Mr. Powers when she set this all up. This was the most exciting thing that's ever happened at this bank."

Actually, Anne could, but she knew the bank officer was enjoying himself. She made an effort to be patient and let him finish whatever revelations he had in mind.

"As I already mentioned, she was an American spy in World War I. And she was also in Paris for a time. I shudder just to think of how much danger she was in."

"She must have been a very brave woman. My great-aunt Edie admired her immensely," Anne said.

Mr. Sanders had a faraway look, almost as if he were reliving an adventure of his own.

"I get chills just thinking of how much danger she must've been in," Anne said. "How long was she in Paris?"

"Longer than expected. Her aunt who lived there had amassed quite a few valuable pieces of jewelry, but her aunt was ill."

In spite of her need to return to the library, Anne was mesmerized hearing Lois Stover's story.

"Lois managed to bring the jewelry into this country. She was a little vague about how she'd done it. I had the impression some people high up in the government had helped her, a reward for some valuable information she brought back."

"What did she do with the jewelry once she had it back here?" Anne was pretty sure she knew, but she loved hearing it from Mr. Sanders.

"Nothing at first. But after her aunt passed away, Lois wanted to do good with her inheritance. Above all else, she valued education, especially giving women the chance to study traditionally male subjects as she had."

"She sold the jewelry?"

"Yes, she took it to a New York auction company and did very well. That's what she invested with us to finance the scholarship fund. Now I have a surprise for you." He stood up grinning and handed over the envelope. "Open it."

Anne's hands weren't steady, but curiosity helped her slide some papers from the envelope. The first sheet was a copy of the sheet she and Ben had found. The other was an accounting of the investment for the last sixty years. Anne's jaw dropped, and she didn't have words for the figure she saw.

"Nice, isn't it?" Mr. Sanders said. "I think the interest alone will fund the scholarship fund for years to come."

"I never expected anything like this," Anne said, counting the numbers to be sure there really were seven in a row. "She must have sold some wonderful jewelry."

"That, and when funds have decades to grow, the result is significant," Mr. Sanders said, looking as pleased as if he'd donated the money himself.

Only one thing was nagging at the edge of Anne's consciousness.

"What if Ben hadn't discovered the secret hiding place? What if the bequest was never revealed?"

"Ah," the bank officer said. "That would be a problem, but knowing Lois only briefly, I'm pretty sure she left some clues to find it. She had a lively sense of humor to go with her puzzle mania. Somewhere there's a clue or clues. But you're right. It might have been years before someone else worked it out. You should be very proud of your son."

"I am," Anne said. "What happens next?"

"I'll be happy to start things in motion here. The bank directors will want to appoint a board to administer it, a responsible group to decide who gets the scholarships and what criteria they'll have to meet to keep them. If you're willing, I'll nominate you for their consideration. Ms. Stover's instructions said that if the finder of the bequest is qualified, he or she should serve on the board. Since your son is obviously too young, that would fall to you."

"I wouldn't know where to begin," Anne said, feeling overwhelmed by his offer.

"Neither will anyone else in Blue Hill," Mr. Sanders said. "I'll volunteer to be a nonvoting advisor if my superiors agree. Meanwhile, these are copies of the documents for you to read as a likely board member."

Anne took the envelope he handed her without really registering what she should do with it. There was a lot more in the envelope than she had started with from the compartment in the statue.

The elderly bank officer walked her through the ornate lobby to the door, nodding at the security guard standing nearby. Anne wanted to give Mr. Sanders a big hug for all the help he'd given her, but she settled for taking his hand when he offered it.

Outside in the bright sunshine, she dug in her purse for her sunglasses. It wasn't the sudden heat and light that made her feel disoriented. She was thrilled and shaken. Her little boy had found a secret hiding place for a document that made college scholarships available to deserving young women.

She walked several car lengths before realizing she was going in the wrong direction.

As she drove home, she thought of what she would tell Wendy and Maggie. She could imagine squeals of surprise and pleasure and couldn't wait to call them. She especially hoped to see Alex and tell him in person.

Now if the statue would turn up, she could go back to her normal routine, untroubled by mysteries plaguing the town she loved.

Chapter Twenty-Nine

The scholarship news was so special Anne decided not to blurt it out on the phone. Instead she hurried to the bakery for one of their key lime pies and invited Wendy and Maggie to come to her home after the kids were in bed.

"What's up?" Wendy asked when she arrived that evening.

"I'll tell you when Maggie gets here," Anne said, enjoying her secret. "How's your family?"

"The kids are all fine, but Chad still has a cough. He refuses to see a doctor. He says the hot sun at football practices will sweat it out of him. Meanwhile, he keeps me awake half the night with his hacking."

Wendy had dark circles under her eyes, but Anne was certain the good news would perk her up.

Maggie didn't keep them waiting very long. Anne heard her soft knock on the downstairs door before she finished steeping some soothing jasmine tea.

"I got here as soon as I could," Maggie said. "My husband's vehicle is in the garage, so I had to wait for him to get home with mine."

"I could've picked you up," Wendy said.

"I didn't know you were coming here too," Maggie said. "In fact, I don't know why I'm here. Does it have something to do with the document you found?"

"It has everything to do with it," Anne said. It wasn't like her to be coy, but she was enjoying every moment.

"Tell us," Wendy urged her. "Did you take it to the bank today?"

"I certainly did. I showed it to a bank officer who worked on the final details of the endowment when the statue was dedicated. The good news is that the bequest is absolutely genuine."

"And the bad news?" Maggie asked, sounding a bit skeptical.

"There is no bad news," Anne said, grinning from ear to ear. "Come sit down at the kitchen table and have some tea and pie. I got your favorite, Maggie, key lime."

"I can't swallow a bite until I know what you're not telling us," Maggie said.

Anne grinned and took the accounting sheet off the counter to pass around to them.

"Is this what I think it is?" Wendy asked, rereading it over Maggie's shoulder.

"That's a big number at the bottom," Maggie said. "Is that the amount available for the scholarship fund?"

"Yes," Anne said, her eyes dancing with pleasure. "Lois Stover sold her aunt's jewelry and invested it. The bank has been managing it all this time. That's why it's grown to such a large sum."

"I never expected something like this," Wendy said. "What happens now?"

"According to the terms of the bequest, Mr. Sanders is going to propose my name to be on the board that administers the scholarships. I'd love to give him your names too if you don't mind."

"I'm not sure I'm qualified," Wendy said.

"Would it be the board's job to pick who gets the scholarships?" Maggie asked.

"Yes, although you know as much about it as I do right now. I'd love to learn the job with you two," Anne said.

"Well, I'm game," Maggie said, although she sounded a bit anxious about the responsibility.

"If you two are going to serve, I'll give it a try too," Wendy said.

"All for one, and one for all," Anne said, lifting her tea to clang the other two cups in a toast.

"I have one question," Maggie said. "What if Ben had never found the secret hiding place? Would the money stay in the bank indefinitely with none going to worthy students?"

"Mr. Sanders didn't know, but he suspected Lois had left other clues to locate the document," Anne said.

"There's one person who might know," Maggie said. "That is, if we can catch him in a lucid moment."

"Arlen Buchanan," Wendy said. "Do you think he knows of other hiding places that are part of Stover's puzzle?"

"If anyone does, he does," Maggie said. "The big question is whether he remembers."

"I don't think it would hurt to visit him and ask," Anne said. "He seemed to like the attention he got at the park."

"I guess it's too late to go tonight," Maggie said. "The residents of the retirement home go to bed pretty early. What about tomorrow?"

Anne visualized the chart of volunteer helpers and knew her best time to get away was early afternoon the next day. She suggested it to her friends. They agreed to meet at the residence at two.

"I do have some news," Wendy said as she got ready to leave. "After your bombshell, it's pretty mundane."

"What is it?" Anne asked.

"The police questioned Derek and Mitch Umsted again earlier today. Chad heard about it from one of his players."

"Why?" Maggie asked.

"I expect they were following up on the information about Derek taking Alex's truck overnight," Wendy said, "but I think the questioning shook them up. It's impossible to know whether the police have any real evidence against them, or they're just fishing for information."

"Should the bank release the scholarship story to the newspaper, or do you want to?" Maggie asked.

"I thought I'd call Grace Hawkins first thing in the morning. I'll tell her to interview Mr. Sanders for her story. It seems only fair that he gets the credit for managing the fund so well for so long."

"If he wants it," Wendy said. "Bankers can be a secretive bunch."

"I guess it's because they know so much confidential information about their clients," Anne said. "More pie anyone?"

Both her friends declined and left, but Maggie had another thought on her way out.

"Maybe I should call the mayor and let him know," she said. "He likes to be kept in the loop."

"Good idea," Anne said.

Both her friends agreed, disappearing down the stairs with a promise to lock the door on the way out.

Anne was too excited to sleep. She took a warm bath, put on her pajamas, and read in bed until her eyes ached. Even after she turned off the light, she couldn't get Lois Stover out of her mind. She was creative, adventurous, and compassionate, all traits Aunt Edie had. Anne could understand why her great-aunt had admired the architect so much.

Both were nourished by their deep roots in Blue Hill, and Lois would be remembered by many generations for her generous scholarships. Edie had followed suit with her legacy, leaving her house and savings to establish the library where Anne worked and lived. Anne couldn't help but wonder how much Lois had influenced her aunt's bequest. Or maybe they both felt a deep debt of gratitude to the town for starting them on their life paths.

Before her kids woke up in the morning, Anne crawled out of bed and remembered to call her friend Grace. She didn't know whether there was time to put the scholarship news in this week's paper, which would come out tomorrow, Wednesday. Maybe as editor, Grace could delay it to print the big story. Anne wanted to give her a chance for a scoop before rumor spread the news.

"Sorry if I woke you," Anne said when a sleepy voice answered her call. "But I think you'll want to know the news I have for you."

Grace woke up quickly and extracted every bit of information from Anne.

"You can get the full story from Mr. Sanders at the bank," Anne suggested. "He should get the credit for managing the account so well."

"The bank won't open until nine," Grace said. "I think Mr. Sanders is going to have a guest for breakfast—namely me. He and my father were friends, so I don't think he'll mind."

With two hours to go until she had to open the library, Anne was tempted to grab a little more sleep when Ben walked into the kitchen.

"What's for breakfast?" he asked, rubbing sleep from his eyes.

"How about scrambled eggs and raisin bread toast?" She felt as sleepy as he looked.

"I don't like the raisins in the bread," Ben protested.

"You've always liked them before," Anne said, trying to remember when Ben had started having such strong opinions about what he ate.

As the children got themselves ready for the day with only minor help from her, Anne thought ahead to visiting Arlen Buchanan at the nursing home. He had a tendency to ramble, but his rambles could be interesting.

The morning at work seemed to drag as Anne anticipated her visit, but she had a surprise visitor just before noon.

"How about lunch?" Alex asked.

"I'd love to," Anne said, especially welcoming a chance to tell Alex all she'd learned about Lois Stover's bequest.

He had his truck with him, and he helped boost her up to the high seat on the passenger side.

"What are you in the mood for?" he asked, sliding behind the wheel. "Fish, fowl, or fresh vegetables?"

Anne responded to his high spirits and told him to surprise her.

"There's a new place on the south side," Alex said. "The owner and chef is a former army cook. I think it might be worth trying. As a matter of fact, I have a coupon for a couple of dollars off. I think it's still valid if you want to look for it in the glove compartment."

The glove compartment had enough stuffed in it to be a mobile office. Anne started pulling out all the paper to sort through it on her lap when her fingers touched something metallic.

"Oh my," she said, almost dropping the nest of papers as she pulled out a familiar metal object. "Did you know there's a bolt from the statue in your glove box?"

"I don't see how that's possible," he said glancing at the bolt in her hand. "The police searched my truck."

"It was wedged inside your owner's manual and buried at the back. They must have overlooked it." Anne wrapped it in a tissue from her purse and held it out on her palm.

"Well, it's not something I want to drive around with. Whoever borrowed my truck must have left it. We can throw it in the next trash can we see."

"We should save it," she said. "There could be fingerprints or other evidence. If we can learn who put it there, we'll know who stole the statue."

"Maybe," Alex said, sounding unconvinced. "If you want to keep it, that's okay with me. But let's get it out of my truck."

Anne slipped it into her purse, unsure what to do with it.

Their luncheon began with forced cheerfulness helped along when the burly owner/chef came to their table to welcome them to his restaurant. Anne had crab cakes so delicious they topped any others she'd eaten. Alex had chicken fried steak with cheesy mashed potatoes, a meal that suited him perfectly when he had a long afternoon of work ahead.

They left, assuring the cashier they'd be back again.

When Anne returned to the library, she still had a little time to spare before meeting her friends at the retirement home. She checked on her library volunteer, then hurried up to her living quarters to put the bolt in a safe place until she could take it to the police.

CHAPTER THIRTY

Anne knocked as softly as possible on the senior Buchanan's partially open door. She wasn't ready for the booming voice that came from inside the room.

"Where's my red pencil? How can a man get anything done without a red pencil?" He was sitting at a small table by the window with paper and pencils laid out in front of him.

"I'll look for it," Anne said, spotting it under his chair.

Wendy and Maggie inched forward while Anne stooped to retrieve the pencil.

"Here you are, Mr. Buchanan," she said handing it over. "Do you remember me?" She gave him her name and her friends', but he was too occupied with his drawing to acknowledge them.

"Is Gavin here? Tell him to come in here. I'm not mad at him." He pressed down so hard with a green pencil that the lead snapped.

Anne saw a sharpener and offered to put a new point on it. As she sharpened the pencil, she mused on why the aging sculptor kept talking about his dead younger son. What kept the old man going back to him again and again?

"Can't draw her eyes without the green," Arlen Buchanan muttered, taking the newly sharpened pencil from Anne.

Maggie was the first to edge her way behind him. She gasped when she looked down at the portrait he was drawing.

"It's Lois Stover," she said.

"Of course it is. She was an inspiration. Sorry about the statue. When I get better, I'm going to make one to rival the Statue of Liberty."

Anne gazed at the drawing with a heavy heart. She knew this was his permanent home for as long as he lived. Even if he did have the knowledge to cast another statue, it was highly unlikely he still had the strength or skill.

The elderly sculptor suddenly stopped drawing and held the portrait up to the light.

"No, that's not her," he said, ripping his art into small pieces. "I can't seem to get her eyes right. The eyes are the doors to the soul, you know. Lois's were like emeralds lit from behind with knowledge and wisdom."

Anne hadn't expected anything so poetic from Harold's father. Was there any chance he knew about other clues or the contents of the time capsule?

"The statue showed how lovely she was," Anne said.

"It was her insides that were beautiful. Don't know why this town meant so much to her, but she loved it as if everyone here were her child."

"Did she choose what to put in the time capsule?" Wendy asked.

"We did it together. Bunch of silly stuff, really."

"What silly stuff?" Anne asked.

Instead of answering, he pushed all his pencils off the table, some of them going as far as his bed. Anne started retrieving them with help from her friends.

"Mr. Buchanan, you've dropped all your pencils again." One of the residence's nurses came into the room with a pill for Arlen. She wore a colorful top with a butterfly print, a far cry from nurses in starched white or green scrubs.

Anne exchanged a look with her two friends. It was hard to tell if the elderly artist was playing games with them or genuinely had trouble remembering. She thought the latter.

"I think it's time for a little nap, Mr. Buchanan," the nurse said as she patiently waited for him to swallow his pill.

Anne took it as a sign they should leave. She led her friends outside without commenting. It was obvious they wouldn't learn anything about other clues from Harold's father—at least not today.

As she parted from her friends, she knew she needed to talk with Harold as soon as possible. Surely he could explain his father's secrets if anyone could.

Time ticked by on the big wall clock behind the checkout counter. The afternoon seemed to drag, but it gave Anne time to think of what to say to Harold. Both Wendy and Maggie had other commitments that evening, so she was on her own.

Anne planned to let the volunteer close the library so she could make a quick visit before picking up her kids.

Before she could get inside her car, a familiar truck pulled to a stop on the street in front of the library. She smiled at Alex and started walking toward him as he got out of the cab.

"I didn't expect to see you again today," she said in a cheerful voice.

"I had a strange call an hour or so ago," he said sounding serious. "Harold Buchanan wants to borrow my truck."

"Your truck? Does he even know how to drive it?"

"I asked him that. Apparently he has Mitch Umsted lined up to drive it. I have no idea why or where."

"I was just going to go talk with him," Anne said, giving Alex the details of their visit to the bank.

"I don't think you'll find him at home. He gave me directions to meet him at a deserted barn. Why don't you come with me?" Alex said.

"I'll follow you so you have a ride home if you decide to trust your truck to him," Anne said, happy to have someone to go with her.

* * *

The barn wasn't hard to spot, although nature had taken over the land around it. It was an old one with the bottom five feet or so made of rocks cemented together. The wood above it had once been buttermilk red, a paint favored by many older farmers in the county. Now it was mostly weathered to silvery bare wood.

Anne cautiously followed Alex down a dirt and gravel path with small weeds beginning to take it over. By the time they stopped and got out of their vehicles, two men appeared in the open doorway.

"Come in, come in," Harold said walking out to meet them. "Do you both know Mitch Umsted? He'll drive the truck if you agree to let me use it."

"About that..." Alex took the hand the young man offered, but the puzzled expression on his face only intensified.

"I didn't expect to see you, Mrs. Gibson," Harold said.

"I came because I have good news, and a question for you." Anne quickly told him about the secret compartment Ben had found and the bequest inside, leaving her question unasked for the moment.

"Lois never got over being a secret agent in the war," Harold said with admiration. "She loved mystery and intrigue. I wonder what would've happened to the scholarship fund if no one discovered her secret hiding place."

"We wondered too — Wendy, Maggie, and me. Mr. Sanders at the bank seemed to imply she must have left other clues. We were hoping you have some ideas — but of course, putting her endowment to good use is the most important thing," Anne said.

"According to my father, she thought small towns like Blue Hill were the best possible places to raise children." Harold sounded proud of her. "Lois always said it shaped her future by making everything seem possible."

"About my truck," Alex said. "I have to know why you want it and where you'll be taking it. I'll need it for work tomorrow morning."

"Actually," Anne said, "I think I know why Harold needs the truck."

"I don't doubt that you do," Harold said. "I've thought repeatedly that you've been close to figuring it all out."

"Not all of it," Anne replied. "I think all the pieces of the puzzle are coming together about what happened, but I have no idea why."

Alex looked at Anne like she had started speaking Greek. "What on earth are you talking about?" he asked. "Why do Mitch and Mr. Buchanan want my truck, and why do you know all about it?"

Alex sounded anything but happy.

"Thanks to Mr. Buchanan's graphic design class, I have a good job over in Deshler," Mitch said. "When he needs a favor, I'm his man."

Anne saw him exchange a look with Harold. The older man nodded.

"Mitch has been telling me it's time we fess up," Harold said in an unhappy voice. "I can't keep covering for my brother the rest of my life."

"I suspect you took the statue with Mitch's help," Anne said. "And I'm pretty sure you did it to help protect your younger brother. But why?"

"My younger brother, Gavin, was always in trouble with Dad. They were like oil and water when they were together. He thought it would be a good joke on our father to hide the original statue before it was installed in the park. He planned to plant it in the middle of the river, but he didn't make allowances for an especially rainy spring in 1990."

"Let me guess," Alex said. "The current caught it and dashed it on the rocks."

"Yes. By the time Gavin and his friends caught up with it, it was battered and broken. They removed the time capsule from inside it, and then they weighed the statue down with rocks and let it sink to the bottom.

"Your father must have been devastated," Anne said.

"He never knew. I was in charge of putting the statue in place in the park. He'd made an earlier casting using cheap, poor-quality bronze. That's what I had installed, and I put the time capsule exactly where Dad and Lois Stover wanted it. The early casting looked all right when it was new, but with all the weathering, it was in pretty sad shape. It wasn't apparent how bad it was until I cleaned it up. Large sections of it stayed tarnished and corroded despite my best efforts. It wouldn't fool my father for a minute if he saw it still tarnished after it had been cleaned. He would have recognized it as the practice cast. And then I would have to explain it all to him."

"So you took it so he wouldn't see it?" Alex asked.

"My original idea was to clean it as best I could and cover tarnished spots with a special paint I mixed. It didn't work. The statue looked even worse. That's why I had to remove it in secret. I knew my dad would want to see it one more time in the park."

"And he'd know immediately it wasn't the real one," Anne said. "You went to all that trouble to cover up for your brother."

"No, to save my father the sorrow of knowing his original statue was lost forever. All it would take was one quick look and he'd recognize the poor quality casting."

"So how did the time capsule end up at Franklin's Antiques?" Anne asked. "Did you secretly drop it off there?"

Harold nodded sheepishly. "Yes. It was the best way I could think of to let someone discover it. I never had any intention of tampering with the time capsule or its contents."

"So where is the statue now?" Anne asked. She stared into the gloomy interior of the old barn, but there wasn't enough light to see whether the statue was inside.

Again Harold and his former student exchanged glances.

"It's in this barn," Mitch said.

"The owner was glad to rent it before he tears it down and sells the siding to a decorator," Harold said. "I guess he'd rather see it serving a useful purpose than losing it forever."

"What's your plan now?" Alex asked.

"To take it back to town," Mitch said.

"I've already talked to the police chief," Harold said. "I don't think he believed my story about taking it for more restoration work, but he said the case was closed."

"You know they suspected me because paint from my truck was on the post," Alex said frowning.

"I'll make good on whatever you had to pay to repair it," Harold said.

Anne knew Alex was more concerned about his reputation than the scratch.

"If I loan you my truck, does that make me an accomplice in this whole business?" Alex said. He looked at Anne.

"From what Harold has said, it sounds like the case is closed," she said.

She and Alex both looked at the retired art teacher, who nodded and gestured to follow him inside the barn. Anne didn't believe in haunted houses or barns, but the gloom inside the ancient structure was downright creepy. She brushed aside a cobweb that caught in her hair and was thankful when she managed not to fall over a bale of rotted hay. Behind her Alex shone the flashlight from his truck to light her way.

The barn was much larger inside than it looked from the outside. There was an odor that made her cover her nose.

"It smells like mice," Alex said. "I wonder how long this place has been abandoned."

"The owner had three sons who served in the military," Harold said, sounding more comfortable as he told the history of the barn. "When they got back, none of them wanted to farm. They took advantage of the G.I. bill that let them go to college. One became a dentist and one a stockbroker."

"What about the third?" Anne asked.

"He went to the police academy," Mitch said, chiming in on a story he thought was interesting. "Now he's Blue Hill's police chief."

"And he just wants to let old stories stay untold," Anne filled in.

After they passed the stalls where animals had once been confined, they stepped into a broad area with rusting farm equipment put to rest.

All three men played the light from their flashes over what looked like a junkyard of discarded implements. Anne had to catch her breath when she caught a glimpse of the fallen statue.

"There it is," she said excitedly. Light streamed in where part of the roof had caved.

Anne picked her way carefully to the prone statue and immediately saw what Arlen had meant by inner beauty. The features on her face were angular with a rather sharply pointed nose, but her eyes softened all her other features. It was lying on a low platform with wheels, the kind mechanics used to work under a car.

"Where do you want to take it?" Alex asked while Anne was still admiring the artistic rendering of the architect.

"My place," Harold said. "I think there are still a few things I can do to improve it. First I need to have a long overdue talk with my father."

"I'd better drive," Alex said. "I don't want any more dings on my truck. Mitch, help me load the statue. You can ride into town with me. We need to have some words about borrowing my truck without asking. Anne, would you mind following with Harold?"

"My car is here," Mitch protested.

"It will still be here when we get this done," Alex said.

Anne used her cell phone to tell the kids' babysitter that she'd be a little late then she went to the driver's side of her car. Harold was already in the passenger seat with the seat belt buckled.

"I'm sorry about this," he said, speaking as Alex positioned his truck as close as possible to the barn.

"I think I understand," Alex said graciously.

"I cleaned up after my brother for most of his life. We lost our mother when we were young, so it was just Dad and us boys. Most of the time he was so busy with his sculpting, we hardly existed for him. Or at least, that's how it seemed to me."

"You substituted the practice statue for the lost one to spare your father the pain of knowing Gavin had trashed the real one." Anne started her engine.

"Yes, he would've spotted the tarnish and corrosion on the restored statue in an instant. He doesn't have many pleasures left in life, but he still takes pride in his greatest work."

"He was drawing pictures of Lois Stover when we saw him today," Anne said, filling him in on their brief visit.

"He admired her even though she was considerably older. I think he especially liked that she gave Blue Hill the credit for shaping her life. You can't tell now, but my father feels the same way about this town. He traveled to places like Italy and Japan to study his art, but he always returned here to work."

Would the town want the inferior casting to go back into the park? Did Harold plan to tell his father the whole truth?

"I have a huge favor to ask of you," Harold said as they reached the town.

"I have to pick up my kids," Anne said, still floored by the statue. Even in the dim light of the barn she'd noticed how unsightly dark patches and other evidence of corrosion stood out on the otherwise polished statue.

"This won't take long. Just swing by the retirement home and come in with me. My dad will be in a better mood if he sees you."

Anne doubted she would have any influence on the sculptor, but she couldn't help sympathizing with Harold. He'd done all he could to spare his father's feelings. Maybe it was too late to get through to him, but she could spare a few minutes to try.

She parked her car at the retirement center and followed Harold through the spacious commons area to the room on the west corridor where his father may or may not recognize his only living son. Anne braced herself for anything, remembering Arlen's explosive voice when she visited earlier. Would he appreciate all his son had done for him, or would he feel betrayed? She fingered the bolt in her purse that had been one of the final clues.

"I hope he's having a good day," Harold said.

The elderly man was reclining in a lounge chair with his feet elevated. His eyes were hooded, and Anne thought he was asleep.

"Dad, are you awake?" Harold asked.

"Course I am. Only babies and old women sleep in the afternoon."

Anne wouldn't have minded a short nap herself, but all she could hope for was a quick visit here so she could pick up her kids.

"I have something important to tell you, Dad," Harold said.

"It's about Gavin, isn't it? I keep trying to convince myself he's alive, but he isn't, is he?"

"I'm afraid not," his son said. "He died instantly in the car crash."

The elderly man's face crumpled in sorrow, and errant tears rolled down his wrinkled cheeks. "I need a tissue," he said.

This was something Anne could provide. She found a box by his bedside and handed it to him.

Suddenly her question about other clues about Lois's endowment didn't seem important. Harold was hesitating, no doubt not wanting to blacken his brother's name or upset his father more than necessary.

"Did you notice the statue of Lois Stover was missing when they held the memorial service?" Harold asked.

"Nothing wrong with my eyesight. I only wear glasses to read."

"Yes, I know, Dad." There was tenderness in Harold's voice that brought moisture to Anne's eyes. "I took it. It's safe."

"It's wherever Gavin left it," Arlen said. "I suspect it's gone for good since you kept the prototype in the park for twenty-five years."

"You know?" Harold stammered the question, and Anne was speechless.

"Sometimes my mind gets a little foggy," Arlen said, seeming to tire in front of their eyes. "I was angry at Gavin at first, but as time went by I had a hard time remembering why. The memorial service at the park brought it all back."

"Why didn't you say something to me?" Harold asked.

"You always tried to get Gavin out of scrapes," he said with a faraway expression. "I never thought you'd go as far as removing the practice copy from the park. Where is it?"

While Harold explained about the barn he'd rented, Anne sighed with relief. Arlen's eyes drooped shut, but he wasn't asleep. Apparently, he still had a few things to say to his older son.

"Gavin was the prodigal son. I loved him even when he did unacceptable things. You're a good brother and a good son. I'm fortunate to have you," Arlen said in a weak voice. "Now if you'll push me down to the dining room, I think it's time for supper. We're supposed to have meat loaf and baked potato. I just hope they don't fill my plate with carrots. Never could abide them."

Anne rocked back on her heels, surprised by the way Arlen abruptly changed the subject.

"I'll meet you at the car," she said to Harold.

He was helping his father into a wheelchair.

"That was a good thing you did with the statue," Arlen said nodding his head up and down as his son put a pillow behind his back.

Anne waited patiently outside, marveling at the sweet reunion Harold had had with his father. She couldn't help but wonder about Gavin. What made one son so irresponsible and the other kind and well intentioned?

She looked across the street at the immaculately maintained houses, many newly painted in soft pastel shades. The entrance to the nursing home was a gleaming white door with the glass panel recently polished.

No matter where she went in Blue Hill, she could see the pride people had in their town. It was no wonder both her great-aunt and Lois Stover had always had pleasant memories of growing up here. Anne hoped her own children would also be nurtured by childhoods spent in the comfort of this town.

Chapter Thirty-One

Y ou both look so nice. I want to take your pictures before we leave," Anne said, smiling at Liddie and Ben.

Her daughter was wearing her favorite pink dress and socks with lace on them. Ben had a new white dress shirt with a cute little green bow tie.

Anne had taken special care with her own outfit for the occasion, choosing a black jersey sheath with a silvery jacket and heels.

She'd snapped two poses before Ben dashed away down the stairs to their door.

"I think Alex is here," he called out.

Anne didn't need to check her watch. Alex was certainly on time, if not early. The big meeting at the bank wasn't scheduled to begin until ten. They'd conveniently scheduled it on a Saturday morning so Ben could be there, although he didn't know that.

"Everyone ready?" Alex asked, looking spiffy in a herringbone sports coat and sharply pressed slacks.

"I thought we could go in my car," Anne said. "Then we won't have to move Liddie's car seat."

"No problem," Alex said, helping to load the kids, including Ryan. He didn't even suggest driving himself, which pleased Anne. It was his way of acknowledging how competent she was.

Only the drive-in window of the bank was open, but Mr. Sanders met them at the front door and let them in. He looked very formal in a charcoal suit, black tie, and white shirt, but Anne smiled when she noticed he was also wearing orange and black socks. It seemed the bank officer had a playful side.

They weren't the last to arrive, and Mr. Sanders invited them to help themselves at a long table placed in the large open space. The bank had provided coffee, juice, and an assortment of pastries and donuts.

Anne got a small cup of apple juice for Liddie and warned Ben he could only have one choice from the platters of treats.

"No chocolate," she warned. "You don't want to spoil your new shirt."

She knew why it was important he stay neat, but it was too soon to let him know.

Several people she didn't recognize came to the front door next. When they were inside, she was introduced to the bank's board of directors and what seemed to be the entire town council. Her friends followed them almost immediately, Maggie and Reverend Tom, Wendy and Chad.

"What's up?" Wendy whispered to Anne. "We got a printed invitation to come this morning, and we don't even have an account here."

"I guess we'll have to wait and see," Anne said, watching as Ben started to devour a bear's claw, easily the largest on the tray.

Two men came from the back of the bank, Mr. Royer, the bank manager, and the mayor. Anne did hope the mayor wouldn't make a long speech. Her children would get too restless if they had to sit a long time.

The bank manager invited everyone to sit on one of the folding chairs lined up in front of a podium. Anne guided her children to the front row, catching sight of one more person arriving, Grace Hawkins. Apparently, whatever was going to happen would be newsworthy.

After introductions and formalities, Anne, Wendy, Maggie, and two people Anne didn't know were invited to go to the front.

"It's my privilege to ask the five of you to serve as a board to administer Lois Stover's scholarship endowment. Ms. Stover's bequest stated that the board should have a majority of local women of good character along with whoever found the hidden bequest. Mr. Sanders will be the bank's representative and a nonvoting member."

Anne looked out and caught Alex's eye. She expected her appointment, but she loved his pleased grin.

"Now for something special," the mayor said when they were all seated again. "Ben Gibson, would you come to the front, please?"

He looked at his mother. She nodded, and he took it as permission.

"Without Ben's talent for solving puzzles, none of this would be happening now," the town official said. "The bank's instructions were to release the funds in 2050 if no one discovered the document before then. Thanks to Ben, many of our most promising students will be able to attend college now."

Anne grinned broadly, watching her son. He looked stunned at all the attention, but there was more to come.

"On behalf of the bank and the town fathers, I'd like to present you with this medal."

Ben's jaw dropped as the mayor stepped over to him and hung a medal on a chain around his neck. Grace stepped forward and snapped several pictures in quick succession, then gave him a moment to compose himself and say thank you.

Ben's smile grew as he took in what had just happened. He hurried back to his seat at the front and showed his medal to Ryan, then to Anne and Liddie.

"There's one other item I'd like to bring up." Harold Buchanan spoke from behind the chairs, a latecomer to the meeting. "With the town's permission I'd like to reinstall the prototype statue that stood in the park for twenty-five years. I've done all I can to restore it, but it will never measure up to the original one that was lost many years ago."

"I guess that's a decision for the town council," the mayor said. "Let's see if we have a quorum."

He counted by pointing his finger and concluded that all but one member was there.

"All in favor say 'aye,'" he said.

The council members agreed with one voice, and the mayor declared that the proposition had carried by acclamation.

Alex carried Liddie through the crowd to the front door while Ben chatted nonstop beside his mother.

"Am I going to be in the paper?" he asked.

"I wouldn't be surprised," Anne said, catching a wink from Grace on her way out.

"Now can Ryan and me go metal-detecting on our own?" he asked, trying to read his name on his award as they walked. "Maybe I'll find some real treasure this time."

"You are a treasure," Anne said smiling down at him. "We'll talk about the metal detector later.

She was certain her son would hold her to it.

"Now who wants pizza?" Alex laughed.

"I do," Anne said, smiling at him.

About the Authors

Emily Thomas is the pen name for a team of writers who have come together to create the series Secrets of the Blue Hill Library. *Frozen in Time* was written by the mother-daughter writing team of Pam Hanson (daughter) and Barbara Andrews (mother). They have had more than forty books published together, including many for Guideposts. Pam's background is in journalism, and she previously taught at the university level. She and her college-professor husband have two sons. Previous to their partnership, Barbara had twenty-one novels published under her own name. She began her career by writing Sunday school stories and was a longtime contributor to antiques publications. She makes her home with Pam and her family in Nebraska.

A Conversation with the Authors

Q. *What is one treasure from the past that you hold dear?*

A. Barbara: My father's rolltop desk. It sat in his drugstrore for many years. It's been my "command center" since Pam and her siblings were young!

A. Pam: My grandma Rock's old hardcover mysteries, of which I have a few. She was a big reader and passed that love on to my mom and to me!

Q. *If you were preparing a time capsule to be opened by your descendants fifty to one hundred years from now, what would you put inside?*

A. Barbara: Some of my collage art (postcard sized), my grandmother's opal ring, a piece of Fiestaware, one of our books (Grace Chapel Inn series), and one of my mother's fancy silver plates, spoons, or coins.

A. Pam: My laptop! My grandmother's wedding ring (given to my mom), pictures of my sons, and one of my Lowell Herrero cow wall calendars, which I've hung on my kitchen wall for more than a decade!

Q. *In what way do you see yourselves most like Aunt Edie?*

A. Both of us would say in our many varied interests and activities.

RECIPES FROM THE LIBRARY GUILD

Mrs. Covell's Lemon Bars

2 sticks butter

½ cup brown sugar

2 cups flour

1 teaspoon salt

4 eggs

2 cups sugar

6 tablespoons flour

½ cup fresh or bottled lemon juice

Melt the butter and mix the brown sugar, two cups of flour, and salt into it. Pat into a nine-inch-by-thirteen-inch lightly greased pan. Bake approximately fifteen minutes at 350 degrees.

Remove from oven.

In a separate bowl mix eggs, sugar, six tablespoons of flour, and lemon juice. Pour mixture over crust and bake another twenty-five minutes. Dust with powdered sugar while still warm and wait to cut until cool.

FROM THE GUIDEPOSTS ARCHIVES

This article by Sabra Ciancanelli originally appeared in
Guideposts magazine.

"Team Ria will find the loot!" my niece Regina declared. She brandished a compass and a journal, items from the treasure-hunting kit her mother, my sister Maria—Ria for short—had assembled as a Christmas gift. Now we were putting them to good use. Somewhere amid the browning oak trees and rocky shores of Catskill Point Park was a golden doubloon that had lain hidden for seventeen years—and we wanted to find it. We needed to. *God, we need something to keep our minds off missing Ria,* I prayed, holding back tears as I watched Regina look under benches and picnic tables with my sons and my brother's children. Had it really been six months since Ria died, so suddenly, so utterly unexpectedly, in her sleep? I took a deep breath of the chilly autumn air and touched the photograph of her that I kept in my coat pocket. How I wished she were still here with us. Ria was all about treasure hunts and family time.

A few days earlier, my sister Laura had sent me an e-mail with the subject, "Want to look for treasure?" I followed the link in the e-mail to a newspaper article, "Treasure Hunt Unsolved For Nearly Two Decades." Officials in nearby Greene County had created the treasure hunt back in 1991 to promote tourism to Catskill, New York. Although there had been plenty of interest at first, over the years the treasure had been forgotten by all but a few dedicated hunters. The prize that Greene County had put up for finding the golden doubloon—a specially-made jeweled crown valued at over ten thousand dollars—seemed like it might never be claimed.

Ria would have loved this! I thought. She loved everything about the ocean: waves, seashells...but especially pirates. Every summer our families rented a cluster of cottages on the beach in Wellfleet, Cape Cod, and on our last vacation, Ria planned an elaborate treasure hunt for the kids, burying clues and making a large X in the sand with rocks and flotsam above a big treasure trunk filled with goodies. She even threw Mom a pirate-themed birthday party complete with skull-and-crossbone hats, swash-buckling outfits and plastic swords. It was nutty...but that was Ria. Life was one big adventure, full of hidden clues and joyful surprises.

The picture in my pocket was from Mom's party—Ria dressed like a regular Captain Hook. It seemed like her goofy ideas and energy were what brought our family together, our center of gravity. Who else but Ria could get us all digging through sand for clues to buried treasure or wearing eye patches, laughing as we did our best pirate shouts: "Avast Matey!" Now that she was gone, every family gathering was tinged with sadness. Her oldest daughter's graduation, Regina's birthday. I even dreaded Christmas, because we always spent it at Ria's. The treasure hunt was the first thing we'd gotten excited about in a while. We were all in: my husband, Tony, my two sons, Solomon and Henry, my brother, Paul, my sister, Laura, and their families. Even Mom, who had been hit the hardest by our loss.

As the kids searched, decked out in pirate swag, I thumbed through the treasure story concocted by the tourism office, which held the clues to finding the now-legendary doubloon. Mom, Laura, and I had read it earlier. "Captain Kidd and The Missing Crown" was filled with details of the infamous pirate's travels, and about the cargo, crew, and supposed longitude and latitude of his stops. I reread the ending, which said the treasure was buried "somewhere on the banks of the Hudson River." The hand-drawn map depicted Catskill Point but lacked the usual X for buried treasure.

All day we scratched around in the dirt. Lifted up rocks. Searched behind buildings and through bushes. But every shiny glint turned out to be a crushed soda can, a penny, a gum wrapper. "That doubloon could be anywhere," Mom said. I nodded. In seventeen years, no one had found it. Had it been washed away somehow, irretrievably lost like Ria?

We resumed our search the next weekend. Team Ria gathered at a restaurant called, of all things, Captain Kidd's. We'd learned from the locals that the restaurant had once been owned by an organizer of the treasure hunt. Aha! Was the doubloon hidden on Captain Kidd's property? Regina tore ahead to a larger-than-life statue of the captain himself. Pushing aside leaves, we looked to see if there was a hidden compartment. "Is that a doubloon on his boots?" Solomon asked excitedly. No, just gold-colored buckles. We joked at how silly we must look. How would we explain ourselves if the owner came out?

Laura was sure she had it figured out when she spotted a big pig statue across the bridge from Catskill Point. The clues were filled with references to St. Anthony, who, according to our research, was often accompanied by a fat pig. But we checked it out and discovered that the statue had been a promotion for the movie *Babe*...and had been placed there seven years after the hunt began. "*Arrgh*," we said.

Later that week we got together at Laura's and went over the story, the map, and our notes. "Maybe there's a hidden code," someone suggested. Taking out Scrabble tiles, we rearranged the letters of the names of the story's characters. Among the many combinations possible, one stood out: "low tide marker." We decided to zero in on the Hudson's shoreline at low tide.

The next few weekends were filled with trudging the shoreline of the park and even taking kayaks out on the river, searching land only accessible at low tide. The kids splashed each other and had a great time, but we still came up empty. It's just a silly treasure hunt, I tried to convince myself. Inside though, I ached for Ria's presence in my life. *Lord, will it always feel like this?* I asked.

I came home from hunting one day to find my refrigerator on the fritz. Great, just what I need. Tony pulled the refrigerator away from the wall and fiddled with the back.

"Look what I found!" he said, holding up a postcard. On the front was a treasure map, on the back, "We already miss you guys! Can't wait for next year. Love, Ria." She had sent it from Cape Cod last summer.

I shook my head and smiled. "Who else would send a postcard to the people she had just vacationed with as a surprise for them to come home to?"

All of a sudden the fridge hummed back to life. Tony scratched his head and looked puzzled. "I didn't really do anything yet," he said. I stuck the postcard to the front of the fridge with a magnet. We had to keep looking. Ria would have wanted it.

By our next outing, only a few stray leaves still clung to the trees as our crew of fifteen, ages two to sixty-two, hiked through a nature preserve just north of Catskill Point. The sun retreated behind a steel gray cloud, as if to hide from the rain that soon began. We trudged along, tugging our hoods over our heads, and I couldn't help but laugh. What other family does this? The laughing spread to my brother and sister. Ahead on the trail, Regina giggled with her cousins. Hiking in the rain in search of buried treasure? We had to be nuts, as nuts as Ria.

Oh, Ria!

It didn't feel as if we were missing something. We were celebrating all the joy and optimism that was my sister. It didn't matter if we found the doubloon. This was the way to get past the sadness: living our lives a little bit like Ria had.

Back at the car, sopping wet, I whispered a prayer of thanks.

A few days later Laura called. "Are you sitting down?" she asked.

Her husband, Michael, was walking their puppy that morning. "He felt guided to look under a big rock buried in the riverbed," Laura said. There wasn't any one clue, any logical explanation as to why he picked up that particular rock of the hundreds of large rocks on the edge of low tide. But when he did, the doubloon—worn and blackened by years underwater—was underneath.

Our family was awarded the jeweled crown right before Christmas. It had been kept for seventeen years in an old cake box under the bed of one of the organizers of the hunt. It's in a safe-deposit box now, though Mom keeps the box it was stored in at the top of her stairs. "It makes me smile every time I see it," she says. Me too.

Hunters who had searched for years sent us e-mails and phoned us, from as far away as California. "How did you find the treasure?" they asked.

"We had lots of help," I tell them. A sister nuts for pirates and treasure hunts. An encouraging postcard at the right time. A nudge toward a certain rock. And the crown wasn't the most precious treasure we found. We discovered Ria's joyous spirit, alive in all of us.

Read on for a sneak peek of another exciting book in
Secrets of the Blue Hill Library!

The Not-So-Civil War

Anne Gibson ran a brush through her five-year-old daughter's unruly curls, but Liddie kept wriggling, making it impossible to clip a barrette in place.

"Hold still, honey," Anne said.

Liddie stiffened in her chair and stuck both arms and legs out straight. "Please hurry, Mommy. I want to see the war."

Anne smiled. "We won't see any fighting today. They'll just be setting up the soldiers' camp in the park."

The town of Blue Hill was hosting a group of Civil War reenactors for the weekend. While the major events in Rosehill Park wouldn't take place until Saturday, Anne's children were eager to see the bustle of the preparations.

"Besides, it's not a real war," Ben said as he poured himself more juice. "It's just one battle, and it's not real."

"There will be lots of other things to see, besides the battle," Anne said. "The reenactors are going to live in tents and show us how people did things in the old days." She slid a pink plastic barrette through Liddie's hair and clamped it shut. "All done. Get your jacket and backpack. We don't have much time before school."

Ben gulped down his juice and stood. "I'm ready." He picked up his backpack of books from the floor and slung it over his shoulder.

They went down the back stairs and out the private entrance of the big, old Victorian house. Most people in town knew it as the public library, but for Anne and the kids, this was also home. They climbed into her car, and she drove to the park, where she helped Liddie out of her booster seat and closed the car door.

"Hurry up, Mom," called Ben from near the back bumper where he waited for them. "I want to have time to see everything before we have to leave."

"We're coming." Anne was glad to see that he was enthusiastic. Ben's teacher had assigned his fourth-grade class a project on the Civil War. Ben didn't like the research part, but he seemed happy with this portion of the homework.

Anne took Liddie's hand and joined him. They walked across the park to where people were setting up canvas tents, and a truck was towing a Civil War cannon on its carriage into place.

"Wow, is that a real cannon, or is it a prop?" Ben asked.

"I think it's real," Anne said. "They'll probably fire it during the battle tomorrow."

Ben seemed properly impressed as they followed along behind the cannon, toward the field where dozens of people were already bustling about. The leaves on the oak trees were turning golden, and the maples at the edge of the park showed scarlet and peach on their foliage. Anne hoped they would have perfect October weather for the weekend's events.

"They won't have everything ready yet, but tomorrow we'll see it all," Anne assured the children.

"I know," Ben said, "but I like to see how they do things. Can I watch them set up the cannon?"

"I guess so. Just be sure to stay back out of the way."

"I will." Ben dashed ahead toward the encampment.

* * *

When they had surveyed the encampment and reenactment site and it was almost time for school, Anne called for Ben to join them. As she, Ben, and Liddie walked toward the parking lot, Anne spotted George Franklin, who owned an antiques shop at the far end of Main Street, talking to a man she didn't know. The reenactment was certainly bringing a lot of out-of-towners to Blue Hill.

George saw her and waved. Anne waved back.

"Hey, Anne! Got a minute?"

"Not really," Anne said with a smile, but she slowed and veered toward the men. "I need to have the kids at school within fifteen minutes."

"Oh. Well, I was going to introduce you to Nash Tyburn." George glanced at the man next to him. "This is Anne Gibson, our librarian. Anne, Mr. Tyburn has an antiques shop in New York. Specializes in Civil War artifacts."

Anne shook Mr. Tyburn's hand. "How do you do. Is that what brought you here? The reenactment?"

Tyburn, whose dark hair was sprinkled with gray, nodded. "I like to travel a little in the summer and fall and set up a booth at events like this. I meet a lot of people who are interested in the Civil War period."

"And you never know when you'll meet someone with an artifact to sell, right?" George said with a chuckle.

"You got it." Tyburn reached into his shirt pocket and pulled out a business card. "I'm especially interested in Civil War weapons."

Anne took the card, wondering if she ought to look through the attic to see if Aunt Edie had anything like that among her treasures. "I'll keep it in mind."

"My booth will be right over there tomorrow." Tyburn pointed to the spot. "I've brought a small selection of items that I thought might appeal to the crowd here. Come by and take a look."

"I will," Anne said.

"Nice meeting you." Tyburn strolled away, and George walked beside Anne toward the parking lot. The children ran ahead, and Anne clicked the automatic opener on her key fob to unlock the doors for them.

"He didn't tell you everything," George said with a glance over his shoulder.

"Oh?" Anne stopped walking, sensing that he was about to divulge something confidential.

George nodded. "He's looking for a particular weapon."

"What do you mean?" Anne asked.

"Tyburn told me he'd heard that someone in Blue Hill has an antique pistol that once belonged to an officer in the Pennsylvania Volunteers."

"That's a Civil War regiment?"

George nodded. "And I know where it is too."

Anne eyed him in surprise. "Did you tell him?"

"Nope."

Anne smiled. "Competition, huh?"

"You might say that. But I don't think the owners want to sell the gun that Tyburn's looking for. I've been asked about it before, and I approached the family then."

"And they want to keep it?"

"That's right. They're quite proud of it. But if I tell Tyburn who has it, he'd offer them twenty thousand dollars, sight unseen."

Anne's jaw dropped. "Really? They must be awfully fond of that pistol."

"It's a family heirloom. But Tyburn says he knows a collector who would buy it immediately."

"What are you going to do?"

"First I'm going to tell the owners about Tyburn. I don't want him learning about them from someone else and ambushing them." He glanced around again and then leaned closer. "It's Nellie Brown and her sister, Betty Warring."

"Wow. I didn't know they had a special heirloom like that, though they have some interesting things in their house." The elderly ladies were regular patrons at the library. Both were in their seventies, and their minds were sharp, but they could be opinionated. The refusal to sell an heirloom sounded right on target for those two.

George nodded. "I figure they ought to be prepared, in case this New York smooth talker gets wind of it and decides to pay them a visit." He looked at his watch. "Almost time to open my store. Better run."

"Oh, me too," Anne said.

George eyed her with speculation. "I don't suppose you'd want to carry the message over to the Warring sisters for me?"

"I suppose I could, after I drop the kids off at school."

"Would you? I'd really appreciate it. I think they ought to know as soon as possible, but I want to open shop on time because of all the visitors in town. Can't afford to lose business this weekend."

"Sure. I'll be on their doorstep in twenty minutes. Don't you worry about it."

"Terrific." George stepped away with a wave. "See you later, Anne."

Anne hurried to her Impala. Ben was buckled in and was helping Liddie with her seat belt.

"Thanks, guys. Mr. Franklin wanted to tell me something private." She checked Liddie's belt, got into the driver's seat, and drove to the school.

She checked Liddie's seatbelt, got into the driver's seat, and drove to the school. Anne pulled into a parking space and helped Liddie get out and settled her backpack on her shoulders. Then, she watched them enter the school building while the final bell sounded. She climbed back into her car and headed toward Betty's and Nellie's house.

The three-story brick home was set back from the street. Though built in the same era as Anne's home, its appearance was very different. It looked solid and welcoming. Flower beds along the walkway held chrysanthemums that bloomed in orange, yellow, and gold this time of year. A large oak tree spread its October foliage over the lawn on each side of the walk. Anne climbed the steps to the covered porch and rang the bell.

Nellie Brown, clad in a becoming plum-colored pantsuit, opened the door and grinned at Anne.

"What a wonderful surprise. Won't you come in? I was just about to pour myself a cup of tea."

"I think I have time." The library wasn't due to open until nine-thirty, an hour away, so Anne followed Nellie into the cozy parlor of the old house. Nellie and her husband had lived here for many years, and after Mr. Brown died, Nellie's sister had moved in with her. Between them, Betty and Nellie had decorated the house with a combination of modern furniture and beloved antiques. The startling abstract painting over the fireplace always surprised Anne. The sisters, it seemed, had eclectic tastes.

Anne carried their teacups in from the kitchen for Nellie. She set the tray on the glass-topped coffee table, and they settled on the beige sofa.

"Where's Betty today?" Anne asked.

"She's gone with Georgia Winters on a ramble," Nellie said. "They both wanted to get up into the mountains and see the foliage."

"What fun! The colors will be lovely up there."

"I expect they will. Next month, Phyllis Oster and I are going to drive to Corning, New York, and tour the glassworks. That way we each get an outing of our choice, and the house isn't left empty."

"I hope you both have wonderful trips." Anne sipped her tea.

"Are you going to the reenactment tomorrow?" Nellie asked.

"Yes. The kids are all excited about it. In fact, we stopped by the park this morning to see them setting up the soldiers' encampment. There are already quite a few tents up, and Ben got to watch some of the men who were bringing in a cannon for the skirmish."

"Oh my, I expect he enjoyed that. Phyllis and I are going over tomorrow."

Anne set down her cup. "As a matter of fact, I saw George Franklin at the park a few minutes ago, and that's why I stopped here. He had a message for you and Betty."

"Oh?"

"Yes. You see, there's an antiques dealer in town this weekend, and he's been asking questions about Civil War artifacts, particularly weapons. George told me in confidence that he knew you and Betty had a family heirloom that fits the description."

Nellie straightened her shoulders. "He means the Colt Dragoon pistol."

"I expect so. George said a pistol, anyway. He wanted you to know that he didn't tell Mr. Tyburn about it, but that it's possible someone else might. He wanted you and Betty to be prepared, in case Mr. Tyburn came here asking about it."

"Well, thank you. That was thoughtful of George, but the pistol is not for sale."

Anne smiled. "That's what he said. He didn't want the dealer from New York to come and bother you about it, so he didn't say a word. But now you know what's going on."

"Yes. If he comes here, I'll put him in his place. These dealers assume everything has a price. Oh, not George so much. He understands how folks feel about family things. But I've dealt with plenty of those greedy people in my day."

"I'll bet you have."

"Of course, Betty might not see it that way," Nellie said.

Anne waited, curious. She knew both sisters were proud of their Civil War heritage. She had heard mention of their illustrious ancestor before.

"The two of you don't agree on this?" Anne asked.

"Oh, we both love the pistol, but I'm afraid Betty might see it as a way to help pay for the new roof this house needs. She talked about selling it once before, when the car needed repairs, but I put my foot down. We don't want to sell our heritage!"

"I see. Well, if it makes any difference, George said that Mr. Tyburn might offer as much as twenty thousand dollars."

Nellie had reached for her teacup but stopped with her hand in midair. "As much as that?"

Anne nodded. "Is that more than you expected?"

"A lot more. We had speculated a thousand or two. What do you know?" Nellie smiled. "It's very special. Have you ever seen the pistol?"

"No, I don't believe so," Anne said.

"Would you like to?"

"Certainly, if it's not too much trouble." By this time, Anne was curious about the pistol, and she sensed that Nellie would love to have a chance to show it off.

"Not at all. Let me get it." Nellie pushed herself up off the sofa. "It belonged to our great-great-grandfather, you know. He was a colonel in the Civil War. And it's in mint condition. Never fired."

Anne arched her eyebrows. "Never fired? You mean he never used it in combat?"

"Oh, he didn't get it until after the war. His general gave one to him and five of the other officers in the regiment as a sort of souvenir gift. A presentation piece, they call it. Silver chasing on the handle, and each one is engraved with their names. Let me show you."

Anne rose and followed her into the next room, where Nellie went to a wooden cabinet. It was a fine old cherry piece, with glass-fronted doors on top and drawers below.

Nellie paused before it, and a look of chagrin crossed her face. "Oh, I'll need to go upstairs and get the key. Have to be cautious, you know."

"Where is the key?" Anne asked. "Perhaps I could get it for you."

"It's up in Betty's room." Nellie turned to face Anne, and she nodded toward a framed piece on the wall. "Did we ever show you that? Your aunt Edith made it."

"Really? I don't think I've ever seen it." Anne stepped closer. "It's your family tree!"

"Yes. Edie used to do a lot of genealogy, and she was into calligraphy for a while there, too. She put Betty and me here at the bottom, see? And then our parents, our grandparents, and all the way back to the colonel."

"It's beautiful." Anne gazed at the colorful scrolls and fancy lettering. "It's almost like an illuminated manuscript."

Nellie smiled. "Edie was so talented. And she knew how much we esteemed Great-grandpa. That's why we hung it in here—so it would be near where we keep the pistol."

As she spoke, Nellie touched one of the doorknobs on the cabinet and tugged gently. The door swung open. She stopped short and stared at it. "Why—it isn't locked. Well, I never!" She pulled both the double doors back and peered into the shelves of the cabinet. She turned and faced Anne, her face pale.

"It's gone. The pistol isn't here!"

A Note from the Editors

We hope you enjoy Secrets of the Blue Hill Library, created by the Books and Inspirational Media Division of Guideposts, a nonprofit organization that touches millions of lives every day through products and services that inspire, encourage, help you grow in your faith, and celebrate God's love in every aspect of your daily life.

Thank you for making a difference with your purchase of this book, which helps fund our many outreach programs to military personnel, prisons, hospitals, nursing homes, and educational institutions. To learn more, visit Guideposts Foundation.org.

We also maintain many useful and uplifting online resources. Visit Guideposts.org to read true stories of hope and inspiration, access OurPrayer network, sign up for free newsletters, download free e-books, join our Facebook community, and follow our stimulating blogs.

To learn about other Guideposts publications, including the best-selling devotional *Daily Guideposts*, go to ShopGuideposts .org, call (800) 932-2145, or write to Guideposts, PO Box 5815, Harlan, Iowa 51593.

Sign up for the Guideposts Fiction Newsletter

and stay up-to-date on the fiction you love!

You'll get sneak peeks of new releases, recommendations from other Guideposts readers, and special offers just for you . . .

And it's FREE!

Just go to Guideposts.org/newsletters today to sign up.

Visit ShopGuideposts.org or call (800) 932-2145

Find more inspiring fiction in these best-loved Guideposts series

Secrets of the Blue Hill Library

Enjoy the tingle of suspense and the joy of coming home when Anne Gibson turns her late aunt's Victorian mansion into a library and uncovers hidden secrets.

Miracles of Marble Cove

Follow four women who are drawn together to face life's challenges, support one another in faith, and experience God's amazing grace as they encounter mysterious events in the small town of Marble Cove.

Secrets of Mary's Bookshop

Delve into a cozy mystery where Mary, the owner of Mary's Mystery Bookshop, finds herself using sleuthing skills that she didn't realize she had. There are quirky characters and lots of unexpected twists and turns.

Patchwork Mysteries

Discover that life's little mysteries often have a common thread in a series where every novel contains an intriguing mystery centered around a quilt located in a beautiful New England town.

Mysteries of Silver Peak

Escape to the historic mining town of Silver Peak, Colorado, and discover how one woman's love of antiques helps her solve mysteries buried deep in the town's checkered past.

To learn more about these books, visit ShopGuideposts.org